PRAISE FOR THE N
WRITING AS

"York's combination of werewolves, romance, suspense, science fiction, and fantasy is a winning one." —*Booklist*

"Rebecca York delivers page-turning suspense."
—Nora Roberts

"[A] quick pace and dangerous overtones ensure that readers won't be disappointed!" —*RT Book Reviews*

"Action packed . . . and filled with sexual tension . . . A gripping thriller." —*The Best Reviews*

"A steamy paranormal. Brava." —*Huntress Book Reviews*

"A compulsive read." —*Publishers Weekly*

"York delivers an exciting and suspenseful romance with paranormal themes that she gets just right. This is a howling good read." —*Booklist*

"Mesmerizing action and passions that leap from the pages with the power of a wolf's coiled spring." —*BookPage*

"Delightful . . . [with] two charming lead characters."
—*Midwest Book Review*

"[Her] prose is smooth, literate, and fast-moving; her love scenes are tender yet erotic; and there's always a happy ending." —*The Washington Post Book World*

"She writes a fast-paced, satisfying thriller." —UPI

"Clever and a great read. I can't wait to read the final book in this wonderful series." —*ParaNormal Romance*

Books by Rebecca York

KILLING MOON
EDGE OF THE MOON
WITCHING MOON
CRIMSON MOON
SHADOW OF THE MOON
NEW MOON
GHOST MOON
ETERNAL MOON
DRAGON MOON
DAY OF THE DRAGON
DARK WARRIOR

BEYOND CONTROL
BEYOND FEARLESS

Anthologies

CRAVINGS
(with Laurell K. Hamilton, MaryJanice Davidson, and Eileen Wilks)

ELEMENTAL MAGIC
(with Sharon Shinn, Carol Berg, and Jean Johnson)

DARK WARRIOR

REBECCA YORK

BERKLEY SENSATION, NEW YORK

THE BERKLEY PUBLISHING GROUP
Published by the Penguin Group
Penguin Group (USA) Inc.
375 Hudson Street, New York, New York 10014, USA
Penguin Group (Canada), 90 Eglinton Avenue East, Suite 700, Toronto, Ontario M4P 2Y3, Canada
(a division of Pearson Penguin Canada Inc.)
Penguin Books Ltd., 80 Strand, London WC2R 0RL, England
Penguin Group Ireland, 25 St. Stephen's Green, Dublin 2, Ireland (a division of Penguin Books Ltd.)
Penguin Group (Australia), 250 Camberwell Road, Camberwell, Victoria 3124, Australia
(a division of Pearson Australia Group Pty. Ltd.)
Penguin Books India Pvt. Ltd., 11 Community Centre, Panchsheel Park, New Delhi—110 017, India
Penguin Group (NZ), 67 Apollo Drive, Rosedale, Auckland 0632, New Zealand
(a division of Pearson New Zealand Ltd.)
Penguin Books (South Africa) (Pty.) Ltd., 24 Sturdee Avenue, Rosebank, Johannesburg 2196, South Africa

Penguin Books Ltd., Registered Offices: 80 Strand, London WC2R 0RL, England

DARK WARRIOR

A Berkley Sensation Book / published by arrangement with the author

PRINTING HISTORY
Berkley Sensation mass-market edition / September 2011

Cover photo of man by CURAphotography/Shutterstock.
Cover photo of cathedral rock and Oak Creek Canyon by Mike Norton/Shutterstock.
Cover design by SDG CONCEPTS, LLC.

For information, address: The Berkley Publishing Group,
a division of Penguin Group (USA) Inc.,
375 Hudson Street, New York, New York 10014.

ISBN: 978-0-425-24370-1

BERKLEY SENSATION®
Berkley Sensation Books are published by The Berkley Publishing Group,
a division of Penguin Group (USA) Inc.,
375 Hudson Street, New York, New York 10014.
BERKLEY SENSATION® is a registered trademark of Penguin Group (USA) Inc.
The "B" design is a trademark of Penguin Group (USA) Inc.

PRINTED IN THE UNITED STATES OF AMERICA

10 9 8 7 6 5 4 3 2 1

CHAPTER ONE

SHE WAS TWENTY miles from safety when disaster struck.

The desert had cooled off, and Sophia Thalia was driving along Blissful Canyon Road, back to the spa where she and the other women of her ancient family ran a luxury retreat for the rich and privileged.

Sophia had always lived there, always accepted the responsibilities that had fallen on her from an early age, but tonight's contentious meeting of the Sedona Business Association had worn her out.

As she emerged from a stand of junipers, she leaned forward, watching her headlights cut through the desert darkness.

At night on this desolate stretch of road, she was always a little on edge until she reached the turnoff to the resort. This evening it was worse because she couldn't shake the feeling that danger lurked around the next outcropping of red rocks.

When she spotted the small white sign for the Seven Sisters Spa, she sighed with relief, until her premonition slammed into reality. Something came hurtling out of the darkness toward her SUV, and she swerved past the shoulder, almost plowing into a piñon pine before she regained control of the vehicle.

The car rocked back and forth, then settled into a pocket of loose, dusty soil. Her gaze shot to the windshield. Whatever had zoomed toward her had vanished.

Had a bat changed course at the last minute? Or had she managed to dodge whatever it was?

When she tried to drive back onto the road, the wheels spun, digging the vehicle further into the unstable surface.

"Hades," she muttered as she cut the engine. A tow truck could pull her out, but she'd have to wait here for hours.

She made a low sound of disgust, thinking this was the perfect ending to her trying week at work. The new massage therapy and meditation rooms she'd been pushing for were going to cost a lot more than the original bid. She'd been trying to get some of her sisters to agree that the extra expense was worth it, but so far her point of view was losing.

Then the supplier of the handwoven rugs they sold in the gift shop had gone bankrupt, just when they were running low on stock. Which meant she'd have to find another alternative—quickly.

Fumbling in her purse, she found her cell phone, but when she tried to get a signal, nothing happened. The phone was dead, although it shouldn't be. She'd made a point of charging it that afternoon when she'd gotten the bad news that she was going to the meeting in town.

It had been her younger sister's turn to take that duty, but Mrs. Finlander, one of their frequent guests, had made a special request to have Tessa give her a before-bed massage. Really, anyone could have done it just as professionally. But Tessa had developed a rapport with the woman, and she'd asked Sophia to go to the meeting.

Now she was stuck about three miles from the spa. An

easy walk. Too bad she was wearing a creamy yellow suit and high heels. But a pair of running shoes was in the trunk. And a T-shirt and shorts, come to that.

Once she changed her clothes, getting home would be no big deal. Out here in the desert, the moon and stars were brilliant, more than enough to light her way. Yet the idea of climbing out of the car sent a shiver up her spine.

As she peered out the window, she saw headlights in the distance. Someone was coming, and hopefully she could get a ride.

She climbed out, waving a manicured hand as the lights approached. Whoever was in the other car roared past, leaving her standing in his backwash. Did he recognize her? Was he one of the people in town who thought the Thalia sisters and cousins were witches because of the way they retained their youth and beauty?

She allowed herself another curse as she walked to the back of the vehicle and clicked the trunk release. The casual clothing was where she'd left it, in her carry bag. After changing into the running shoes, she reached to shrug off her suit jacket, then changed her mind. The idea of getting undressed on the side of the highway had her nerves jumping again.

To calm herself, she took a deep breath of the desert air. It smelled clean and fresh and reassuring, and she wondered why she was so spooked.

After slinging her purse over her shoulder, she started up the road, her eyes fixed on the white sign for the turnoff to the spa. It was a refuge for her and the other women of the Ionian Sisterhood who had come here long ago, seeking a place where they could practice the ancient arts they had brought from their home in Greece.

As she walked, she heard the crunch of footsteps on the gravel shoulder behind her, and all her vague fears came crashing down on her.

She started to run, wondering if there was any chance of getting away from whoever was stalking her.

He answered the question by streaking past her at speeds no normal human being could attain, stopping about twenty yards in front of her, blocking her path.

In the darkness, she couldn't make out many details, but she saw he was wearing a white T-shirt and tight-fitting jeans. His hair was dark, but the shadows hid his features as he walked slowly toward her, young and cocksure in the moonlight.

In that terrible moment, she knew who he was. Not his name. But everything about him told her that he must be a Minot, one of the men who had hounded the Ionians down through the ages, since they had made a devil's pact with the ancient warriors.

None of them had attacked the Sisterhood in years, and perhaps that had made them too lax in their security measures. Of course there were wards around the property and a guard at the gate, but now Sophia was alone and vulnerable on a dark desert highway. Like in that Eagles song.

Her throat was so tight that she could barely breathe, but she kept her eyes focused on the man who advanced toward her. Even while she kept him in sight, she sent her mind toward the resort, hoping to get a silent message to Tessa, her real sister, the one who was closest to her in all the world.

I'm on the highway. Just a few hundred feet . . .

Before she could say more, he raised his hand. He was holding a small cylinder, and when he pressed on the top, a mist whooshed out and drifted toward her.

The second she breathed it, her head began to spin, and her body stopped obeying her commands. Her mind told her to turn and run, but her legs wouldn't move. She was rooted to the spot, like a desert animal frozen in the headlights of an advancing vehicle.

The man waited a moment for the cloud of gas around her to dissipate. Then he tossed the cylinder away where it clanked against a rock as he walked purposefully forward, his gaze never leaving her.

When he stepped in front of her, she should have been able to see his face better, yet each feature was blurred. Still, she sensed that his eyes were large and dark, his brows heavy, his lips curved into a smile that was as arrogant as it was sensual. If she had met him at the spa, she would have seen him as a vital, desirable man.

And she might have made love with him. Totally on her terms. Because that was the Ionian way.

Yet she wasn't the one in control here, and she knew she was in danger.

"I have you now," he murmured, touching her lips with one long finger.

She tried to speak, but no words came out of her mouth, and sending a mental message to her sisters had become impossible.

All she could do was stand facing him as his hand moved to her cheek in a sultry caress.

He smiled again, showing her his gleaming white teeth, while his hand slid down her neck, pressing against the pulse pounding there—and sending a shiver over her skin.

She hated responding to him, but sensuality was part of her being, and she was helpless to fight against the waves of sexual energy rolling off of him—augmented by the paralyzing mist he'd sprayed on her. She knew it was affecting her senses—and her judgment.

Making a tremendous effort to speak, she managed to say, "Leave . . . me . . . alone."

"That's not what you really want, is it?" he answered in a confident voice as he slid his hand lower, pushing back one side of her jacket so that he could cup her right breast through her blouse. "You're a sexy, dynamic woman who needs a man to complete her. At his pleasure, of course."

She closed her eyes, trying to shut him out as he rubbed his thumb back and forth across her nipple, making it stiffen.

Don't. Please don't. She shouted inside her mind, but she couldn't make the words slip past her lips.

This was so wrong. It wasn't the way any woman should be treated—being aroused against her will.

Somehow she managed to speak again. "Get off me . . . you . . . bastard."

He laughed, a rough, grating sound, and moved in closer. Keeping up the maddening caress on her breast, he slid his other hand lower, finding the juncture of her legs, then pressing through her skirt against her clit, sending an unwanted jolt of sensation through her body.

"You're as lovely as I knew you'd be. But all your sisters are so tempting. So young. So vital. So desirable."

What was he planning to do? Rape her out here on the highway?

She prayed that another motorist would come along and see what was happening.

Or was this like so many instances of modern life when strangers weren't going to get involved? Even if you were lying on the sidewalk bleeding.

Teeth clenched, she steeled herself against the man whose hateful touch sucked her into a vortex of his making.

Desperately, in her mind, she said one of the ancient supplications that had sustained her Sisterhood throughout the centuries. Once they had prayed to the Greek goddesses, but their thinking had evolved so that they had come to see one divine force in the universe.

Spirit of the Earth
Hear my plea
I am but a mortal woman
Standing before you.
But I humbly ask for your aid
In the hour of my need
As the Ionians have done through the ages.

Even as she clung to the ancient words, she could feel herself falling further under the attacker's spell, bending to his will no matter how she struggled against the unwanted arousal coursing through her body.

He tipped up her head, staring into her eyes, and she heard him gasp. "You're not . . ."

Before he finished the sentence, everything changed with the suddenness of a lightning bolt spearing out of the sky.

CHAPTER TWO

SOPHIA CAUGHT HER breath as another man came streaking out of the darkness and into the scene. Like the attacker, he was dark haired and well muscled, although he wasn't close enough for her to see his face.

His voice was loud and commanding. "Take your dirty hands off her."

"What the hell?" The attacker whirled to face the newcomer.

"Get away from her."

"You dare interfere." It wasn't a question, it was a statement of outrage.

"I do."

"I think you've made a mistake. She is mine."

"No." He bit off the one syllable as he charged forward, his fist flashing out, striking a blow to the first man's chin.

At least she thought she'd seen the punch, because it happened in a blur of motion, the way both men had come out of the desert.

The man who had attacked Sophia struck back, but her champion was prepared for the counterassault, dodging aside to avoid the fist before leaping onto his opponent, throwing him to the ground with bone-rattling force.

They rolled together in the red dirt, like two ancient warriors fighting without the need of weapons, each testing the weaknesses of the other and grappling for advantage. They moved with the speed of the wind, so fast that Sophia could barely follow the action. One slammed the other into the dirt with enough force to break the bones of an ordinary man.

When he picked himself up and sprang back into the fray, she knew it could be a fight to the death if they both kept up the intensity.

She heard the breath rushing in and out of their lungs, felt bits of grit spray in her direction as they kicked and scrabbled for dominance.

One heaved himself away. She couldn't tell which it was, but she saw him scramble to his feet. While his opponent was still on the ground, he took off across the desert, running as fast as a speeding train, then climbing into the red rocks. The other clambered up and followed, putting on a burst of speed, almost catching up. They raced up a steep outcropping, taking a route that would have sent any other man toppling to the ground.

Sophia watched until they disappeared from view. She still didn't know whether the second man was really her champion or simply trying to steal what the first one wanted, but she must take this chance to get away. Before one or the other came back to claim his prize.

With every ounce of will she possessed, she struggled against the effects of the gas that had immobilized her, dragging in great lungfuls of the clean desert air as she strove to clear her system of the poison.

To her relief, she found she could move her arms, then her legs. She shook her head and shoulders, before taking a couple of wavering steps away from the spot where she had been rooted.

But she was still out in the open, and she knew she didn't have the strength to run. The best she could do was get back to the car. Lock herself in. Then use her powers to call for help, if she could make her brain function well enough. And pray that the vehicle would be enough protection until some of her sisters could come from the spa.

Doggedly, she staggered back the way she'd come.

As she wove her way toward the vehicle, she struggled to reach her sister's mind and caught a stuttering of contact, as though she had almost closed the circuit but couldn't quite do it. Not in her present condition.

What she needed was to get back to the safety of the spa where the collective power of her sisters would protect her.

With gritted teeth, she picked up her pace, hurrying to the vehicle as fast as she could. But not fast enough, apparently.

When she heard a sound to her right, like wind rushing down a canyon, she felt her heart thud in her chest.

One of them was coming back.

Which one? And did it matter?

She was reaching for the door handle when a voice spoke out of the darkness. "The bastard's gone, but you won't be safe until you get back home."

The words were both gentle and forceful. She knew that it was the one who had saved her from rape or worse. But she still didn't know *his* intentions.

Since there was no point in trying to evade him, she turned, backing up so that her hips were pressed against the car door as she and the man stared at each other across three yards of charged space.

He appeared to be standing in shadow, if that was possible, when the world was all darkness except for the stars and moonlight shining down. All she knew was that she couldn't see him any clearer than the first one.

Still, she could make out his dark hair. The outline of his head and the shape of his supple body. Like the other man, he radiated an aura of power and raw sexuality. Yet he stopped a few yards from her, keeping his distance, making no attempt to dominate her.

"Are you all right?" he asked.

She flicked her gaze into the distance, then back. "Yes. Where did he go?"

"He ran away. Like the coward he is." He spoke in a low, grating tone as though he were worried about her discovering his true identity from his voice. He paused, then added, "You should not be out here alone."

Although she'd had the same thought earlier, she raised her chin. "I take orders from no man."

"Sorry. I was just making a practical suggestion."

She swallowed, remembering what he had done for her. Risked his life, she was sure, to free her from the man who had stopped her on the road. Now he was keeping his distance.

"I should thank you."

"No need."

"Who are you?"

"A friend."

She wanted to tell him that no Ionian was friends with a man. She settled for "Impossible."

"Why do you doubt me?"

"Because I know what you are."

"Maybe. Maybe not. But I will never convince you with words."

"Or any other way."

"We'll see."

Moving slowly, he took a step closer, then another until he was standing only a few feet away.

He was so close that she should be able to see him clearly now, yet clarity of vision was impossible. Her senses were still muddled, perhaps by the gas.

Cautiously, as though he were trying not to spook a frightened animal, he lifted his hand, touching her hair, running his fingers through the silky strands.

The other man had touched her, too. An unwelcome touch. But this was as different as the taste of wine and beer. She sensed that this man meant her no harm, although that could be as much of a trick as anything else that had happened in the last half hour.

A half hour?

Was that all the time that had passed since the car had gone off the road? She didn't know for sure, but she suspected that she hadn't been out here much longer.

When he massaged his fingers through her hair and down to her scalp, she felt something that she had never felt from a man. Something unique. It was almost as if she could sense his thoughts. Almost, but not quite. They were blurred—like her vision. Yet she hovered on the brink of a marvelous discovery. One that she knew would mean more to her than anything she had encountered in this life or any other.

Every instinct had commanded her to shrink from the other man's touch. Now she craved what this one offered.

A hum of sensuality flooded through her, and she clenched her hands at her sides to keep from reaching out and pulling him closer.

"Who are you?" she whispered again. "We haven't met before, have we?"

"No."

He continued to caress her, his touch so different from the earlier one. The first man had been arrogantly possessive. This one was no less sure of his purpose, yet she felt need coursing through him as he touched her. Or was she only projecting her own feelings onto him?

His face was close to hers. He could have taken her mouth if he wanted. Instead he bent to press his cheek to hers, that touch as erotic as any kiss. When he slowly pulled her body against his, the breath caught in her throat.

She had thought the first man had aroused her. It was nothing to what she felt now.

Her senses whirled. Her mind spun. Her blood pumped hotly through her veins. She couldn't speak, but she felt a question form in her mind.

What do you want? she asked, the way she might speak to one of her sisters over a distance.

Again, she felt a flicker of something coming from his mind.

Everything.

Had he silently answered?

Whether he had or not, she felt a flood of longing coursing through her.

Or was she so off balance that she couldn't judge her own responses?

He pulled her more tightly against himself, and she could feel his erection pressing against her middle and the heat of his body overwhelming her.

"Sophia," he murmured.

"You know my name?"

"Yes."

"How?"

He laughed softly. "Modern technology. The spa has a Web site."

"Oh. Right."

And she was pictured there, with the others. Maybe that was a mistake they should correct.

She started to pull away.

"Not yet."

She turned her head—to look at him. And he turned at the same time, so that his mouth brushed hers. An accident.

But she was helpless to draw away as sensations assaulted her. She marveled at the softness of his lips, marveled at the currents of sensation surging through her as his mouth settled on hers, moving, pressing, urging her to open for him.

She accepted the invitation, drinking in the taste of him as his tongue pressed beyond her lips, teasing her and then withdrawing.

It was the most erotic kiss she had ever experienced, and it made her want more. So much more.

Somehow, she knew it was the same for him. They belonged together, in a way she could only dimly understand. But she would. She was sure of it. As sure as she was that he was going to make love with her here and now.

She wanted that. So much.

Before she could raise her hands to pull him closer, he let his arms drop to his sides and stepped back, putting a foot of space between them. As the heat of his body left hers, she felt such a sense of profound loss that she had to steady her hand against the side of the car.

"Not like this. It must be right."

The words were so low that she barely heard them, as though he were talking to himself.

Turning away, he walked to the rear of the SUV. "You need to get back to the spa."

"The . . . car's stuck," she managed to say.

"I'll take care of it. Step back."

When she'd done as he asked, he grasped the bumper with both hands. As she watched, he bent and braced his legs in the shifting soil, then began to rock the car, moving it back and forth, freeing the vehicle from the unstable surface. With a mighty heave, he shoved the SUV back onto the road.

CHAPTER THREE

JASON TYRON STOOD with his heart pounding, watching Sophia, wondering what she would do. He had already dared too much, gone too far, yet nothing could have stopped him from gathering her into his arms when they'd finally been alone.

He'd simply wanted to hold her. Then he'd almost lost his sense of purpose in the heat of the moment. Somehow he'd had the strength to step away from her before shoving the car out of the dirt and onto the road so that she could leave.

Now the front of his body felt cold where her warmth had left him. At the same time, he still felt her imprint along every one of his nerve endings.

For a charged moment, he thought she might return to his arms, drawn back by the need that had sprung up between them and started to blaze out of control. She shouldn't do it, but he saw it in her eyes as she stood facing him. Felt it in the intent radiating from her like the blast of a furnace.

Sanity told him this was the wrong time and the wrong

place to take this any further. She was in danger out here. And so was he if he let himself succumb to the sensations that were already making him dizzy.

"What just happened?" she asked in a shaky voice.

"We kissed."

He saw her swallow. "You know it was more than that."

"What was it?"

This time, she was the one who looked uncertain, and he was sure she didn't want to examine the strong emotions of the encounter too closely.

She proved the point by changing the subject. "Do you know who that other man was?"

"No. But I'm going to find out."

"Who are you?"

Although he could have given her a lot of answers, he kept them all locked behind his lips. It would be easier to reach for her again; but if he did that, he was as bad as the other guy, the one who'd forced her off the road.

"You should go."

"I won't leave until you explain what's going on."

He almost laughed at the typical Ionian reaction. Even now, she was making herself the one in charge.

"Don't put yourself in any more danger."

"From you?"

"Of course not!"

He burned to prove it to her. Instead, before he could do anything he was going to regret for the rest of his life, he turned and ran from her as swiftly as he had arrived, disappearing into the desert darkness, putting on a burst of speed that made his lungs burn.

Her thoughts seemed to reach out to him, calling him back. Or more likely that was what he wanted to believe.

Calm down, he told himself.

You'll get what you want, but not if you push too fast.

To distract himself, he thought about the other man who

had stopped her on the road. Had the other guy known who she was? Or had he even cared which one he captured?

Had he studied the Ionians the way Jason had?

He'd acquainted himself with all of them—from afar. Fallen a little in love with all of them. Longed to have one of them to bond with him in the way his parents had bonded.

A few minutes ago he hadn't known which one it would be. Perhaps he hadn't even cared. But when he'd gathered Sophia close, he'd felt a special thrill. As though it was meant to be *her* all along.

His roiling emotions almost made him stop and turn around. If he went back to her, he could. . . . They could . . .

No. Not yet. He had time. And carefully considered plans.

STILL feeling dazed, Sophia stared after the man who vanished into the darkness, leaving her standing alone beside the car.

Moments ago, she'd had no way of leaving this place, except on foot. Now she'd better get away before someone came speeding along and smashed into her.

Or would the car even start?

Still coping with the enormity of everything that had happened, Sophia turned the key in the ignition.

She felt a surge of relief as the engine sprang to life. With a jerky motion, she flicked the transmission into drive and lurched forward, then remembered to turn on her lights.

Although she hadn't been able to contact Tessa after the attacker had sprayed her with that gas, it had worn off. Maybe she could reach the high priestess, Cynthia. The woman who had led the Sisterhood for almost thirty years. She was in her seventies now, but like the rest of them, she had the Ionian genes that gave her the appearance of a much younger woman.

Under ordinary circumstances, Sophia would never

presume to try and contact the high priestess mind to mind without permission, but fear had her reaching out for help now.

Cynthia, I need your strength. Please open yourself to me.

In her highly emotional state, she caught the border of the other woman's consciousness. But she knew at once that Cynthia was in her bedroom—and not alone.

A sudden vision filled her brain, of two people rolling across a wide bed, their hands moving frantically over each other's naked bodies as they exchanged hot, savage kisses.

One of them spoke low, erotic words.

Sophia couldn't tell which. And she didn't want to know.

Mortified that she was seeing this encounter, she desperately tried to pull away from the bedroom, but she was held captive, perhaps because of her own encounters in the desert.

She saw the woman take command, pushing the man to his back and climbing on top of him. The foreplay had been frantic. As soon as they were joined, she changed the rules of engagement so that the encounter suddenly became languid.

Cynthia and her lover, Matthew Layden.

Sophia clenched her teeth, knowing that she had overstepped the bounds of Ionian propriety.

She had known Layden was at the spa, and she should have been smart enough to realize that Cynthia would probably be with him after her duties were finished for the day. Yet Sophia's desperation and her own muddled state had sent her hurtling into territory where she should not have ventured.

She'd heard whispered comments about Cynthia and her lover. Unflattering comments. Since the Ionians' long-ago flirtation with the Minot, the women had vowed never again to be dominated by men. Over the centuries, they had used the opposite sex for only two purposes. For procreation and for their own pleasure—and at their own pleasure. They never married, because their loyalty was to the ancient order. But Cynthia had developed a relationship with her current lover that appeared to go beyond those bounds.

For a few moments, Sophia was caught and held by the bedroom scene.

Making a tremendous effort, she wrenched her mind away, but she had the awful suspicion that the high priestess had sensed the intrusion.

Which wasn't going to make things any easier when Sophia told her sisters about her encounter on the road. With *two* Minot.

Only a few of the Ionians living at the spa now had dealt with *any* Minot.

But she'd learned about them in the classes that she and her sisters had taken after their regular schoolwork. Almost two thousand years ago, the Ionians had been like blond goddesses in a country of dark-haired people. Until they'd found themselves smack in the path of a barbarian invasion of Greece. Because there was no other way to escape the hordes, they'd turned to the Minot for help.

The warriors had defeated the barbarians in a fierce battle and escorted the Ionians into what was now Albania—where they'd crossed into Italy. For a while, the men had stayed with them, until the warriors had tried to dominate the proud priestesses. The women had used their mental powers to escape and never looked back.

Sophia had heard of various plots hatched by the Minot to assert their power over the Ionians again. They'd never succeeded, partly because all of them were alpha males, which made it difficult for them to work together, although they must have done it in ancient times.

But what about tonight?

Had something changed? Why were two of them in the desert waiting outside the spa?

The first one fit the profile she'd learned from childhood. Arrogant. Aggressive. Sexually potent. Bent on having his way at all costs. The second one had been aggressive and sexy, but he'd kept his arrogance under control.

Sophia clamped her hands on the wheel as she drove

through the night, trying to shake off the notion that a man was out there, running like the wind. Keeping pace with the car.

Over the years, some of the Ionians had argued that they should hide from the Minot. But that had proved to be impractical, and they had relied on their defenses. Now she wondered if that was enough. And wondered if the Ionians really understood the Minot. How much of what she'd been taught was fact? And how much was fiction?

She breathed out a sigh as she reached the gate.

Miguel, who was on duty, stepped out of the guardhouse and greeted her. "Are you all right, Miss Sophia?"

"I'm fine. Why do you ask?"

"You're late coming back from your meeting."

"I stopped to chat with some friends," she lied, not wanting to get into anything with him.

She'd thought that driving onto the grounds would ease her tension, but as she started thinking about relating the night's events to her sisters, her stomach clenched.

After parking in the staff lot, she sat staring at the adobe wall in front of her and collecting her thoughts.

The spa was a beautiful place, with low buildings that blended into the southwestern landscape and gardens filled with native plants. At night, spotlights set off some of the trees and bushes.

The Native Americans had known the spiritual properties of this Red Rock Country for centuries, and Sedona had suited the Ionians because the desert vortexes intensified their own power. They'd felt safe here. Would they still?

Sophia hurried across a bridge that spanned an artificial creek and into the private part of the compound. When she saw a man striding along the path, she froze, wondering what he was doing there. Then she realized it was just Bobby Ames, the maintenance man. He'd come to the spa after the previous handyman had been killed in an automobile accident, and he'd been with them for about four months.

He was carrying his toolbox, and she supposed he'd gotten a call to fix something.

He nodded deferentially and walked quickly past.

Sophia continued toward the building where she and eighteen of her sisters lived in private rooms grouped around garden courts. The older women had more luxurious apartments, but Sophia's room was comfortable enough.

Most of the Ionians stayed together at the spa, but the High Priestess had given some of them special protections and permission to go out into the world. Elena Thayer, a news anchor on one of the cable networks, was one of them, for example.

The Sisterhood did their utmost to accommodate their guests during the day, but it was always understood that they had their evenings free, except for the three on duty at the spa and the two who stayed with the young girls in a separate building. The rest would be relaxing in the private solarium filled with flowering plants that had been brought from some of the previous locations where they'd lived. Cyclamen from Greece and orchids from Machu Picchu.

As Sophia stepped inside, Tessa glanced up, then sprang from her lounge chair and hurried toward her to ask the same question as the guard at the gate.

"Are you all right?"

"Yes," she murmured. "Now."

"No you're not. I sensed . . . something," she said as she took in Sophia's disheveled appearance and what must be the look of fear in her eyes.

CHAPTER FOUR

OUT IN THE darkness, Jason Tyron swiped a large hand through his dark hair, fighting his own frustration.

He'd told Sophia she shouldn't be out alone at night. Until tonight he hadn't known how dangerous it was.

Another Minot was sniffing around the Ionians. One who was simply going to take what he wanted and the hell with the consequences.

Jason raised his head, scanning the darkness. The other guy had been too cowardly to stay. Probably he wasn't coming back tonight. But if he did, Jason was ready for him.

He began to stalk through the red, dusty soil, prowling the edges of the compound, keeping out of view of the cameras that were part of the defense system.

Once the Ionians would have relied on their own powers for protection, but in the modern age, they used anything that they found practical.

He lived only ten miles away, cross-country. An easy run

through the desert for him. He'd been too wired to go home after he'd freed Sophia's car from the dirt. And too worried about her. He might have disappeared from her view, but he stayed where he could keep track of her all the way back to the spa, pacing her car until she'd entered the gate. He felt a rush of relief when she was safely inside. Relief that she was out of reach of the man who had attacked her.

He also felt a sense of loss. He couldn't reach her either, and he suspected that she wouldn't be coming outside the compound on her own any time soon.

Would she recognize him again when she saw him? He'd been too focused on the unfolding emergency to think about that problem when he'd come to her rescue. But the bastard who'd attacked her had done something to her senses to protect himself. And Jason was hoping that protection might extend to him.

He switched directions, circling the wall, thanking the ancient gods that he had been out that night.

He'd settled here to get close to the Ionians, and not just physically. If he only wanted that, he was sure he could capture one of them and bend her to his will, the way Minot had done down through the ages. But he had something very different in mind.

He'd laid his plans carefully, first with research on the Web, then local snooping, asking questions about the women who ran the fancy spa outside of town.

It was amazing what people thought.

They were seen as clannish or elitist, and maybe arrogant. Some people remarked about the absence of husbands, although girl children were born to them every few years—only girls. That was another mystery. And some wondered if they gave up boys for adoption or murdered them at birth.

There was a rumor that they were lesbians. Or maybe witches. The more conventional detractors saw them as charlatans who charged exorbitant prices at their spa because they pretended to have psychic powers. Still others admired them for their beauty, their business sense, their intelligence, and their values of peace and harmony.

Except where Minot were concerned, of course.

He'd listened and learned and tried to ignore his longings as he'd worked out his plans to get onto the spa compound.

Tonight, pulling Sophia close had made his longing a thousand times worse. He'd felt so much as he'd held her in his arms—too much. Physical sensations like the silky texture of her golden hair. The twin pressure of her wonderful breasts against his chest. Her belly molded to his almost painful erection.

But it was the deeper level that had affected him more profoundly. He'd almost read her thoughts. Almost, but not quite.

Would it be possible if they were more intimate? Or was he just making up justifications for what he wanted most? Because now that he'd held her, the need for consummation burned inside him like a fire devouring him from the inside out.

He'd been warned about the effect an Ionian would have on a Minot. He hadn't been prepared for the rush of need that had bordered on madness. Somehow he'd managed to step away from her before he did something that would damage their relationship forever.

A relationship? Well, not yet.

That was putting too much faith in a chance encounter. But he was sure of one thing. He and Sophia could have something important with each other, if they both wished it. If they had the courage to cut through all the ancient myths that separated them.

He looked up at the nearest camera, waiting until it swung around to point in the opposite direction before darting in and reaching out to grasp the fence that surrounded the compound. The first time he'd done it, he hadn't been prepared for the jolt of sensation that shot through his body. As though electricity were coursing through the metal, although he knew it wasn't actually wired. Now he was used to the tingling.

It came from a psychic barrier that was designed to keep a man like him out. Although he was pretty sure he could break through, he knew that was exactly the wrong approach tonight. He couldn't take this place by force, only by patience and stealth. Which meant he had to repress all the Minot impulses that urged him to seize what he wanted by force and the hell with the consequences.

When the camera began to swing toward him again, he stepped quickly back, out of range.

The Ionians saw the Minot as hard-driving, unhappy, dominating males. Jason was going to prove them wrong—at least about himself.

Or die trying?

That could be the way this quest turned out, because after holding Sophia in his arms, he knew that if he didn't succeed in his goal, he would long for death. The way his father had.

EUGENIA, one of the senior women, stood up gracefully and came toward Sophia.

It was Eugenia who had been there at so many of the pivotal points in Sophia's life. Really, Sophia felt closer to her than to the high priestess, although she had never said so aloud.

When the older woman held out her arms, Sophia came into them. She hadn't realized the effort she was using to hold herself together until she began to shake, struggling against tears.

"It's all right," her mentor crooned. "Just tell us what happened. Everything's going to be all right."

Would it? Or would anything ever be the same again in the world as Sophia knew it?

When she thought she could speak without breaking down, she said, "Something bad happened on the road."

Eugenia inclined her head toward Ophelia, who looked to be the same age as Sophia but was actually ten years older. "Bring her a cup of tea. Peppermint and lemon balm, I think."

Ophelia went to the small kitchen area at the side of the room and got down a mug, then measured crumbled herb leaves into a tea ball.

As she poured in boiling water, the peppermint-lemon scent drifted toward Sophia.

Ophelia set the mug on an end table, and Sophia sat down. When the drink cooled a little, she clasped her hands around the white porcelain, her thumb tracing the spa crest, an ivy and laurel design, on the side.

In a voice she struggled to hold steady, she told about the attack.

"Did you call for help?"

She clenched her fists. "I tried to. But he sprayed a drug in my face."

"How did you get away?"

Sophia swallowed. "I think he would have forced himself on me, but another one came rushing out of the desert. They fought until the attacker took off, and the second one followed." She stopped and dragged in a breath. "He came back, lifted my car, and shoved it onto the road."

"Was that all?" Eugenia asked.

Before she could answer, a voice from the doorway said, "All right. We know enough to understand that we have a serious problem."

They all swung around as Cynthia entered, wearing a silky dressing gown. Her golden curls were tousled. And she hadn't bothered to put on any underwear or makeup. Still she looked both feminine and commanding. And also perceptive.

All of the women dipped their heads, giving her the respect she was due as their leader.

"What did you tell your lover?" Eugenia asked.

Under other circumstances, it might have been an impertinent question, yet they needed to know the answer.

"Nothing. When I sensed there was a matter that needed my attention, I worked a sleeping charm on him." She tipped her head toward Eugenia. "Thank you for handling this for me."

"How much did you hear?"

"I picked up most of it. On the way here, and then as I stood in the doorway." She gave Sophia a direct look, making her clench her hands in her lap. She knew from the way Cynthia was staring at her that she'd caught the intrusion into her privacy.

There was another moment of silence, as the women looked from Eugenia to Cynthia and back again. The high priestess was supposed to keep her finger on the pulse of the spa, but over the past few months, Cynthia had slipped away from her duties more than once.

Most of the women thought that she and Eugenia were heading for a confrontation. Cynthia might retain her position as high priestess, or she might not. Only time would tell.

Cynthia walked toward Sophia and gave her a close inspection. "Could it have been your imagination?"

Sophia blinked at her. She had never considered that—not for a moment. "Why do you ask?"

"You've always been emotional and imaginative, and I know you've had a bad week. Could you be reacting to that?"

She clenched her teeth, abashed that Cynthia had even asked the question in front of her sisters, yet she understood. Better to have one hysterical woman than a real crisis.

"I'm sure it was real," she answered.

"Then it is well to have respect for the power of your enemies. Too bad we've lost some of the knowledge that would help us deal with them."

"What should we do?" Ophelia asked.

"I believe we must join together to consult the ancient powers," Cynthia said in a steady voice.

There were murmurs of agreement.

"Lysandra should stay in the spa, for she has the experience to act quickly in case of trouble," Cynthia said. She looked at Tessa. "Tell Vanessa and Rhoda to join us in the temple."

She turned and led the way to a dressing room with lockers lining the walls. Each of the women took off the clothes she was wearing and placed it in a locker.

There was no modesty among them. Sophia glanced around at her sisters and cousins, seeing the perfection of their naked bodies. They were all excellent specimens of womanhood. All the envy of the guests who came to the spa for meditation, wellness, and healing treatments.

Once undressed, each of them donned the white gowns that transformed them from women of the modern world into their real personas—the descendants of ancient priestesses.

Since they came this way only on solemn occasions and in times of trouble, Sophia could feel tension rippling through the group. When they were all clad in their ceremonial garments, Cynthia approached the far wall, which was made of marble blocks. The rest of the group spread out on either side of her, joining their hands to make a chain of power. Cynthia was the focus. Sophia felt a surge of energy course through them and concentrate in the high priestess.

As she stared at the solid wall in front of her, it began to thin and fade until there was an archway in the middle leading to a flight of stairs.

The women dropped hands to file inside, descending the steps into a secret temple that workmen had built when the spa was first constructed a hundred and seventy years ago. After the structure was finished, the women had wiped the knowledge of the place from the workmen's minds. Since then, none but an Ionian had come this way.

Sophia knew the temple had been carved out of the bedrock under the desert, then roofed over with a massive stone ceiling.

As she descended, she felt cool air drifting toward her, the first touch of this sacred place on her soul.

Below her was deep darkness, until one of the Sisterhood lit a torch, and flickering light sprang to life, revealing three-foot-high marble bas-reliefs, many of them very ancient and carefully preserved.

They depicted the history of the Ionians, with the earliest ones taken directly from their temple in Greece that the barbarians had destroyed.

Those early pictures showed the high priestess kneeling at the altar, asking the ancient goddesses for wisdom and power.

Next came scenes of the barbarian invasion. The Minot fighting them off. The battle with the Minot, and scenes from some of the places where the women had lived. Macedonia. Albania. Xian in China.

And finally, there were pictures of this place, showing the women with their guests at the spa or gathering for private meditation in the gardens and worship in the temple.

Cynthia knelt at the altar now, asking for help and guidance.

For the first time since the frightening encounter, Sophia felt a sense of peace, knowing she was surrounded by her Sisterhood, protected by their joint power.

As Sophia felt the energy of the group sweep through the room, Cynthia turned toward her.

"Come forward."

She stepped toward the altar and turned to face her sisters, with Cynthia beside her.

"We must discover who attacked you. And who . . . rescued you."

Could they? Long ago, powerful men had come from the corners of the earth to consult them, and they had given wise counsel. They had seen things in visions that no ordinary person could know, but that power had faded over the years.

Could they discover their enemies now? Or was that task beyond them?

CHAPTER FIVE

AS CYNTHIA CLASPED a hand on either side of Sophia's head, she closed her eyes.

"Show us the man who forced your car off the road," the high priestess murmured.

She hated to relive that moment in the desert. Still, she struggled to focus on her captor's face, but the gas had blurred her vision.

"Go back to before the gas hit you," Cynthia ordered.

She did as the high priestess directed, and the man's image came clear, making her heart start to pound. Not because he was ugly or horrible but because he was a young, handsome man with almost jet-black hair, hooded dark eyes that burned with ambition, lips that proclaimed a simmering sensuality.

She heard some of her sisters gasp and knew they were seeing the image that had formed in her mind. But it was more than a picture because all her emotions were in play.

Once again, she experienced her own fear, her defiance, and finally her unwanted response.

She felt naked and vulnerable as she stood before the Sisterhood.

"Do you know his name?" Cynthia asked.

Sophia struggled to answer that question, but there was nothing he had done or said that gave her a clue.

When she shuddered in defeat, the high priestess caressed her temples with gentle fingers, soothing her, but only to a degree.

"There was another one?"

She spoke through trembling lips. "Yes."

"He freed you from the first."

Once again she subdued her own needs for the needs of her sisters. For the good of the group, showing them the second encounter.

Although she couldn't see the man's face, she experienced anew all that she had felt when he'd touched her, pulled her body against his.

Arousal surged through her. It should have been a private moment, but being an Ionian meant surrendering privacy.

She stood before her sisters, knowing they were all staring at her and feeling the blood pumping hotly in her veins. She was helpless to hide her reaction from them and helpless to keep from bringing back more subtle aspects of the encounter.

For an instant, she had almost sensed his thoughts. Sensed his need for her.

"Impossible." It was Cynthia who had spoken. "That must be an illusion. Or an effect of the drug."

Sophia didn't answer. Out in the darkness, it had seemed real, but Cynthia had to be right. How could an Ionian sense the thoughts of a man? And not just any man, a Minot.

"Don't focus on the illusion. Do you know *his* name?" Cynthia asked.

Once again, she struggled to obey but only succeeded in summoning a sense of failure.

"Could he have been at the meeting tonight?"

She went back to all the men who had been there. She knew them from her dealings with the business community. He wasn't among them.

"No," she answered, wanting to scream at Cynthia to release her.

Mercifully, the high priestess dropped her hands. As the physical contact snapped, Sophia had to stiffen her legs to keep from falling.

"I think we are finished here," Cynthia said.

Sophia and Cynthia were the last to leave the temple.

"I'm sorry that was hard for you."

"Did I have a choice?"

"There are always choices."

"Even for Ionians?"

"Yes. Even for us," the high priestess answered, and Sophia knew that the woman was thinking about her own personal life and the man who was presently sleeping in her bed.

Neither of them discussed that as Sophia helped the Ionian leader put out the torches before they climbed the stairs.

Cynthia turned, raising her hand, swinging it from left to right, as though she were signaling to someone far away.

The wall solidified once again.

When they were dressed in their street clothes, they joined the others again in the lounge.

As Sophia looked around the room, she wondered if they were an anomaly in the modern world.

Perhaps, but they still had the power and the will to remain true to their traditions.

And what if they didn't? Would that mean disaster for the world? They had been taught that the stability of their order was tied to the fate of the universe. Was that true or only a myth designed to reinforce their will to continue traditions established in ancient times?

Her thoughts were interrupted as Tessa came up to her.

"That was brave of you," her sister whispered.

"We all do what we have to."

"Sometimes I think I'm not strong enough."

"You are," Sophia answered fiercely, even when she wondered if it was true.

Cynthia began to speak, cutting off the private exchange.

"For a long time, our order has enjoyed a period of peace. But it seems clear that danger is gathering around us. We must all be on the alert to make sure that it does not . . . overwhelm us."

Some of the women gasped.

"Can it?" Ophelia asked.

"Not if we are strong and united."

"Our heritage is our strength," Eugenia added.

There were murmurs of agreement.

"But this may not be as serious as it appears," Cynthia continued. "You all remember that the Minot crave us like a drug. It's been in their blood, ever since they rescued us in ancient Greece and lived with us for a time. They wanted more than we were willing to give them. This may simply be an attempt by one of them to separate an Ionian from the group and make her his slave."

Adona spoke up. "Unfortunately, they've passed that down through the generations. Why is that?"

"It may be their pride," Cynthia answered.

It seemed like more than pride to Sophia, but she couldn't come up with a better explanation.

"There were two of them," Adona said.

"Working against each other," Cynthia responded.

"Unless it's a trick to make us think that one of them is . . . different," Tessa answered.

Sophia listened to the conversation swirling around her, longing to get up and go to her own room.

Then a question from Denada riveted her attention. "Did an Ionian and a Minot ever have a good relationship?"

"No," Cynthia said emphatically, but there was something in her voice that made Sophia wonder if it was true.

CHAPTER SIX

RAFE GARRISON'S BICEPS bulged as he pulled himself up on the parallel bar in the Sedona house he'd rented. His heritage had given him a fantastic body, but he never took it for granted. He had thirty-pound weights around his ankles, and after lowering himself to just above the floor, he pulled up again, moving with slow control, making the exercise as difficult as he could.

He was a silent partner in energy companies and firms that made everything from computer hardware and software to sports equipment. In addition, he was heavily into the financial markets.

He would never have to worry about money, and if the world blew up in a nuclear holocaust or went down in a sea of biological contamination, he had huge shelters waiting where he and his descendants could weather any disaster.

But he wasn't going to conceive his children with just any woman. It must be an Ionian. He wanted children with their ancient talents and their ancient wisdom. He would raise them to be loyal to him, and that would give him advanages no Minot had ever possessed.

His plan had been going perfectly until some bastard had come charging out of the desert and screwed everything up.

He could have taken the guy. He'd opted to disappear into the night and regroup. Maybe that was for the best. In fact, maybe fate had chosen a strange way to keep him from going down the wrong path.

He had wanted to cut Tessa out of the Ionian herd, but it had turned out that the woman whose car he'd driven off the road hadn't been her.

"Blood of the gods!"

It should have been Tessa. The woman he wanted above all the others. She'd been scheduled to go to that meeting. Somehow there had been a switch at the last minute, and he hadn't realized it at first.

Because they were all similar types—willowy, blue-eyed blonds just a little above average height. He could have settled on any of them, but Tessa had drawn him most strongly. Tessa.

She wasn't more beautiful than the others, but she had a quality that attracted him. She doubted herself, and he knew he could give her the confidence that had always eluded her. Tied to his power, she could be more than she ever hoped for as simply one of the Sisterhood.

He knew he could help her. Mold her. Teach her. More than that, he burned to possess her.

He'd thought he had her, until a flicker of uneasiness had made him look at her face more closely.

And he'd known that it wasn't her. It was probably her sister, the one named Sophia.

At the very moment doubt had shuddered through him, another man had barged in and changed everything.

Another Minot, sniffing around the Ionians because he couldn't help himself where they were concerned. Sometimes he thought it was a cruel trick fate had played on his race. Or maybe it was something the women had done long ago just before they'd fled the Minot. They'd cursed them with the burning need for what they would forever be denied.

"Damn them to Hades!"

He understood that maddening desire all too well, but he knew how to use it, knew how to turn it around and get exactly what he wanted. He was going to have more than hot sex with one of the hottest women in the world. He was going to use her to become the most powerful man—the most powerful Minot—in history.

But now he must be more careful because they would be on guard. And there was another guy out there, screwing up his plans.

He had to find the other Minot and kill him.

Stamping out of the exercise room, he went to his computer and started looking through property records to see who had bought or rented a house in town in the last couple of months.

When he didn't find anyone who fit, he fought the impulse to throw the monitor across the room.

Maybe the guy was staying at one of the luxury hotels in the area. That would make him harder to find. Or could he be camping in the desert?

Probably the other guy was looking for him, too. Using the same methods. But he wasn't going to find him. Rafe had had one of his men rent the property as a vacation retreat for company executives. Which effectively hid his involvement in the transaction.

SOPHIA hurried to her room, the one place in the spa where she could be entirely alone.

Once she'd closed the door, she leaned back against the barrier, thankful to have some privacy at last after everything that had happened.

She was still hurting, and she wished for a moment that she could summon a man to her bed and lose herself in his arms. Like Cynthia.

Only a few men lived at the spa. One was Tex Somerville, the gym instructor. But some of her sisters were already sleeping with him. Probably he was in one of their beds right now.

And he wasn't the man she wanted anyway.

Without even realizing what she was doing, she went into a little fantasy, imagining herself with the second man from the desert. Here in her room, with the door locked so no one could disturb them. They'd undress each other slowly, sensually, standing beside the bed. Then she'd push him onto the flat surface and roll on top of him. After they'd both come, she'd talk to him about what had happened tonight. He'd kiss her and stroke her and tell her everything was going to be all right. And she'd believe it, because she was with *him.*

Who was he? He must live around here, because he'd come roaring out of the desert when she'd needed him. Could she ask questions in town? Find out who he was?

She drew herself up short, abruptly canceling the plans she was making. What was she thinking? She could have any man she wanted for sex. She couldn't turn to one for comfort. Or a relationship.

Those things must come from the Sisterhood.

She had given up the life an ordinary woman would seek, but she had always known she was blessed to be a member of the ancient Ionian order.

Eugenia had said their heritage was everything, and Sophia had always lived that way, without questioning her loyalty to the greater good.

She didn't usually dwell on the past, but tonight scenes from her life leaped into her head. Like the first time, at the age of eight, when she had read the thoughts of one of her sisters and felt a burst of pride that she'd mastered the ancient skill.

She'd run to Eugenia to tell her, and the other woman had scooped her into her arms, hugging her and sharing her pride.

She'd gathered the group, taken everyone to the temple, and thanked the gods for Sophia's new power.

That had been an amazing moment for her. Other memories were not so happy.

Like the day when Daphne, her mother, had been killed in a rockslide in the desert, and she knew she would never see her again.

There were so many moments when she'd missed her mother terribly. The morning when Sophia had gotten her first period, she had been excited and also terrified by the blood she had found in her underwear, even though sexual information was always part of the Ionians' training, and she'd known the meaning of the flow.

With no mother to go to, she'd sought out Eugenia.

The older woman had hugged her again. "You are coming into your womanhood. And we must take you to the temple to bless this event."

That was the second time she had stood before the Sisterhood, wearing the traditional white robe, receiving the blessing of the high priestess and of the other women of the order. And in the ceremony, Cynthia had reminded her of her duties and responsibilities.

"You can bear children now, although you would never be asked to do that at such a young age. And you will want to wait a few years before you choose your first sexual partner."

She had nodded gravely, feeling very grown-up.

"And when you do, you will come to your sisters first, for no man will ever take the virginity of an Ionian."

She knew what that meant. At least in a vague way, but she put it out of her mind for the time being.

She was dutiful and thoughtful in her life choices. She hadn't looked for a sexual partner until she'd been sixteen, and a young man named Cole had come to the spa with his parents. They'd been attracted to each other and they'd met in the gardens, kissing and touching and driving each other wild with wanting to go on to the next step.

She knew he was the right choice for her first sexual encounter. He was young and attractive. And he wouldn't be staying at the spa when his vacation was over. She could enjoy him in the way of the Ionians, then let him go.

But she also knew what she must do before she could make love with him.

Once again she came to Eugenia, struggling to keep her voice even as she said that she wanted the freedom to enjoy herself with a man.

"I take it you mean a guest at the spa."

"Yes."

"Which one?" Eugenia asked.

"Cole Donovan."

"He's handsome?"

She nodded.

"You've played sex games with him?"

She felt her face heat, although she knew she shouldn't be embarrassed. Sex was a natural part of life, and the Ionian women were free to enjoy their bodies to the fullest. "Yes."

"Does he know how to give a woman pleasure?"

"I think so." He'd aroused her powerfully, and she'd gone back to her bedroom to find her own release because she'd known she must submit to the will of her sisters before she went to bed with Cole.

He wanted to see her that evening. She'd told him she had duties, but she'd see him tomorrow. Then she went with Eugenia to the sisters' private lounge. Cynthia was waiting for them there. And three of the other women, Adona, Denada, and Ophelia.

Sophia felt herself trembling as they'd led her into a ceremonial chamber near the temple and closed the door.

The room was lit by flickering torches. The air was rich with a spicy scent. And thick Oriental carpets softened the stone floor. She had never been here before, but she had been told about this place.

To her right was a high narrow bed. She tried not to look at it and focused instead on soft light wafting from one end of the room where she could see an opulent marble bathroom.

"Disrobe," Eugenia said, her voice commanding and at the same time curiously gentle. How many times had Eugenia been here, performing this ceremony? It wasn't Sophia's place to ask. And she knew she was only posing the question to distract herself.

Willing her mind and body to steadiness, she took off her jeans, then her bra and panties and stood before the other women.

"We start with a ceremonial bath to relax and cleanse you. Climb into the tub."

She walked to the large marble tub and climbed in, sinking into the warm water, her hips resting on the bench at the center and her head cradled by the cushion at one end.

"Discard all your tensions," Eugenia murmured. "It's always better if you let yourself enjoy this."

Could she? Should she think of Cole?

Eugenia must have caught her wavering thoughts.

"Think of your loyalty to your sisters."

"I'm afraid," she whispered.

"Don't be. Just trust us to do what you need and let yourself respond. Every one of us here has done this ceremony before you and understands what you are feeling."

She knew that, and it helped to give her the courage to surrender.

The women clustered around her, slicking their hands with soap.

They washed her body, their hands gliding over her wet skin, moving quickly to intimate places.

She closed her eyes, letting herself enjoy the attention, feeling her nipples tighten and her sex throb.

Denada stroked her with one finger dipping into her vagina, then up to her clit, and she was helpless to do anything besides press her hips forward, striving for release.

But the erotic caress stopped before she was satisfied, making her whimper.

"You're ready," Cynthia murmured.

They helped her out of the tub and toweled her dry, then led her to the high, narrow bed covered with silk sheets.

When she was lying down with her head on a soft pillow, one of them held her arms above her head and two of them held her legs open.

She knew that the position was symbolic—of her subjugation to the will of the Sisterhood, and she didn't fight to free herself.

As three of them held her down, two more aroused her again, one of them tugging and twisting at her nipples and the other standing between her open legs, teasing her clit and the entrance to her vagina until she was writhing on the bed, panting.

It was Cynthia who brought her to climax, stroking two fingers against her clit and into her vagina as Sophia's hips rose and fell, giving her the stimulation she needed to send her flying off into space.

As the climax ebbed, she felt a jolt of pain and cried out, even when she understood what had happened.

"It's done. You're a woman now, free to take any man you desire as a lover."

She opened her eyes and looked at the women standing around her, smiling down at her.

Eugenia kissed her on the cheek. And Cynthia came up to the head of the bed, holding aloft the polished marble phallus that the Ionians had used down through the centuries to deflower their young women.

As she stared at her blood on the shaft, she felt a sense

of pride. She had done what her loyalty to her sisters demanded. And it hadn't been as bad as she'd feared. They had made it good for her, as good as it would be with a man.

Now she was free to enjoy the man who was eager to become her lover.

SOPHIA blinked, coming back to the present. She knew Tessa saw her as some sort of ideal member of the Sisterhood, since she'd always followed the rules.

Once she'd even said that Sophia might be the high priestess one day. Sophia had scoffed at that suggestion, but she had always been loyal to her sisters. Always done what was best for the order. She had expected to do it again in the future. When it was time for her to bear a child to carry on the Ionian traditions, she would find a man who pleased her—and one with the right qualities—and use him for procreation.

Before one of his sperm could penetrate her egg, she would submit to another ceremony in the temple in which the high priestess made sure that the child she carried would be a girl. Even in ancient times, they'd known that it was the man who determined the sex of his child. And they'd used that knowledge to conceive only female children.

Was having a child the best thing for her, or not?

She wasn't used to thinking about what was best for her. But perhaps she should do that now. Before it was too late. Which meant what, exactly?

She was bound to the order in a way that no outsider could imagine. Her life had been written out for her before she was born, and there was no way to change it.

Still she felt powerful stirrings inside herself. The encounter on the road had changed her. For better or worse?

CHAPTER SEVEN

SOPHIA SPENT THE next few days waiting for Cynthia to call her in for a private talk about her eavesdropping.

Even though Cynthia said nothing, she felt nervous every time she saw the high priestess with Matthew Layden. She'd never focused on them before, but now she saw what some of the others were saying about the way Cynthia was wound up with him and neglecting her duties.

But there was more.

Her thoughts kept returning to the man who had rescued her in the desert. Not just her thoughts. Her reactions to him. She couldn't shake the sexual longing and heightened sense of arousal that he had kindled when he'd pulled her into his arms and kissed her.

In an effort to regain her sense of equilibrium, she turned back to her duties, spending more time than she needed to at the tasks she'd been assigned.

She had a master's degree in finance from Arizona State, and she was the sister who took care of the books.

And while Ophelia was in charge of the riding program, Sophia had responsibility for the business aspects of the stable. The previous vet who'd been hired by the spa had been getting old and coming to check the horses less and less often.

She'd used the local business e-mail loop to advertise that she was looking for someone new and had received résumés from several candidates.

The man she favored would be at the spa that afternoon, after the time when guests could take horses out, and she wanted to meet him and observe his work habits. She'd pored over his background, almost as though she was obsessed with him. He was thirty years old, unmarried, and from northern California. And he had an excellent academic background.

After school, he'd gone to the L.A. area, where he'd worked with a company that provided dangerous animals for TV and movies, and he'd been extraordinarily successful in working with big cats and wolves.

Most applicants had included a picture. He hadn't, and she was curious to find out what he looked like.

At five o'clock, she finished balancing the books. After grabbing the folder with the application, she walked down to the corral area.

A blue pickup truck was already pulled up in front of the barn, and she could see a tall, well-muscled man, with a very nice ass, leaning over the fence, feeding a carrot to Becka, one of the gentle saddle horses suitable for guests who were less skilled at riding. It was a casual pose, but she could see that he was nervous. About the interview?

"Dr. Tyron?" she called out.

She watched him suck in a breath and let it out before turning slowly, a bit reluctantly, and in that moment, she *knew*. It was *him*. The man who had come roaring out of the desert to save her from the marauder.

She took in the wary expression in his dark eyes. Yet she knew he was bold. He had dared to come here into the midst of the Sisterhood, where they could do gods knew what to him.

As they stood regarding each other, she felt her heart pounding. She should turn and run back to the main building and inform her sisters that a Minot was on the property. One of the Minot from a few nights ago.

Or was it him? How could it be? No Minot could get past the wards that protected this property.

That thought calmed her. What evidence did she have, really, besides her own jumping nerves? Was she going to condemn this man on a vague suspicion?

She'd never been in this situation before, making a life-and-death judgment, because she knew full well that Cynthia could have him killed in a way that no one would suspect was anything besides natural.

Which meant she had to find out more before she called her sisters for help.

The thought of Cynthia ordering his execution sent a shiver over her skin.

"Are you all right?" he asked.

"Yes."

"I appreciate the job interview," he said, wedging his hands into the front pockets of his jeans.

She gave a little nod, trying to remember what she had been going to say to him. Was she basing her judgment on her reaction to him? Which was strong. Strong attraction, to be exact, as if there was already something between them. Which could be true, if he was the man.

She had never been more unsure of herself, but she couldn't let him know that.

She stopped focusing on her own turmoil and managed to say, "Your academic work looks excellent. And you worked with a doctor"—she stopped and consulted the file—"a doctor Benjamin Hastings at home . . . in Half Moon Bay."

"Yes."

"He gave you a good recommendation."

"We worked well together."

"Why did you decide to relocate to Sedona?"

"I always intended to start my own practice. Half Moon Bay's a small place, and I didn't want to cut in on him."

She nodded, still studying him, still wishing some lightning bolt of intuition would strike her.

Arousal was interfering with the conversation, at least on her part. Was it the same for him?

Realizing that seconds had passed, she threw him one of the professional questions she'd planned to spring.

"What causes thrush on a horse's hoof?"

Without missing a beat, he answered, "Standing in mud, manure, or water."

"What's the standard interval for trimming and shoeing?"

"There's no standard interval. The average time is six to eight weeks between visits from the farrier, but you and your vet need to decide what's best for each individual horse."

She went on to ask him more questions in rapid succession, all of which he answered quickly and to her satisfaction, and she knew he wasn't just some guy pretending to be a horse vet. He knew the subject inside and out.

Did he know her just as well? Know how she was reacting to him? She hoped not.

"We expect our vet to take the initiative and come here frequently to make sure the horses are healthy."

"Yes."

"You seem to have a good handle on the field," she said.

"Thank you."

They discussed payment for services before he asked, "Do I have the job?"

It was a blatantly leading question.

She could have told him she was considering other candidates. But she'd favored him from the first. Because his background was the strongest or because of something else?

"I haven't made up my mind yet."

"All right," he answered, his tone telling her that he knew she was lying. Or was she reading more into the exchange?

She was so off balance that it was hard to keep standing on her feet facing him. He would make the perfect anchor if she rested her hands on his shoulders.

No. That was crazy. She had just met this man. Or had she?

And what if they *had* just met? An Ionian woman was free to take a man she barely knew, if she wanted him.

The thought was still flickering in her mind that she should run from him—run to her sisters—but something had happened to her during the desert encounters that had changed her in ways she was only beginning to understand.

The first man had made her determined not to lose control. The second one had left her feeling defiant.

"I have one more requirement."

Knowing she was picking an odd way to end an interview and wondering if she was playing with fire, she turned and walked into the barn, sure that he would follow.

Most of the horses were in the corral. A few were in their stalls.

Inside, the earthy scent of the stable enveloped her. Some people didn't like it. She always had, and today it added to the feelings rising in her. She walked directly to the hayloft ladder, aware that Jason Tyron was following.

Before she could question her own motivation, she began to climb.

She was breathing hard as she reached the top and stepped back, not because the exertion had winded her. Her excitement mounted as she watched Jason Tyron gain the upper level, then stand facing her.

She wasn't afraid of him, yet her heart was pounding so

wildly that she thought it might break through the wall of her chest.

In the desert, he'd been in charge. She couldn't let that happen now. She must be the one in control.

He didn't speak. Didn't ask why she'd brought him here. And she didn't make him wait for an answer. She closed the trapdoor that sealed the loft, then reached for him, clasping the back of his head, bringing his mouth down to hers for a greedy kiss.

There was no resistance on his part. Far from it.

He slanted his mouth over hers, devouring her like a man who had gone days without food and suddenly had been invited to a banquet.

She reveled in his response, feeling uncensored emotions surge through her—and through him. It was as though the two of them had been waiting for this moment for centuries.

And she couldn't stop now, not when she sensed how much the two of them could mean to each other.

That was a subversive thought. No man could mean more to an Ionian than her bond with her sisters.

But Sophia had lost the ability to reason as his hands moved restlessly up and down her back, gathering her close, sealing them with heat.

They swayed together, and she knew she was in danger of pitching into the straw.

"I want you naked," she gasped out.

"Oh yeah. And you."

He reached for the hem of his T-shirt, pulling it over his head and flinging it into the straw.

She did the same, getting rid of her bra almost as quickly. His hands were busy with the button at the top of his jeans. She followed suit, both of them tearing off their clothing faster then she would have believed possible.

She stared at his wonderful body with its lean lines and taut muscles before focusing on his magnificent erection.

"You're beautiful," he said in a thick voice.

"So are you," she answered as she pulled him into her arms, swaying in the straw with him, then dragged him down with her, flopping to her back and tugging at him so that his body was splayed on top of hers, his cock pressed against her thigh.

He stayed there for a long moment, then drew in a shuddering breath and rolled to his side so that he could take her breasts in his hands, squeezing and shaping them before plucking at the hardened tips.

She lay back, closing her eyes, letting herself enjoy his touch. When he found one sensitized nipple and sucked, she couldn't hold back a sob.

He stroked his free hand down her body, pausing to run his fingers through the crinkly hair at the top of her legs before sliding lower into her folds.

She was already slick and swollen for him, and her hips rose and fell as he plunged two fingers into her vagina, then slid upward to her clit, repeating the maddening stroke, sending her close to the edge.

Her hand found his cock, and she measured his girth with her fist, squeezing and teasing, loving the wonderful feel of him. He was huge, and she grew wetter as she anticipated how he would feel inside her.

When he moved into position between her legs, she guided him into her, thinking that she would instantly push for climax.

But the unexpected happened. It was as though she caught his thoughts—the way she had in the desert. He wanted more from this than just a quick tumble in the hay.

When his needs tugged at her, she brought herself up short.

She had been trained not to worry about her partner's satisfaction. Sex was simple for men. Once an encounter began, the man would take the inevitable path to climax. And the woman must make sure he didn't leave her behind.

But this was different. She cared as much about his pleasure as her own.

When she gasped, he slid his hands under her, tipping her hips so that he could plunge more deeply into her.

He stopped moving then, staring down at her, stirring emotions she had never felt before. Intimacy on a deeper level than she had ever thought possible.

"What do you want from me?" she gasped.

Everything.

Had he said that on the road? Had he spoken aloud?

"I can't."

"Don't fight what you feel." He spoke the words aloud, but she thought she heard them in her head, too.

If she had been the one on top, she might have pulled away. But he had changed the rules before she realized what was happening.

He held the eye contact until her vision blurred as he drove her toward climax with hard, piercing strokes, sending her spinning out into space, more out of conrol than she had ever been in her life.

As she came, she silently called his name.

Jason.

And she heard his silent answer.

Sophia.

From his mind? How could she get into his mind?

Then she was herself again, her heart racing and her breath coming in great gasps.

She had imagined the mental contact. She must have. Because what she'd thought had happened was impossible with a man.

She pushed at him with both hands. "You're heavy."

"Sorry."

He rolled to his back and turned his head to look at her.

Desperate to distance herself from him, she clipped out, "Don't say anything dumb like—was that as good for you as it was for me?"

"I don't have to. I know."

The arrogance of his response gave her the excuse she needed.

Briskly she stood and began gathering her clothing.

She felt a spurt of triumph when she saw hurt and disappointment flash in his eyes. "Where are you going?"

"I have work to do," she answered, knowing that the brusque words gave away her own uncertainty.

She saw him swallow. "Don't go."

"I have to."

"Tell me if I have the job."

"Because you're a good lay?"

"*You* said you had one more requirement."

She struggled not to grit her teeth. She *had* said it. "You have the job," she answered. "But not because of this." She swept her hand across the hayloft.

He looked as if he wanted to say something more, but he was smart enough to keep his mouth shut. Instead he only watched as she dressed and pulled up the trapdoor so that she could escape.

JASON pushed himself up and looked around, shocked that he was in the hayloft. And shocked at what he'd been doing.

He had only a vague memory of following Sophia up here. Lust had wiped everything from his mind but his need for her.

Well, lust was part of it. He knew damn well it was so much more. And she knew it, too, or she wouldn't have gotten dressed and walked away from him.

Had she recognized him from the desert?

He thought so, but she wasn't admitting it. Or had she rushed off to summon a squad of her sisters to strike him down?

He reached for his pants and pulled them on, then the rest of his clothing. When he descended the ladder, only the horses were in their stalls.

He strode past them to his truck, climbed in, and drove toward the gate, trying to sort out his emotions.

The night they'd met, he had vowed not to make love to her until everything seemed right. Then she'd led him up the ladder, and he'd followed like a stallion after a mare in heat, breathing in her tantalizing scent.

No. They'd both been in heat, and the sex had been as mind-blowing as he'd imagined it would be.

But maybe he should have played hard to get.

He laughed. Hard to get! Yeah, he'd been hard all right, and he'd been thinking with his cock, not his brain.

He'd been arrogant like all the Minot. He thought he could control his craving for an Ionian. He'd been wrong. As soon as he'd taken her in his arms, he'd been lost.

His father had told him it was like being offered a drug designed especially for you. His father had been a rational man, and Jason had thought he was just trying to scare his son into caution, but his need for Sophia was everything he'd been warned about.

Yet he wanted so much more than mere sex. He wanted a relationship, and he wanted to find out if that could change everything for him.

He might have blown his chances by following her up there. Worse, by taking control of the encounter.

That was something else he'd learned from his father. The Ionian women thought they had to be in charge in the bedroom, and when they weren't, they would back away.

He clamped his hands on the wheel. No. He wouldn't believe that he had lost her. Lost everything.

He would start again, slowly and patiently. He would let Sophia set the pace.

Of course, she'd done it this time. She'd been fast and direct, and he'd responded without even thinking. Until the moment when her mind had opened to him. And his to her.

He felt a jolt of excitement.

That mind-to-mind communication had been real.

Opened by the sexual intimacy, even though he was sure she would find some way to deny it, until she was ready to accept what the two of them could mean to each other.

"Careful," he muttered. "You've planned everything else in your life. Don't let this be the one time you screw up."

CHAPTER EIGHT

RAFE GARRISON NEVER let moss grow under his feet. After the disaster on the road, he'd chewed out his contact at the spa.

The guy had the skills to do his job at the facility and enough charm to disarm the women. In addition, he was willing to do things for money that most guys would balk at, but that was what made him useful.

Rafe didn't like working through a surrogate, but he was stuck with the inconvenience because there was some kind of barrier that kept him out of the spa.

Not something artificial like he had at home. Something they generated with their psychic powers.

When he'd tried to get in, he'd almost had a heart attack. So he'd given up and found someone to work for him. Too bad the guy wasn't the sharpest tack in the drawer.

The jerk claimed he hadn't known about the change in meeting plans until after Sophia had come home. Rafe didn't like it. He was paying big bucks for information, but he understood that the women could make last-minute changes in their assignments, because they served at the whim of the high priestess or the mother superior or whatever you wanted to call her.

Instead of shouting curses into the phone, he'd gritted his teeth and given the guy another chance to get it right. This time, they were going with a more direct plan. No chances of mistaken identity on the road. And the man knew that if he screwed up again, he was dog meat.

Rafe went to bed feeling satisfied that the situation was under control, even if he hadn't made any progress in locating the other Minot. Nobody who fit the profile had moved into town in the past couple of months. But that didn't mean he was going to give up looking.

He switched his thoughts back to the man at the spa. He had more control over *that* situation. As he lay on his soft Egyptian cotton sheets, he amused himself by thinking about ways to punish the guy if he fucked up again.

He felt peaceful as he'd drifted off. He even got a few solid hours of sleep.

Then he sank into another one of his damn dreams. The dreams that had dogged him all his life. Well, not when he was a boy, thank the gods. Then he might have grown up insane. The torture had started when he'd hit his late teens, and he'd never told anyone about it.

In the dreams he was always a Minot. He wasn't sure how he knew that. But he was sure he was always another man who had lived in an earlier age. And each time the guy ended up with his ass in a sling.

Tonight's was particularly bad. In this version of the old story, he was a man named Dean Conrad from an Arizona mining town called Thunder Hill. The year was 1832. He owned the bank, the hotel, and the livery stable, and with the silver mines outside of town going great guns, he was doing really well. He'd moved to the area because he'd been keeping track of the Ionians. And he knew they were in Sedona, less than thirty miles away.

In the dream, he breathed a sigh of relief because everything was finally going his way.

He had money and power, and he was plotting how to capture one of the women and take her to a ranch he had out in the desert, where he could do anything he wanted with her.

Just as he was about to kidnap the next one who showed up in town for supplies, outlaws came riding up the mudhole of a street—and shot him before he could duck for cover. Townspeople killed two of the gang members and chased away the rest. Some of them carried the wounded Dean Conrad to the doctor's office. But he'd been shot bad—in the guts. There was nothing the doc could do to save his life. He'd lingered on for most of a day, cursing his fate, and died in horrible pain.

Rafe woke in a cold sweat, still feeling the agony of the massive wound. Teeth gritted, he climbed out of bed and stood naked for a moment, staring at the darkness outside the window, before hurrying down the hall to his office, where he booted his computer and looked up Dean Conrad. As he'd suspected would be true, Conrad was a real person whose life and death conformed to the dream.

He'd lived in Arizona. Been the leading citizen of a town called Thunder Hill, and been killed by outlaws invading the town. Only in the official version, he'd died fighting them off.

As far as he knew, that part wasn't true. He didn't even have the satisfaction of justifying his death.

But even if a few details were wrong, how the hell had he dreamed about the man—when he'd never heard of him until tonight?

Struggling to keep his hands from shaking, Rafe switched to a Word file that he'd been keeping for the past few years and added Conrad's name and a bit of information about the guy.

He joined a list of twenty other men who had haunted

Rafe's dreams. Each was a Minot who had done well for himself in the world—then died at the peak of his powers.

None of them was a figure he'd made up from his own imagination. Each of them was real. He'd confirmed that through computer research, each time hoping that the guy wouldn't turn out to be a historical reality.

Stanley Weston was a businessman in Philadelphia in the eighteen hundreds who had been swept away in a flood when he'd gone to inspect a cotton mill he was thinking of buying.

Will Tilden was a railroad executive at the turn of the twentieth century who had died of some terrible illness. Probably of appendicitis.

Ben Gunderson was a German beer maker who'd come to Milwaukee and cornered the brew market—before he'd gotten killed in an accident at one of his own plants.

There were more, but he didn't need to scan the list. He'd memorized it long ago.

He wasn't sure how he knew they were Minot. But he was certain of it, all the way to the marrow of his bones.

To be truthful, he didn't even know what made a man a Minot—not really. Genetics, he supposed. Probably they had a bunch of dominant genes that were passed down from father to son. They must be sex linked, because he'd never heard of a female Minot.

Did all of them dream of long-dead men who had come to grief? He couldn't shake the feeling that he was supposed to learn something from their failures.

And he had!

They'd made him realize that he didn't have complete control of his life. Still, he was determined not to let their failures happen to him all over again.

He'd like to ask the others about their dreams. The problem was, Minot weren't real approachable.

They fought for what they wanted, and that extended to fighting each other. To avoid the conflict that was building between himself and his father, he'd never lived at home after he'd gone away to college and never come back for more than a few days. Even when he'd attended the old man's funeral, he hadn't stayed in the house for long.

Too bad the Minot couldn't join forces the way they had in ancient times. If they could team up, surely they could defeat the damn Ionians.

Maybe the last time they'd worked together was when they rescued the Ionians from the barbarians. The way he'd heard it, after the big blowup over the women's escape, the Minot had all blamed each other. They'd been too angry to work together again, ever. Maybe the damn women had cursed them. And even if they could now join forces, then what? Each of them would want the spoils of victory for himself, and only one of them could climb to the top of the heap.

Of course, he did have a line on someone who he thought would join him in the current project. A man who'd had reasons to hate the Ionians.

That made the guy vulnerable, and Rafe was going to pitch his case to him once he had Tessa safely away from the compound.

BEFORE dinner, Tessa tiptoed down the hall and slipped into the private library that the Sisterhood maintained. After stepping into the darkened room, she closed the door quietly behind her, breathing in the atmosphere of the room.

In the public part of the spa, there were books that guests might read, novels or interesting nonfiction.

But this small room was different. These books held the wisdom of the Ionians. Some explained how to work ceremonies and cure illnesses. Others described psychic powers and how to cultivate them. A few even had information on the Minot.

Some of the sisters were transcribing the information

into electronic form, but she suspected that one book would always be kept in writing.

It was a volume that Demeter, their teacher in Ionian studies, had shown them in one of their indoctrination classes.

Tessa hadn't thought of the lessons that way when she'd been a little girl. Instead she'd been fascinated by the history of the Ionians and the training in using their psychic powers.

Now she knew that the special schooling had been designed to make the girls want to grow up and take their place as members of the Sisterhood.

She'd been intrigued by this particular book all those years ago but hadn't questioned any of the information. Now she thought it might be pertinent.

After Sophia had come home from the attack on the road, Tessa had asked Cynthia if any of the Ionians had left the order. The high priestess had answered in the negative, but Tessa couldn't stop wondering if that was really true.

She turned on the light, then scanned the library shelves and didn't see the book she was looking for.

Taking a deep breath, she forced herself to give the room a closer inspection and found a locked cabinet under the shelves opposite the window. The lock might have stopped her, but she was too determined to give up. Again she searched and found a small gold key in a drawer above the cabinet doors.

It fit the lock. Inside the cabinet was the book she remembered, bound in white leather.

Crossing to one of the comfortable armchairs, she sat down and began to turn the pages. It was a list of all the Ionians, down through the ages, copied from old scrolls and kept up to date by the order. The first entries were in ancient Greek, and she couldn't read them. Then they switched to modern languages. Spanish. Albanian. Chinese. Now they were in English.

As a girl, she'd been thrilled to see her own name and

date of birth in the list. And saddened to see the notation on her mother's death.

But what if an Ionian had been born into the order who was missing from the sisters at the spa, and there was also no record of her death?

Turning backward through the most recent entries, she began looking for the births of all the women currently here.

She could account for all the Ionians now at the spa, until she came to an entry that stopped her.

Linda.

Tessa's heart began to pound.

Apparently she'd been born in the first years of the twentieth century. According to the book, she hadn't died. But she wasn't here, either.

Which must mean that she had left the group and not returned.

Unless there was some mistake in the book, which Tessa couldn't believe, not when all the records had been kept so meticulously.

So where was Linda? Had she died under mysterious circumstances? Was she AWOL?

Tessa shivered. Or had something worse happened?

She kept looking and found another name. Chandra. She had been born in the mid-1940s and never died either, as far as the record was concerned.

The last name she found was Julia, from the late 1940s. Again, missing in action.

Who were they? Had they all met the same fate? Did Tessa dare ask about them?

CHAPTER NINE

FRUSTRATION HAD JASON plunging back into the search he'd started for the other Minot. He could imagine the guy was doing the same thing, plowing through property records, looking for the rival who had foiled his plans in the desert.

But Jason was sure the other guy wouldn't find him because he'd prepared too well. He'd bought his house five years ago, and rented it out until he was ready to move to Sedona. Which meant that nobody was going to find him in any recent property transfers. And if anybody started asking around town, he didn't think they'd connect a Minot with the new vet.

Was the other Minot as methodical?

Jason had made a list of recent property transfers in the area and also rentals, and he'd been checking out the purchasers and renters.

So far he hadn't come up with anything he could take to the bank. But he had lots of time to keep searching.

Or maybe he should go back to the spa and give all of the horses a physical exam—whether they needed it or not. Maybe Sophia would come down to the stable again.

If she didn't, that would be worse than staying away on his own.

WHEN a light tap sounded at Sophia's door, she sat bolt upright in bed imagining that Jason Tyron had somehow come to her room.

But he wouldn't dare!

It must be one of her sisters. Quickly she got out of bed and crossed the tile floor. When she opened the door, she found Tessa standing in the hallway.

"May I come in?" her sister asked.

"Of course."

As Tessa stepped into the room and closed the door behind her, Sophia turned on a bedside lamp.

Her sister peered at her. "I'm sorry I woke you."

"I wasn't sleeping."

Tessa scuffed her foot against the tile floor. "I came to ask you a favor."

"If I can."

"Can you help me see the future?"

Sophia sucked in a sharp breath. "You know that neither one of us was very good at that."

Tessa's voice took on a note of desperation. "I know. But I'm afraid. I feel like everything's changing."

Sophia understood because it was true for her, as well. She'd been lying awake, worrying about Jason Tyron. Maybe this was her chance to find something out.

"I want to feel . . . safe," her sister said.

Sophia understood that, too. Still, she wasn't sure they could accomplish anything.

"The temple would be best, but we can't go down there

alone, and I don't want to talk to anyone else about this," Tessa murmured.

"We can use the altar in here," Sophia answered, gesturing toward the table that sat in front of the window. Since she might bring a lover to her room, it looked like an ordinary piece of furniture. Opening the drawer in front, she took out a length of fine lace, a solid gold plate, and a fat candle.

After spreading the lace along the width of the table, she set the candle on the plate and lit it.

The sisters each knelt on the small rug in front of the table, joining hands and closing their eyes the way they'd done as girls.

Sometimes they'd felt a flicker of future knowledge, but nothing that had ever helped them or made them feel more secure.

She felt Tessa tense and knew she was groping for images of events that hadn't happened yet.

Although she wanted to know her own future, it stretched in front of her like a great void. But maybe she could help Tessa.

She couldn't exactly read Tessa's thoughts, but she felt a mental joining.

"Focus on what will be," Tessa murmured. "On our lives as they unfold."

Sophia tried to do as her sister asked, but she could pick up nothing concrete, only Tessa's desperate desire to discover what was ahead.

She felt the strain—her own and Tessa's. She wanted to give up a struggle that was obviously useless.

Then she picked up something from her sister's mind.

"Who is Linda?" she whispered.

"You caught that from my thoughts?"

"Yes."

"She's someone we don't know."

Sophia was going to ask another question when an image

leaped into her mind. She saw a large building looming in front of her. A church, she thought, but she couldn't be sure. Smoke billowed around it.

"What?"

Tessa gasped, and pulled her hands away.

CHAPTER TEN

SOPHIA'S EYES SNAPPED open. "What did you see?"

"Nothing."

"A church. Burning."

"I'm not sure."

"Then why did you break the connection like that?"

Tessa turned her head to the side. "I . . . don't know."

When she scrambled up, Sophia also stood, then leaned down to put out the candle.

"Tell me what frightened you."

"Nothing specific. Just a vague . . . dread."

That was a lie, Sophia knew. There had been something specific. Something that had alarmed them both.

"About Linda?"

"I don't know." Tessa was already out the door, leaving Sophia shaken.

She'd been in bad enough shape. She didn't need to take on Tessa's burdens as well.

Sophia couldn't go back to sleep. Finally, she got up and went to her office, where she struggled to focus on work.

Did her future merge with Jason Tyron's?

Impossible. Her future was with her sisters.

Yet she was guarding her thoughts from them, lest one of her sisters discover what had happened in the hayloft. She had no shame about enjoying sex with a man and walking away from him.

It was the other part that worried her, the sense of connection with him that she never should have felt.

Worse, she still didn't know who Jason Tyron was. Not really.

If he was a Minot, he could even be the one who had attacked her in the desert.

As soon as that idea surfaced, she thrust it roughly away. She might be looking for excuses to mistrust him, but she didn't have to go that far. She'd have known if it was him. When the attacker had touched her intimately, she hadn't liked it. But she had liked Jason Tyron's touch—very much.

She'd thought again about hooking up with the hunky gym instructor, Tex Somerville, who'd been hired for his sex appeal as well as his knowledge of weight machines, aerobics, and fat-burning routines.

But she couldn't work up any enthusiasm for him, not when she compared him to Jason.

Speaking of which . . .

She looked out the window and saw his blue truck shining in the morning sunlight.

She should be making surprise visits to the stables to see how he was getting on with the horses. In fact, Ophelia was doing that from time to time.

If anyone noticed that Sophia was staying away, they didn't comment. When she got questions about how the new vet was doing, she always answered, "Fine," knowing that sooner or later she was going to have to make a decision about the man.

Like, was she endangering her sisters by not admitting her suspicions? She hated to think that was true.

She had never felt more unsure of herself. Never felt more like she was simply going through the motions of her duties. But even when her heart wasn't in her work, there was no escape from the details of daily life. She had a quick breakfast in the lounge, then went to check on the stock in the gift shop.

Some of the sisters rotated working there, especially the younger ones who had recently been assigned jobs at the spa. Some of them liked selling beautiful jewelry and crafts and reading material to spa guests. Others felt it was a waste of their talents.

This morning, Tessa was behind the counter, and she looked up, catching Sophia's eye, sending her a silent message that she wanted to discuss something.

Was she finally going to talk about the night they'd tried to see the future together? With equal parts anticipation and dread, Sophia walked into the shop.

Two women were there, one in her fifties, the other closer to seventy and leaning on an ebony cane with a silver dragon head.

The older one purchased a couple of books on meditation and gentle yoga and left. The second one, a well-off matron, lingered longer. Some guests were curious about the Ionians and asked a lot of questions. Maybe she hoped to see Tessa and Sophia exchanging a secret handshake, because she kept glancing at them as she fingered the expensive silver and turquoise jewelry that the spa took on consignment from local artists.

Sophia also examined the stock, seeing that they were getting low on books about the Sedona area and on natural healing. Moving to another section of shelves, she rearranged some of the herbal products that the sisters made at the spa, lining up jars that patrons had moved around.

The customer had walked over to a display of crystal pendants.

"Which do you think looks best on me?" she asked Tessa, holding two up.

"I think the white quartz. But you might think about what effect you want from the crystal."

"Such as?"

They went into a discussion of the properties of the various specimens, after which the woman bought the white one that had first caught her eye.

When the guest had left, Tessa shook her head. "Do you think working in a gift shop fulfils my destiny as an Ionian?"

"It's not the only thing you do here. You give a lot of the treatments, and some of our guests specifically ask for you."

"But clerking in the shop always feels so superficial. I should have gone to college the way you did. Then I could help with the accounting or something."

"You could start taking classes at the university, if that's what you want to do. Or tell Eugenia you'd like to be more involved in . . . management," she said.

"I don't like to ask for changes in assignments."

Sophia understood that, too. She wasn't going to try to get out of overseeing the work of the vet. But maybe her reasons were different. Maybe she wanted an excuse to go down there.

But not yet.

Tessa glanced toward the door, then spoke again. "It makes me question . . ."

"Question what?"

"What we're doing here. I mean, have the Ionians outlived their purpose? And they're just going through the motions."

"I hope not," Sophia murmured, remembering she'd had similar thoughts herself.

"You really believe we have some vital function in the world?" Tessa whispered. "Like keeping the balance between powers or something? Maybe we did when rulers came to consult us. Running a spa doesn't feel quite so important."

Sophia shrugged. Again, she'd had the same thoughts.

Tessa looked toward the door, then back again.

"When we were trying to see the future, you asked me about Linda."

"Who was she?"

"She's like Julia and Chandra. You don't remember any Ionians with those names, do you?"

Sophia shook her head.

"We need to talk about them."

"Why?"

"They could be important."

Sophia opened her mouth to say something else, but before she could, Tex Somerville came in.

"I'm looking for a piece of jewelry," he said. "I want it to be special."

Tessa nodded. "I'm sure I can help you."

"We can talk more later," Sophia said to her sister, wondering if it was some kind of omen that Tessa had wanted to discuss some of the same topics that had occupied Sophia's mind for the past few days. Or did this happen to all Ionians when they got into their late twenties?

For years, she'd never questioned her way of life. It was just the path of her existence. Then the encounter on the road had shaken the foundation of her world.

As she left the gift shop, she saw Bobby Ames, the handyman, come in through an outside door, carrying his toolbox. He paused and looked toward the gift shop entrance and stopped for a moment. It seemed like he was looking at Tessa.

When he saw Sophia, he nodded. "I got a call on a stopped-up sink."

Before she could reply, he continued down the hall.

She hadn't seen him since the night she'd come back from

the desert. Was it a bad omen that she had met him again now? Or was she looking for signs and portents in everything that happened?

Maybe it would be more constructive to go down to the stable and confront Jason Tyron.

And say what?

Perhaps it was better to see what *he* had to say.

She left the main building and walked down the hill to the stable. Jason had his medical bag with him, and he was examining the hoof of one of the horses as she approached.

With his back to her, she had a chance to study him, taking in his broad shoulders, narrow waist, long legs. He was a perfect physical specimen. The kind of man she'd choose to father a daughter.

The idea took her by surprise. She wasn't thinking about a daughter. Not yet, and maybe not at all. If she couldn't be sure of the Ionian values, how could she teach them to her child with any kind of integrity? She was glad she wasn't involved with teaching any of the young girls in the order. What would she say to *them* if they asked her any questions?

As those thoughts flashed through her head, she saw Jason's shoulders stiffen, telling her he knew someone was behind him. Probably he was hoping it was her. Or maybe not.

She snorted softly, annoyed that she was making up thoughts for him.

Folding her arms, she let him finish what he was doing before he set down his tools and turned, regarding her with a mixture of caution and anticipation.

Determined to let him make the first move, she remained silent.

"It's good to see you," he finally said.

She nodded, wondering if she should ask if he was the man who had rescued her in the desert.

And why would he tell the truth, if he was?

"You've been avoiding me."

Somehow, unexpected words came tumbling out. "I didn't know what to say to you."

A look she couldn't read crossed his features. "Why?"

She turned one hand palm up. "Things . . . happened too fast between us . . ."

"You could be right. I was thinking the same thing when you left so abruptly. We should have talked, but you made that impossible."

Of course she had. Deliberately. Today she was confronting him in a less threatening situation. "What do you want from me?"

He hesitated.

"Whatever it is, you won't get it unless you're honest."

He kept his gaze even. "Okay. You know there's something between us."

"Sex."

"More than that."

"And your point is?"

"I want a relationship. Not just a roll in the hayloft."

Other men had hinted at the same thing, although none had been so blatant about it. It had been easy to brush them off. Not this time. Still, she wasn't going to explain the Ionian philosophy of man–woman relations to him. That wasn't something they shared with their sexual partners. Or anyone else besides their sisters, come to that.

Instead, she said, "Maybe I'm not comfortable with . . . a relationship."

He lifted one shoulder. "You asked for honesty."

"I'm being honest, too."

"Where does that leave us?"

"I don't know."

If she expected an argument, she didn't get it. "Okay. I won't push you on the personal stuff, but we do have business to conduct. You're my liaison at the spa. How do you know I'm doing a good job?"

"I researched your background. I don't think you'd give us less than your best. Besides, Ophelia is in charge of the riding program. She's got a lot of responsibility for evaluating your performance."

"Okay."

"I could ask someone else to work with you on the business end," she added.

He kept his gaze steady. "You think hiding from me is the solution?"

"I'm not hiding!"

"What reason would you give your boss for trying to get out of the job?"

"What do you mean, my boss?"

"You don't run the spa, do you?"

"Of course not," she answered, ducking the other part of the question. She wasn't going to tell him that any Ionian would understand if she said she wanted to avoid spending too much time with a particular man.

"Have you ever thought about what's best for you?" he asked.

The question took her by surprise. "What do you mean?"

"Do you consider your own happiness when you make big decisions?"

"Why wouldn't I?"

He kept staring at her. "You tell me."

They were getting close to subjects she shouldn't be discussing with him. More than that, it seemed like he was hinting that he knew more about the Sisterhood than he should. What if she asked point-blank if he was a Minot? Not just any Minot, but the one who had saved her from the first guy. Would he even tell the truth?

She settled for, "That's none of your business."

"Maybe it is."

Before he could say something else shocking, an alarm bell began an insistent ring.

CHAPTER ELEVEN

THEY BOTH TURNED toward the spa in time to see a window shatter, followed by smoke pouring into the afternoon sunlight.

"Fire!" Jason shouted, already charging up the hill toward the burning building.

Sophia followed, but he was running faster than she, faster than any normal man could run. Like the night in the desert.

He reached the area around the building and stopped, surveying the scene.

Denada was outside, her arm protectively around one of the guests, a red-haired woman wearing only a large towel. She must have been having a massage when the bell started ringing.

As Sophia joined them, she heard him ask, "How many people are in there?

"Fifteen . . . of my sisters and twenty-two guests," Denada

answered. "I . . . I hope that's correct. I didn't look to see who was checking in this morning."

"We have to make sure they're all safe." Jason headed for the source of the smoke.

Sophia watched Ionians and guests pouring out of the building. She tried to make sure that everyone was safe, but they were moving around, making it difficult for her to keep an accurate count. To her relief, she saw Tex Somerville and some of her sisters helping guests leave, then leading them into the shady parts of the gardens where they sat on benches or stood around in small groups, staring back at the building.

Cynthia came out, looking like she couldn't believe what had happened.

"How did it start?" Jason asked.

Nobody answered, and Sophia wondered if they'd find out.

Cynthia tipped her head to the side as she regarded Jason. "Who are you?"

"The new vet Sophia hired last week. Is everybody out?"

Denada answered. "I think Mrs. McFadden was in the meditation room by herself. She wanted privacy."

"And she's not here?"

Denada craned her neck, looking over the crowd in the garden. "No."

"Where is the meditation room?"

The high priestess gestured toward the entrance. "Down the hall. The third door on the left."

When Jason started for the entrance, Sophia gasped. "You can't go inside."

"I think there's more smoke than fire."

"Smoke can kill you as quickly as fire."

"I'll keep low." He turned and gave her a direct look. "Stay outside, take care of the guests, and find out if anyone else is missing."

When he bent at the waist and charged inside, Sophia's heart leaped into her throat.

He didn't know the woman in there, but he was risking his life because he was at the spa, and there was someone in danger.

She ached to go after him, but she knew that he was right. There was work to do out here. And she suspected he had a much better chance in there than anyone else.

JASON kept his breath shallow as he looked around, making sure he knew where he was. He'd never been inside the spa before, and this was a hell of an introduction.

The woman who had told him where to find the meditation room was probably Cynthia, the high priestess.

He'd seen her picture in some of their advertisements. Of course, they had called her the spa director, but he'd known what that meant.

He'd also seen a layout of the spa and studied it. Just as he'd studied everything else he could about the Ionians.

When he'd gotten his bearings, he started down the smoke-filled corridor, the sound of the alarm bell ringing in his ears, adding to the disorientation of the smoke. His eyes stung, and when he took a breath, he started to cough, but he kept going because he had never given up easily.

If there was a woman trapped in here, he was going to get her out.

As he moved down the corridor, he braced for a wall of fire somewhere ahead, but he saw no flames. It was almost like someone had set off a smoke bomb in order to get everyone out of the building. But who would do that? And why?

The hairs on the backs of his arms prickled. Could the man who had captured Sophia in the desert have gotten in here? And now he was trying again?

He cursed under his breath. He'd left Sophia out in the garden with the guests and the other Ionians. Suppose she was in danger?

He stopped for a moment. Should he go back? But what

about the woman who was still in here? He'd said he'd get her out, and he couldn't abandon her.

And if he was thinking rationally, he'd have to believe that Sophia was okay. The guy from the desert wasn't at the spa. He would give off "bad vibes." And the wards the women had set around the compound would pick them up.

Or could he have sent someone into the compound? Someone who was acting for him.

Those thoughts raced through his mind as he plunged down the hall, trying to finish his mission and get out as soon as possible. Yet he couldn't move too fast because he might miss the door.

The smoke thickened as he went, and he almost missed the meditation room. It was closed, and when he slipped inside, he saw a woman who looked to be in her seventies cowering in the corner farthest from the exit.

When she saw him, she gasped, then wheezed, "Thank God. I closed the door when I smelled the smoke."

"That was the right thing to do. Are you Mrs. McFadden?"

"Yes." Fear and relief warred on her face. "I didn't know if anyone would come."

"I'll get you out of here." He looked around. They were in an interior room with no windows, which meant he'd have to go back the way he'd come.

"What happened? Is the building on fire?" she asked in a trembling voice.

"There's smoke. I didn't see any fire." He crossed the room, slung his arm round her, and guided her back to the door.

"I have a bad hip. I can't run very fast."

"You don't have to. I'm going to carry you. When I say 'now,' take a couple of deep breaths, then hold the last one." He picked her up, cradling her in his arms, and she reached up to sling her arms around his neck. To a man with his strength, her weight was nothing.

"Now."

They both breathed deeply several times. Then he held his breath and started back the way he'd come, moving at superhuman speed but still relieved that the smoke wasn't as thick as it had been.

SOPHIA stared at the people milling outside in a chaotic mass.

She saw Matthew Layden with his arms protectively around Cynthia, comforting her. But he made no move to go back into the building.

Switching her focus from the high priestess and her lover, she began naming each of the Ionians. Most of them seemed to be here. And the young girls were all off to the side with two sisters.

Sophia was starting to relax a little until she realized she didn't see Tessa and gasped.

Ophelia, who was standing beside her asked, "What?"

"Tessa. She's not here."

When she started for the nearest door, her cousin grabbed her shoulder. "You can't go in there."

"I have to. I know where she was. I saw her in the gift shop a little while ago."

"That's on the other side of the building. She probably went out the other way."

"I'll go around."

She left the group, heading for the other side of the spa, when a cry for help crackled in her brain.

Help me. Please help me.

It was Tessa, calling to her.

Where are you? Inside?

No. He's got me.

Who? she desperately asked.

Ames.

That made no sense. Ames? The handyman. Why would

he have Tessa? Had he rescued her, and the smoke had made her confused?

She had to find out what was going on.

Where are you?

The parking lot.

She ran in that direction and saw the man's white van. The back door was open, and Ames was forcing a struggling Tessa inside. A bucket lay on the ground beside the vehicle.

Sophia gasped and leaped forward.

"Tessa's in trouble. Help her," she shouted aloud and in her mind.

Someone streaked up beside her, then tore past, and she realized it was Jason.

Before Ames could close the door, Jason reached the man and grabbed him, yanking him away from the struggling woman.

The handyman grunted and tried to spin around, but Jason threw him to the ground.

Sophia left the abductor to Jason and scrambled into the van, where she found her sister lying across the backseat, her hands and feet bound. A gag in her mouth prevented her from talking, and she stared at Sophia with frightened eyes.

"It's all right. I've got you."

She pulled the gag from Tessa's mouth, then began working on her sister's bonds.

"Thank the fates," Tessa gasped.

"What happened?"

"He came into the gift shop and closed the door. When I asked him what he was doing, he leaped behind the counter and grabbed me. First he stuffed the gag in my mouth, then he put a metal bucket over my head, tied me up, and wrapped me in a blanket. I could smell smoke in the hallway. Did he set a fire?"

"It looks like it."

"When I struggled with him, the bucket fell off, and I reached you."

"Thank providence."

Sophia helped Tessa from the van and gasped when she saw Jason on the ground grappling with the handyman. Jason was breathing hard, and she knew the smoke inside the building had affected him. He was fighting with Ames when he should be flat on his back, resting.

Still, with his superior strength, Jason was winning. Ames managed to wrench away and lunge for his toolkit. Hammers, screwdrivers, and other equipment spilled onto the pavement. Scrabbling through the mess, he closed his hand on a wrench, which he brought down on Jason's head.

Jason went slack, and Ames heaved himself up, his gaze fixed on Tessa.

"Run," Sophia screamed.

She backed away as Ionians who had heard Sophia's call were already rushing toward her. And Matthew Layden, Cynthia's boyfriend, came jogging up. All of them put themselves between Ames and Tessa.

Sophia ran to Jason where he lay on the ground. Blood oozed from his hair, and his eyes were closed.

From the corner of her vision, she could still see Ames looking frantically around for an escape route, as the Ionians surrounded Tessa. Joining hands, they made a circle of power, protecting their sister from harm. Ames cut his losses, and ran back toward the van.

Layden made a grab for him, but he shook the man off, jumped into his vehicle, and roared away, the back door still flapping as he sped out of the parking lot and toward the gatehouse.

The guard stepped out, his gun in his hand. "Stop or I'll shoot," he shouted.

Ignoring the warning, Ames kept barreling toward the gate.

The guard raised his weapon and fired, the sound of the shots like firecrackers, but Ames ducked low and kept going.

As he approached, the guard jumped out of the way, and

the van roared past, snapping the wooden barrier before continuing down the access road in a cloud of dust.

Sophia was torn between her sister and Jason, who still lay on the ground.

"Stay with him," Tessa whispered as she saw the distress on her sister's face.

Sophia had no idea what to do as she crouched over him. Try to wake him? Or was that dangerous?

Bending toward him, she touched his cheek and asked, "Jason. Are you all right, Jason?"

His eyes blinked open and focused on her. After a moment, he answered, "I'm fine."

She looked at the pool of blood that was collecting under his head.

"Your head is bleeding. You need to go to the hospital," she murmured.

"No. I'll be okay." His voice sounded groggy. He reached up to touch his scalp, then brought his hand back, his fingertips smeared with blood. "Remember, I'm a vet. I know head wounds bleed a lot."

"And you know you were unconscious. You might have a concussion."

He shrugged, then winced.

When he tried to sit up, she put a firm hand on his shoulder. "Lie still."

Paramedics, who had arrived with the fire trucks, came trotting up. "Out of the way, miss." They began working over Jason, and Sophia took several steps back, watching his eyes follow her.

"They'll take care of you," she said, then added, "Thank you for saving Mrs. McFadden—and Tessa." She knew that the thanks were inadequate. He'd risked his life twice in the space of a few minutes for women he didn't even know.

She could see he wanted to talk to her, and she wanted to talk to him, but how could they say anything personal in front of the gathered Ionians? As far as anybody knew, he was only the new vet. Nothing more to her than that.

And what was he to her, exactly?

She wanted to find out, but that was impossible now.

"Later," she mouthed, then turned to her sisters.

Cynthia was speaking to Tessa, asking what had happened, and Tessa repeated the story.

"I think this is like the attack on the road," she finished. "When a Minot went after Sophia. Only it was supposed to be me."

Cynthia glanced at the crowd around them, not just Ionians, but guests and also Layden.

"We will talk of this later," she said, obviously aware of the listening ears. "I have . . . other duties."

"Of course," Tessa murmured.

The circle of Ionians closed around her again, and Sophia knew that they were sending her reassuring thoughts, but they would have to discuss this later.

As Sophia thought about the implications, she shivered.

Ames had tried to kidnap Tessa. Did that mean Tessa had really been the target the other night, since she was supposed to go to the meeting? And only chance had put Sophia in harm's way?

Cynthia strode over to one of the firemen, asking what he had determined about the origin of the smoke.

"It was definitely arson," he said. "We found a pile of wood shavings and other debris that had been set on fire, but it looks like it was designed to create more smoke than flames."

"I guess that's lucky," she answered.

To get everyone's attention, Sophia thought. So he could go after Tessa. And he obviously hadn't cared if someone else—like Mrs. McFadden—died in the attempt.

Cynthia and the fireman continued to talk, as Layden came up beside her.

She glanced at him, then back at the man who was giving

her information. Her stiffness must have conveyed her disapproval, because Layden stepped back. It was obvious to Sophia that the high priestess didn't want to deal with her lover while she conducted urgent business.

An expression of annoyance crossed his face, but when he saw Sophia looking at him, he quickly rearranged his features.

Sophia turned toward Tessa. She wanted to comfort her sister and get more information from her. At the same time, she wanted to go to Jason and make sure he was all right.

From the corner of her eye, she saw the medics load him in an ambulance. And then he was gone, and she was left with her sisters. The Sisterhood that had sustained her throughout her life. She'd always felt sheltered and comforted by them. Not now.

CHAPTER TWELVE

THE EMERGENCY WAS under control. There was minimal fire damage to the spa, and the Ionians were taking care of their guests.

When Matthew came up to her again, Cynthia allowed him to draw her into a quiet alcove where they could be alone.

"Are you all right?" he asked.

"No." She looked toward the center of activity. "And I can't stay here with you."

"You're allowed to take a breather," he said in that deep voice that always soothed her. She'd watched women at the spa with their husbands. Sometimes she envied their lives. They could let the man make the decisions, if they wanted to. Leaving them free to relax and have fun. But often it wasn't an equal partnership. The man would have too much power, making the woman weak and needy.

She drew herself up taller. "I have to stay on top of the situation."

He nodded with resignation. She'd told him some things

about the Ionians that few outside the Sisterhood were aware of, like their status as the descendants of an ancient religious order. But he didn't know any of their real secrets. She'd kept them from him, and at the same time, she felt guilty about telling him too much.

He'd started at the spa as just one of the guests. Most of their clients were women. But some men came, partly because they were attracted to the Ionians. Which suited them perfectly because they had their pick of the crop.

When she'd shown interest in him, her sisters had deferred to her. She'd begun an intimate relationship, thinking that she would use him the way all the women in the order used men.

When he'd gone away, she'd been lonely—and delighted when he showed up again. He'd come back every few months, and their relationship had developed over time.

Now she didn't know what she would do without him. Which was a bad position for her to be in. As the high priestess, she must give her complete allegiance to the Sisterhood. She would owe her sisters that, even if she were just one of the ordinary women in the order. Well, none of them were ordinary, but few had achieved her status.

Would she be happier if she gave up the leadership? Sometimes that was tempting, but it wouldn't solve her feeling of divided loyalty. And it would give her less power. Suppose Eugenia were high priestess and demanded that Cynthia give up her lover? What would she do then?

"Are you going to have a meeting?" Matthew asked.

"Yes."

"Come to me after that."

"If I can," she said, pulling away from him and going back to her duties.

RAFE Garrison was a master of keeping his emotions to himself—when it suited him. It made him an excellent poker player any time he sought that kind of relaxation.

This was the day he'd been waiting for. The day Bobby Ames was going to bring Tessa to him.

Then he'd get rid of the man, so there would be no one to talk about what had happened. But he'd dispose of him in a humane fashion, as a reward for a job well done.

When Ames called, Rafe knew at once that something was wrong.

"You have the package I ordered?" he asked in an even voice, unwilling to spell out his business over the phone in case someone was listening—or recording the conversation. He didn't know who that might be, but he wasn't going to take a chance on saying anything that could be used against him later.

"There was a problem."

"You'd better get over here."

"I . . ."

"Don't think about running," he advised. "If you do, I'll track you down, and when I find you, you'll wish I hadn't."

"I'll be there in a few minutes."

Rafe paced back and forth, his hands balled into fists. He was fair with his employees, but he had given an assignment to Ames, and the man had failed him—twice. There must be a steep price to pay.

When Ames's van came trundling up the driveway, Rafe stepped outside to meet him, grasping a metal cylinder in his hand, but holding his arm down by his side, the way he had after he'd forced Sophia's SUV off the road. But this was a different formula. Something designed to put Ames out for an hour or so.

Ordering himself not to rush forward, he eyed the bullet holes in the front and side of the vehicle.

What the fuck had happened?

When Ames got out and approached him, he said, "That van I bought's all shot up, and you don't even have Tessa, do you?"

"I had her." He began to talk rapidly. "I set the shavings

on fire, and added the stuff to make them smoke. That worked great, and everybody was running around the spa like a bunch of chickens with their heads cut off. I got into the gift shop and tied her up and put that bucket over her head like you told me to do. But it fell off in the van, and one of her sisters came charging out and stopped me from leaving."

"You idiot! I told you to make sure she couldn't . . ." He stopped. What was he going to say? Make sure she couldn't send a mental message to her sisters? He'd told Ames to use the bucket to confuse her and keep her from seeing where she was going. He couldn't tell him the truth.

Instead, he asked in a deadly calm voice, "A woman kept you from taking Tessa?"

"No. It was a guy. He came roaring after the woman, pulled me out of the van, and started beating up on me. But I whacked him with my wrench and got away. Maybe I broke his skull."

"You had Tessa. Why didn't you take her?"

"They got her out of the van. Those women are weird. You know that. They made a circle around her. When I tried to get through, I just . . . bounced back. All I could do was get out of there."

Rafe glanced at the bullet-riddled vehicle. "Did anyone follow you?"

"I got away clean."

"How?"

"Busted through the gate. It's a piece of shit."

"And the man who fought you? Who was that? Cynthia's boyfriend? What's his name—Matthew Layden?"

"No. It was the new horse doctor they hired. I've seen him around a few times."

"What does he look like?"

Ames thought for a moment. "Dark hair. Dark eyes. Tall. Well muscled. He . . . looks a lot like *you*, actually."

The vet! Was *he* the guy who attacked him in the desert? He'd have to figure out where he could ambush the guy. But at the moment he was busy with this *malaka*.

"What else can you tell me . . . about the incident?"

"That's all. Except . . ." He paused and licked his lips. "You don't have to pay me the rest of the fee. And I'll return the money you already gave me. That's fair."

"You don't have to return the money."

Ames let out a little breath.

"I assume you can't get back on the property, and even if you could, they know it was you who set the fire and tried to kidnap Tessa."

The handyman directed his gaze somewhere over Rafe's left shoulder. "I didn't think I had to hide my face from Tessa. I thought I'd get her out of there without any problems. But then the guy interfered, and the women came swarming around."

"An unfortunate miscalculation on your part."

Ames took a step back, but Rafe had already raised the cylinder and depressed the button on top, sending a cloud of spray into Ames's face. Seconds later, he keeled over and lay still.

Rafe picked him up and slung him over his shoulder like a sack of horse feed, then carried him to the garage and dumped him into a four-wheel-drive SUV. Next he drove the van into the garage. He'd have to get rid of it later, after he took care of Ames. Maybe he'd drive it over a cliff into an arroyo.

With the vehicle hidden, he went back into the house to change.

When he was ready, he headed into the desert, to a desolate area where few ventured.

After unloading Ames onto the red dirt, he sat down in the shade of a cedar tree while he waited for the *malaka* to wake up.

But his mind was busy. He was thinking about the vet—the guy who had fought Ames. Was he really the other Minot?

There was a hitch in that theory. He'd apparently gotten

into the Ionian compound with no problem. More than once, if Ames was telling the truth.

And that would be impossible. Wouldn't it?

"Impossible," he said aloud. Yet if he wasn't the mystery Minot, who was? And what was special about him?

Well, it shouldn't be hard to get the horse doctor's name, then look up information about him, see if he had any background that would mark him as a Minot. Could he capture the guy and find out what the hell was going on?

Before he got rid of him.

He thought back to the encounter in the desert. Not his finest moment. Perhaps it wasn't smart getting close to the man again. Maybe the thing to do was finish his business here and get out. He'd have to come up with another plan for getting Tessa, but he still had a spy on the property—which gave him a source of information.

Finally, after about forty-five minutes in the hot sun, Ames began to stir.

"Where am I?" he groaned as he sat up and rubbed his eyes.

Rafe got to his feet and stood a few yards away. When Ames spotted him, he gasped.

"What's going on?"

Rafe wore athletic shoes. Comfortable shorts and a tank top. He could have been out for a run, except that he was holding a hunting knife.

Fear flashed in Ames's eyes when he spotted the knife.

"Please. Don't," he wheezed.

"I'll give you forty minutes' head start," he said. "You can take that bottle of water lying next to you. If you can get away from me, you're free to go."

"Please, just let me go. I did everything you asked, but it didn't work out the way we thought."

"I would have asked you to leave the state," he lied, "if you'd completed your assignment. It wasn't all that difficult, but you screwed it up. Twice."

"Not difficult! You try getting in there with those bitches. They're all spooky."

"Stop whining and get out of my sight," Rafe spat, "before I change my mind and gut you right now."

With a look of utter terror, the man grabbed the water bottle and ran.

Rafe sat down to relax again. He had no doubt he could track Ames, and when he caught up with the sorry bastard, he was going to have a good time killing him slowly. With the knife.

Then he would make other arrangements for keeping tabs on the Ionians' compound.

CHAPTER THIRTEEN

IT WAS WELL into the evening before the sisters got their guests settled down after the frightening experience with the fire. As it turned out, they'd been lucky. Damage to the spa was minimal, and they'd been able to move all their activities into another wing of the building.

Then all but the women on duty and the mothers gathered in their private lounge.

Nobody had been harmed except Jason Tyron. Still, they were shaken by the experience.

When some of the people staying at the spa had said they were leaving, the sisters gave them full refunds. They didn't depend on the spa's revenues for their income. Long ago they'd invested their wealth in many diversified stocks, bonds, and other ventures. And they also had large stocks of gold and precious jewels.

"We must make security our top priority," Cynthia told the group after the women with daughters had come back from reassuring the little ones. "I think it's safe to assume that Ames created the fire and smoke as a diversion for the attempted kidnapping," she continued.

"Is staying open too dangerous? Should we shut down?" Ophelia asked.

"We'll talk about that in a moment," Cynthia answered.

"I'd feel like I was in prison if we were the only ones huddled in here," Denada put in.

"Yes, we have to be secure without feeling . . . totally confined," Cynthia said.

There were murmurs of agreement around the room.

Sophia glanced at Tessa, who sat in the corner with her back to two walls. Physically she was none the worse for her ordeal, but Ames had almost succeeded in getting her out of the spa, and it was obvious that she'd suffered emotional damage.

Sophia's mind flashed back to the ceremony they'd worked. Tessa had brought up the image of a burning building. Sophia had thought it was a church. Maybe it simply represented the spa.

"The rest of you will be all right," Tessa said in a small voice. "Ames was after me. He was probably sent by the guy who stopped Sophia out on the road. And we have to assume that attack was supposed to be against me, too."

"We can't know that for sure," Eugenia answered, but Sophia wondered if her sister believed the reassurance herself.

The older Ionian looked at Sophia. "The new veterinarian prevented Ames from accomplishing his goal."

She nodded.

"You'd met him previously?"

"Yes."

"Could he have been working with Ames?"

The question startled Sophia, but she understood where it was coming from. "I don't think so," she answered. "When he found out one of the guests was trapped in the building, he ran inside to rescue her. After he brought her out, he heard me call for help and came charging over to the van and grabbed Ames—who bashed him over the head with a wrench. It was a real injury. The hospital's keeping him overnight for observation."

"You checked on him?"

"Yes. I called to find out how he was." She spread her hands. "He got hurt because he was helping us."

"When he's here next time, see how he's doing. And see if you can get a sense that he's what he appears to be."

Sophia nodded. She was thinking that perhaps Cynthia could do the same thing with her lover, Matthew Layden, but she didn't voice the suggestion. Her mind switched back to Jason. She hadn't been sure if she could keep away from him. Now the high priestess was ordering her to check the man out.

Of course, she already had suspicions. But she didn't voice them, probably because she wasn't the same woman she had been since the attack on the road. The old Sophia would have reported everything to her sisters. The new Sophia was more guarded.

And what if Cynthia asked her to stand before them at another ceremony? Could she keep them from seeing what was in her mind?

The question was unthinkable. No Ionian would do that, would she?

Cynthia turned back to Tessa. "You can take some time off from your duties," she said.

"Thank you."

Sophia was startled again. She'd expected Tessa to say she wanted to work to keep her mind occupied. Apparently, she did want time to herself.

"Should we try to read the future?" Ophelia asked.

"We didn't get very far with that last time," Tessa answered in a low voice. "Why should it work now?"

"The last time?" Cynthia asked.

Tessa looked like she wished she hadn't opened that line of discussion.

"I asked Sophia to help me see my own future."

"Did you?" Cynthia probed.

"I saw a fire."

"You saw the spa burning?"

"No, another building. It looked like a church. I would have told you if I saw the spa."

"Yes."

"I didn't know what it meant. I knew it was muddled in my mind."

"Seeing our own destiny was never one of our most reliable skills," Cynthia said.

Nobody challenged her, but Sophia could feel the reaction around the room. They were beginning to doubt themselves, which wasn't helping the situation.

As they were struggling with that, Cynthia dropped another bombshell.

"And I believe that the danger may be greater than we thought. I would like to take a vote on closing the spa for the time being."

There were various responses. Voting was something they rarely did, but in this case Cynthia didn't want to take action unless the majority of her sisters were in favor of it.

Some of the women were against it. Some were startled by the suggestion. Others, especially the women with young daughters, had apparently been thinking along the same lines. After a half hour of discussion, they decided that they would tell the outsiders remaining on the property that they would have to leave. All of them would be offered the opportunity to come back later at the spa's expense. They'd say the buildings needed to be repaired, but really they would be evaluating the safety of having outsiders on the property.

The meeting broke up early, with many of the women staying to talk informally and some of the mothers going back to the children's building. Sophia knew they were disturbed and worried about their daughters.

She didn't want to rehash the day's events. But as she left the room, Tessa caught up with her.

"That bucket," she said.

"What about it?"

"He must have known the metal would keep me from calling for help."

Sophia nodded. She'd thought of that, too.

Tessa changed the subject abruptly. "I wanted to thank you again. You and Jason Tyron. You both risked your lives to save me."

"You'd do the same for me."

"Yes." They walked in silence for a few moments, until Tessa looked over her shoulder to make sure that no one was listening, then said, "I watched you with Dr. Tyron."

A bolt of alarm shot through Sophia. "You mean after he was knocked unconscious?" she asked in a careful voice.

"Yes."

When she heard Tessa's answer, she let out the breath she'd been holding. Her sister hadn't seen them going into the hayloft—or coming out.

Tessa's next words had her on edge again. "He means something to you. When did you get to know him?"

Before answering, Sophia stepped into one of the gardens, and her sister followed.

"I interviewed him for the job. I came down to watch him work."

"And you made love with him."

Sophia caught her breath. Instead of denying it, she asked, "How do you know?"

"It was a guess."

"You tricked me!"

"I thought it was true."

"Why?"

"You were so frightened when he got hurt. So tender with him. You care about him."

She swallowed. "I'm still trying to figure out how I feel about him."

"Maybe it happened before. Maybe the missing Ionians found someone—a man. And that's why they left the spa."

"What are you talking about?"

"When you came into the gift shop, I started to tell you about them. They were in the register of our Sisterhood. Two were born in the 1940s. One in the 1920s. But they're not here. And there's no record of their deaths."

"They could be some of the sisters who have jobs out in the world."

"We know who *they* are. Linda, Chandra, and Julia just aren't anywhere."

"Could they have done . . . something bad? Been . . . killed?"

"You think the high priestess would do that to one of *us*?"

"I hope not."

"Maybe they bonded with a man, and that changed everything for them," Tessa said in a wistful voice.

"Or maybe they were kidnapped."

When Tessa winced, Sophia was sorry she'd said it.

"I should go to bed," Tessa murmured.

"Yes. Try to relax."

Tessa nodded, then walked out of the garden and headed for her bedroom.

Sophia stared after her sister, hardly able to believe the conversation they'd just had.

They were discussing the unthinkable. Bonding with a man. Defection. Kidnapping. But the last had almost happened to Tessa today.

THE next day, Tessa was glad for the excuse to be by herself. At the morning meal, she told Sophia and the others that she wanted to rest, but once she closed her bedroom door behind her, she was too wired to lie down.

She paced back and forth across the carpet, her mind in

turmoil. Had the fire at the spa been what she'd seen in her vision? Or was there something else?

But what?

And what if she were putting the whole order in danger? Was there something she could do about it?

Had the missing Ionians left because they'd had visions of their own futures? Or had they encountered something they couldn't cope with at the spa? And they'd solved the problem by leaving the Sisterhood?

Or maybe they'd left—and then something had happened to them, like an automobile accident. Or what if they'd gone to a foreign country to work with the poor?

It wasn't like their mother, Daphne, who'd died while rock climbing in the desert. She'd been brought back to the spa and buried with all the other Ionians who had lived here.

In some part of her mind, Tessa knew that she was becoming obsessed with the missing women.

Because she'd lost her mother? Almost no Ionians had more than one daughter. Daphne had been an exception. Because she'd known she was going to die early and wanted to leave her mark on the order?

"Stop it," Tessa whispered to herself. But she couldn't keep her speculations from running wild. Suppose one of the women had clashed with the high priestess. Or she'd been in love with a guest, and the only way to break off the relationship was to leave. Or she'd run away with him. There were lots of reasons why a sister might have felt she had to quit the order.

Had any of them planned to come back? But something had happened?

As Tessa contemplated that possibility, her chest grew tight. She wanted to know about the women. Burned to know, but probably she never would. This society was rigid. They might as well have been in some monastic order, except that sex was fine—as long as it was sex in the Ionian way.

And she didn't have to take a vow of poverty, either. The

sisters lived very well. They kept apart from the modern world, but they incorporated modern conveniences into their daily lives. And they kept up with world events.

The only vow they had to take that could really be considered monastic was obedience to the high priestess and the traditions of the order. And that, too, was unspoken. It was something they simply *knew*.

Her mind circled back to the money angle. There was wealth here, and some of it belonged to her. She'd worked for the good of the Sisterhood and always let her earnings go back into the communal pot. But did that have to be strictly true?

Plans began to form in her mind, plans that should be unthinkable. Yet she was considering them because perhaps they were for the good of the order, not just her own.

SOPHIA could have called Jason to find out how he was feeling and when he was coming back to the spa.

There was no reason why she couldn't. But that wasn't the Ionian way, and she wasn't going to do anything that made it look like she was reaching out toward him. Especially after her conversation with Tessa. If her sister had noticed their relationship, others would, too.

But she couldn't stop herself from looking for his truck. When she finally saw it three days after the fire, she felt her heart start to pound.

As she stepped out of the main building and started down to the corral, she had the vague feeling she should tell someone where she was going, although Cynthia hadn't said anything specific. Perhaps she'd been too distracted, but Sophia was willing to take advantage of that oversight, if that's what it was.

Her nerves were jumping as she walked toward the stable, forcing herself to move at a moderate pace in case anybody was watching. When she didn't immediately see Jason, she stepped inside the barn and found him in the storeroom checking the medical supplies.

He heard her come in and turned, his arms at his sides and his expression a mixture of emotions, the way it always was when he saw her. He looked defiant, wary, and at the same time glad to see her.

"I was hoping you'd call," he said.

"I called the hospital."

"How was I?"

"They said they were keeping you for observation. Obviously you passed their tests."

"You were right. I had a concussion."

She winced.

"But they did a CAT scan and some other tests before they released me. I'm fine."

"I'm glad. Should you be at work?"

"I didn't want to just sit around."

"Let me see your head."

"That's not necessary."

"I'd like to see what Ames did to you."

He hesitated, then leaned down so that she could reach the top of his scalp. "There's a bump, but it's no big deal. The doctor said it will go away."

She could see where his dark hair was slightly parted. When she tentatively touched the spot, a rush of dizzying sensations swept over her.

CHAPTER FOURTEEN

JASON MUST HAVE felt it, too, because he tried to wrench away, but she grabbed his shoulder with her free hand, holding him in place.

She'd caught a few of his thoughts when they'd made love. Maybe he'd been able to control her access to his mind before. But he'd been hit on the head and suffered a concussion, which left him vulnerable to her in a way he hadn't been earlier.

She gasped when his thoughts leaped toward her. Suddenly she was no longer able to deny what she'd been trying not to believe since she'd first encountered him at the stables.

"You're a Minot!"

Their positions changed abruptly. When she tried to back away, he grabbed her arm and held her fast.

His gaze bored into hers, and she saw the Minot defiance that was so true of his kind. "Is that a surprise?"

"Yes," she spat out. "It should be impossible for one of your kind to get past our wards."

"One of my *kind*? Is that a racial slur or something?"

"Of course not. I'm stating a fact."

"In the way you were taught to think—by your Ionian teachers. Suppose what you've learned is wrong?"

"It isn't! We've been at war with the Minot for almost two thousand years. You tried to dominate us, and we fought you off. We're still fighting you off. So stop trying to change the subject. How in the name of Hades did you get in here?"

"I guess I must be different."

"Impossible."

She could see him struggle to get a grip on his emotions as he tried to bring the discussion down to a more manageable level. They'd been talking loudly. Would one of her sisters come running in here?

And did she want that?

When he spoke again, his tone was more reasonable. "If you picked up on my . . . heritage, you must also know I'm the man who rescued you on the road."

"For what purpose?" she asked, trying to match his tone.

"To save you from the other guy."

"You're not working with him?"

"Of course not! Again, if you can read my mind—you can see that."

"I can't trust what's in your mind." She was going to tell him to get off the spa property, but she had reached the point where she didn't trust her own judgment. Better to get the others and interrogate him.

"Keep this between us," he said in a low voice.

"Too dangerous."

"I'm not what you assume."

She laughed mirthlessly. "We both know what you are."

"I don't think so. You're right about my father. He was a Minot. But my mother was an Ionian. That's why I can walk in here without any problems."

"That's impossible."

"It's true. My parents had a great marriage, but you've

been brainwashed into thinking their relationship couldn't exist."

"Because no Ionian can ever trust a Minot. If your mother was with your father, he was holding her captive."

"No."

"So you say. What was her name?" she asked, ready to tell him that she would have known about any marriages between an Ionian and a Minot.

"Julia."

As the name registered, she felt the hairs on the backs of her arms prickle. Tessa had told her about the sisters who had been born here but then vanished. One of them was named Julia.

"That doesn't prove she was with your father of her own free will."

"She was. She left the spa because she was unsure of her place in the Sisterhood. She went to San Francisco in the mid-sixties and became a Tarot card reader. When a drugged-out hippie tried to rob her, my father saved her."

"Is that where you got the idea of 'saving' me?"

"Of course not. I was just in the right place at the right time."

They glared at each other, and she saw him making another effort to control his emotions.

When he spoke again, it was in a softer voice. "At first my mother didn't trust my father, but she finally accepted that he wanted a real relationship with her. And when she opened herself to the possibility, she found out how much it could mean to the two of them. Even so, she wasn't going to abandon her heritage."

Sophia kept her gaze on him, trying to judge the truth of his words.

"She came back here to get permission from the high priestess to marry, and she was told she had to choose between the Ionians and my father. She went with him."

"And she's still with him? Can I ask her about her marriage?"

"They're both dead. For a while they were happy. The relationship with my father was new and exciting, and they shared so much, but she started pining for contact with her sisters. I think you can understand that."

"Yes," she whispered.

"Finally she couldn't cope with being cut off from the order. Eventually she died. And after that, my father sort of gave up. He was killed in a sailing accident, probably because he didn't want to go on without her."

"You expect me to believe that story without any proof?"

"It's true."

"Why are you here?"

"Because I saw what my parents had, and I want the same thing."

She laughed again. "Or something else."

He kept his gaze fixed on her. "You can read my mind. You know I'm not lying."

"I can get flashes of your thoughts. Nothing that's sustained. Nothing I can trust."

"I'll do anything you want to prove that I'm telling the truth."

She considered his words and decided to make a request that no Minot could ever accept.

"Put yourself completely in my power."

He answered without hesitation. "All right."

For a shocked moment, she couldn't respond. Then she asked, "You agree, without knowing what I have in mind?"

"Yes."

"Why?"

"Because I have to. It's the only way you're going to trust me."

"It means that much to you?"

"Yes."

"I could have you in my power—and kill you."

"I'll take that chance."

He sounded convincing. Was he telling the truth? Or did he have some trick up his sleeve that she couldn't anticipate?

She wanted to know the answer, and at the same time, she was afraid to find out. Before she could change her mind, she said, "We'll do it now. You come with me into the desert—to a place of power."

He swallowed, and she noted that he didn't look quite so cocky, although he answered, "All right."

Her mind was whirling, but she said in a mild voice, "I want to get some things. I'll be back in twenty minutes. You've got that long to change your mind and get out of here. For good."

SOPHIA hurried back to the spa. In her room she grabbed the knapsack she used when she went out into the desert. After a few moments' thought, she went down the hall to a storeroom that her sisters maintained. She had played with some of the toys here with previous lovers. But it had only been play. Now she was deadly serious as she began filling the carry bag with things she might need. Next she went to another storeroom and got camping supplies.

As she worked, she thought about Jason. He'd said his mother was an Ionian. He'd said his parents were happy together. She had to assume that he knew more about the Ionians than anyone who wasn't in the order—which was unthinkable. Yet the confidence with which he spoke about the Sisterhood argued that it was true.

And what about herself? Was she doing this to prove that she wasn't in his power? Or to discover something that she had longed for and hadn't found with her sisters? She couldn't answer the question. She could only proceed with her reckless course of action.

Although she was probably endangering herself, she hoped she wasn't putting the rest of the order in jeopardy.

She had hoped to get back to the stable without meeting one of her sisters. When she left her room, she passed Ophelia in the hallway. She'd tried to like Ophelia, but the other woman had always been very aware of her position as Sophia's senior.

"I saw the vet's truck down at the stable," Ophelia said.

"Yes. I'm going to talk to him," she answered, sorry for the evasion. She was planning to do a lot more than talk, and the prospect had her blood pounding.

"And report back to Cynthia?"

"Yes," she answered, wondering if it was a lie.

Struggling to keep her own emotions under control, she returned to the barn, where she found Jason standing with his arms folded across his chest, waiting for her.

She gave him a direct look, then laid out the situation in the starkest possible terms. "You said you'd put yourself in my power. You're saying you agree to be my slave—until I find out the truth of your words?"

He licked his lips but answered quickly, "Yes."

"Then you will not speak to me again unless I give you permission."

He answered with a tight nod.

"Come on. We'll take your truck. Give me the keys."

He handed over the keys, and she threw her pack in the back before climbing behind the wheel. When he'd joined her in the passenger seat, she started the engine and headed for the main entrance.

The uniformed guard gave her a questioning look as she pulled up at the barrier. "I was instructed to make sure none of you women go out alone," he said.

"I'm not alone."

The guard glanced at Jason. "He's your escort?"

"Yes."

The man raised the gate, which had been repaired after Ames broke it, and she drove through. From the corner of her eye, she could see Jason shifting in his seat. It looked like he wanted to say something. Maybe he wanted to warn her that they shouldn't leave the compound, but she didn't want his advice.

"What if he's out here?" he blurted.

"You took care of him before."

When he opened his mouth again, she said, "We're five minutes into this, and you're already breaking the rules."

He clamped his teeth together, and gave her a frustrated look.

Before she reached the end of the access road, she turned off onto a dirt track through the desert that circled around toward the back of the compound. Her destination was a huge outcropping of red rock, but they'd have to get out and walk before they reached it.

They drove past familiar desert vegetation, reddish-brown-barked manzanita, clumps of snake grass, and prickly pear cactus that was blooming with yellow flowers. As they headed for a small stand of juniper trees with twisted trunks, she saw Jason eying them.

Had he learned that twisted junipers were a sign of powerful forces in the desert?

She pulled behind a clump of sycamores that would partially hide the truck from the spa.

There were places of power called vortexes all over the Sedona area, which was one of the reasons the Ionians had settled here.

Most of the vortexes were well marked, and the public often visited them to see if they could feel the energy vibrations. This spot was different. It was on land owned by the spa and seemed to affect only the Ionians.

Perhaps it would affect Jason, too.

He was half Ionian, if he was telling the truth. And there was evidence that he might be, like the way he'd driven onto spa property with no problems. And he had said his mother's name was Julia—one of the women Sophia and Tessa had discussed. Which didn't really prove anything; if Tessa had found out about her, maybe Jason had, too.

She couldn't determine anything about him yet. But what about herself? Was she doing this because she was dissatisfied with her life? And Jason had just offered her something more.

No, something different, because if they followed in the path of his mother and father, she'd be cutting herself off from her sisters. And ultimately, that hadn't done either one of his parents any good. Yet he was still longing for what they'd had. That said something about his motivation—if his story was true.

And then there was her ability to dip into his mind—perhaps that did mean something. She'd never read a man before and never heard of an Ionian doing it.

She kept going back and forth, wanting to believe him, then sure that he was only trying to use her, the way they all did. Finally, she broke off the debate. She was getting way ahead of herself. It didn't matter what he told her. Only his actions and his thoughts counted. The Minot were proud men who would never submit to a woman's will. Unless . . .

Cutting the engine, she jerked her head toward Jason. "Grab the knapsack."

He silently climbed out and did as she asked, slinging the bag comfortably over one shoulder.

"We're going up there." She pointed to a red rock formation that was partially obscured by its own shadow.

RAFE was out for a run in the desert. Killing Ames had helped satisfy his craving for vengeance, but it had done nothing to get him any closer to capturing Tessa.

And he would not give her up.

He still had several sources of information about her. One was a guy named Tex Somerville, who was a fitness instructor on the property.

He liked to relax at a bar in town called the Silver Bullet, and Rafe had chatted him up a couple of times, making it look like a casual conversation. They'd gotten into several discussions about the Ionians, although the guy apparently didn't know that word.

But from his own accounts, he was a stud who was fucking a bunch of them, sometimes two in the same bed.

He was happy with the arrangement and didn't want anything besides sex with them, and that was what they wanted, too.

Everybody was happy.

Except not now, because the spa was closed, thanks to Ames's screwup, and Tex was temporarily out of a job.

Rafe's cell phone rang, and he pressed the receive button. But apparently he was too far out in the desert to get anything but a garbled signal.

Was it an important call?

About *what* for Christ's sake?

He looked toward an outcropping of rock in the distance. If he went up there, maybe he could get a signal. Or maybe not.

He'd find out who was calling when he got home. Or maybe he'd better *go* home.

WHEN Sophia started along a rough trail that wound upward through the scrubby vegetation, Jason followed.

She knew he must want to ask her a million questions, but he was abiding by the rules she'd set out. She hoped that was a good sign.

Still, they were out in the wilderness, far from help now, and he was a man whose strength far exceeded her own. If he decided to turn on her, she'd have little chance of fighting him off.

Instead, she'd recklessly brought him out here.

As they climbed the winding trail, small lizards skittered

out of their way, and a jet-black raven landed on a nearby cactus, watching them with appraising eyes.

They entered the shadow of an outcropping. When they stepped to the other side, they were facing a shallow cave that had been hidden from view by rocks that stood between the entrance and the rest of the landscape.

"Put the knapsack down," she said.

He did as she asked, and she took out a flashlight, stepping inside and inspecting the interior, looking for snakes and scorpions.

When she was satisfied that they were safe from any dangerous creatures, she turned back to Jason. He was standing with a wary expression on his face.

"Come here."

He followed her into the cave and watched as she took a blanket from the knapsack and spread it on the ground between them.

"Take off your clothes," she said.

He kept his gaze on her as he pulled off his running shoes and socks and tossed them aside. Then he dragged his T-shirt over his head, revealing his broad, well-muscled chest, with a mat of hair fanning out across the middle and arrowing down toward his waist.

He was staring at her as he unbuckled his belt and unzipped his jeans. She watched him slick them down his legs, revealing most of his firm body. Only his navy briefs remained.

"Those too," she ordered.

He hooked his thumbs under the waistband, pulling the briefs down and kicking them away.

She took her time running her gaze over him, struggling to keep her face impassive as she looked at his wonderful body with its impressive male equipment.

"Lie down on the blanket. Spread-eagle."

He gave her a long look, then complied.

She stood over him for a moment, then returned to the

knapsack, pulling out cloth cuffs, wooden tent stakes, and a hammer.

Kneeling, she slipped a thong over one wrist, attached the end to a stake, and hammered it into the ground. Then she did the same with his other wrist and his ankles until he was staked down at all four limbs like a victim at an ancient sacrificial ceremony.

THE knock on the door had Cynthia sitting up in bed. She was with Matthew, who had stayed when the other guests had left, another precedent-breaking decision.

With no urgent work to take care of, she'd spent a lot of her time with him. No one at the spa would dare to disturb her when she was with her lover, yet the knock sounded again.

He looked questioningly at her. "Who would come here now?"

"I don't know." She reached for the robe she had thrown on the end of the bed. "Just a moment."

When she climbed out of bed, Matthew also got up and went into the bathroom where no one could see him.

Cynthia padded to the door and opened it to find Eugenia standing in the hallway.

She gave the other senior woman a hard look. "You had better have a good reason for bothering me."

"I do. Something's happened. The guard at the gate called me. Since then, I've been turning the spa upside down."

"Because . . ."

When Eugenia began to speak again, Cynthia felt her throat tighten with alarm.

SOPHIA struggled to keep her expression neutral as she watched Jason test the bonds. An ordinary man would not be able to free himself. A man with Jason's strength might well wrench the stakes out of the ground. Did that mean he'd truly given her his trust? There was a way to find out.

She heard him drag in a breath as she turned toward the knapsack. When she came back to him, her right hand was hidden by her side. She placed her other hand on his chest, feeling the beating of his heart.

She spoke low, ancient words, asking the spirit of the universe for guidance, for she knew that this was about more than one man and one woman striving to come to an understanding. It could mean the breaking of traditions that had lasted for centuries. Or perhaps she was throwing away her own legacy.

Her own heart was pounding as she brought out the knife, raising it high so her captive could see it. His gaze shot to the sharp blade, and she heard him catch his breath.

Before she could change her mind, she brought the weapon down in a quick strike, stopping at the last second so that the point barely penetrated the flesh of his chest. His body jerked, but he didn't try to free his hands.

She could have killed him with that one blow. He hadn't tried to stop her, or get away, she thought with dizzy wonder.

It took a moment before she could meet his eyes. As their gazes locked, she saw a flash of anger.

"You don't like to be tricked," she said. "Was it a trick to pretend that the man on the road and the vet weren't the same person? Don't bother answering."

His mouth hardened. She knew he wanted to speak, but he was sticking to her rules.

He had passed one crucial test, but she couldn't base a life-changing decision on that. What if he were only pretending to go along with her? Even a Minot might be able to hide his real self for a short period of time.

But he might still give himself away. Like all of them, he was a proud man. Perhaps he had preferred death to rejection. Could he accept punishment at the hands of an Ionian?

She put down the knife, went back to the knapsack, and took out a small whip with a braided leather handle and thin leather strands at the business end. Keeping her back to Jason, she unbuttoned her blouse. Under it she was wearing a sheer black lace bra. Hiding the whip in the folds of her blouse, she turned back to him. He licked his lips as his eyes went to her breasts. Unable to look away, he watched her take off her shoes, then her jeans, moving slowly, making each action a sensual show.

Even in his restrained position, he reacted as she'd thought he would, his penis coming to attention as he watched her undress. And she was gratified to discover that he was fully aroused by the time she stood beside the blanket, wearing only her provocative underwear.

His magnificent cock stood up straight from his body, and she wanted to kneel down and grasp it, but she only gave him a slow, simmering look, her gaze raking his body and coming back to the main attraction.

She could see his hands clenched into fists as she knelt beside him, leaning over so that her breasts were inches from his face, then shifting her position, touching his chest, sliding her fingers down his body, feeling his muscles jump as she caressed him. His breath hitched as her hand drew near to his penis, but she bypassed that proud shaft, sliding her hand onto his muscular thighs, then down to his ankles and finally his feet, taking each of his toes in turn, pulling and twisting on them as she watched his face.

His breath came in ragged gasps now. His eyes were pleading as she moved up his body again, playing the same game, touching him everywhere except the place where he must ache to feel her hand.

She wanted to caress him there, craved the intimate touch, but she was going to push him to the limit. And push herself, it seemed.

The crotch of her panties was sopping wet. Probably he could smell her arousal, but she kept her face impassive as she reached into the folds of the blouse on the ground and picked up the small whip.

His eyes went wide as he saw it.

She brought the leather cords down on his shoulder in a swift, calculated blow, not hard enough to break his skin, but hard enough to get his attention, judging the effect on him.

"You deceived me," she said in a low voice. "You should be punished for that."

She used the whip on his shoulders, his chest, his thighs, knowing the blows must sting. And as she did, she finally reached out to circle his cock with her fist, squeezing him, drawing a moan from his lips. She closed her eyes, enjoying the sensual contact, then lightening her touch, moving her hand up and down, hearing him gasp as she teased him.

She had planned to keep up the whipping as she caressed him, making him submit to her, even as she stoked his arousal. But something happened that she hadn't expected.

The intimate touch brought a blast of energy to her mind, a blast that opened his thoughts to her. And at the same time, opening her thoughts to him as well.

In this place of power where she had come to test his truthfulness and his resolve, she was suddenly testing herself as well. She felt his need, his desperation, his willingness to do anything she asked if she would only give him a chance to strengthen the bond between them. And she knew he could read her own thoughts—her hurt, her uncertainty, her fear.

She hated him seeing that. And he would know that, too.

She had ordered him not to speak, but words were no longer necessary between them. More than that, words would only skim the surface of this mind-to-mind communication.

When he made a strangled sound deep in his chest, she felt his arousal and his need for her to the depths of her soul. And more. So much more.

The choice was hers. She could flee from him now, or dare what few Ionian women had dared over the centuries.

This was the real test. Not just of him but of herself as well.

His gaze met hers, and she knew that they were both poised on a knife blade of emotions, of possibilities, and of disaster as well.

Did she dare give them what they both wanted? Or was she a coward? And was the coward's way the right choice after all?

CHAPTER FIFTEEN

WHEN RAFE REACHED the front door of his house, he pulled out his phone again.

This time, when he pressed the message button, he was able to get a connection.

There was one message. A man speaking low and fast.

"I don't have much time, but I've got some information you want. Two things have happened."

As Rafe listened to the first part, then the second, a buzz of excitement went through him. Just to make sure he'd heard the message correctly, he played it again.

"I want the payment you promised delivered to my bank account."

"When I get around to it," Rafe muttered as he hurried into the house. He had the information he needed. Now he had to figure out how to act on it.

FROM one moment to the next Sophia made the decision. Swiftly she reached to unhook her bra and pull off her sopping panties.

Jason didn't speak, but her name rang in his thoughts, in gladness and in gratitude as she straddled him, gasping as she brought him inside her.

"Jason."

She went very still. Unable to move. Unable to do more than stare down at him in wonder.

In this time and place, they were one being, their souls joined in a union that should have been impossible for either one of them. He was a man. A Minot. She was an Ionian. Sworn enemies, yet the two of them were no longer on opposite sides of any divide.

It was as though they belonged together, had always belonged together. And she knew in that moment of joining that he had been telling her the truth about himself.

Your mother and father.

I wasn't lying to you, I would never lie to you. Well, except to get near to you, he added ruefully.

Jason Tyron's not your real name.

Jason is. I changed my last name.

He opened himself to her, giving her more.

His father was a Minot named Paul Castle. His mother was Julia, an Ionian who had run away from the order because she felt stifled by life at the spa. Against all odds, she had found a Minot who was different from the rest, who wanted only what the two of them could build together.

But she had craved more. She had wanted her sisters as well, and that had been denied her by the high priestess, who was unable to accept the marriage of an Ionian. Especially an Ionian and a Minot.

For years she had been happy with her husband and her son, but in secret, she had longed for her sisters, and finally the separation had broken her.

As Sophia took in all this, she knew she was opening herself to him just as fully. He knew about the ceremony where the high priestess had deflowered her. He sensed her doubts about herself and about her sister Tessa.

He made a rough sound. *The order confines you. You've lost your way.*

She longed to deny it, but it was impossible to hide herself from him. Not now. Not in this place, with her body joined to his and her mind as open as it had ever been to any human being.

She had been still above him, but all at once she heard a clattering noise as the stakes that had confined his wrists slammed out of the ground. He pulled his hands from the restraints and brought them to her hips, urging her upward and then down again as he moved her above him, matching her rhythm.

She knew that he could have pulled his wrists free at any time. But he had chosen to remain in her power because that was the only way he could win her trust.

Then his hands moved upward, cradling her breasts, skimming his thumbs across the tightened crests. When she cried out in pleasure, he slid his hand around her back, stroking her spine, then pulling her upper body down to his chest as their movements became more frantic.

The intensity swept over them, driving them toward a climax that took them away from reality. At that moment she sensed something more. Something about him that he might not know himself. She couldn't quite grasp it either, and before she could focus on that, her gathering climax made it difficult to think of anything besides the here and now.

Clinging to him, she was helpless to keep from being swept into a world of pure sensation.

This was what she had always longed for yet never knew existed.

The firestorm swept over them, leaving them both limp and breathless.

When Jason wrapped his arms around her and rolled to his side, she realized he'd also freed his ankles.

Still overwhelmed, she clung to him. "Was that real—what happened to us?"

"Yes. It's what I wanted to show you we could have together—if we dared."

"You mean if *I* dared. You knew where we were going. All along. Your parents had that?"

"Yes."

"How? He didn't have Ionian blood, did he?"

"I don't know. It's possible. I know they spent a long time striving to enter each other's minds, and finally they did it. I'd see the joy in their eyes."

He moved his face against her cheek, and she closed her eyes, cuddling against him, enjoying intimacy she had never expected to feel.

"You didn't kiss me," he whispered, bringing his lips to hers for a long, ardent kiss.

She opened for him, reveling in this new sweetness. Between kisses, they spoke.

"The wards didn't keep me out of the compound because of my Ionian genes."

She was still having trouble imagining an Ionian and a Minot together. "Your parents loved each other," she whispered against his lips because she knew it was true.

"Yes. And my mother raised me with her values of love and honor. I grew up feeling blessed and wanting the same thing. Yet I knew how difficult it would be."

Sophia nodded, remembering all the lessons she had absorbed from childhood.

He gestured in frustration. "I saw what my parents had with each other. I also saw what it cost my mother."

"Cynthia, our high priestess, has a . . . boyfriend. He means more to her than other men have. Maybe that's shifted her point of view. Or maybe it makes her more adamant." She pushed herself up, looking down at him. "How do you know so much about us? We keep so much hidden. Even your mother must have been cautious."

"She was. I told you, she taught me her values, although she didn't give away any important secrets. My parents made it clear I could do anything I wanted with my life. My father left me plenty of money, so that was never an issue. I picked a profession that gave me a chance to get close to you. I moved to Sedona. I found out as much as I could about the order."

"And you wanted one of us. Not necessarily *me*."

"I knew as soon as we met on the road that it was *you*."

She had felt it, too, although she hadn't dared explore her feelings for him. Not really. But he had understood his goal.

"I studied *you*, too," she murmured. "What you'd put in your résumé. Then I looked you up. I couldn't get enough."

He grinned. "Good." Reaching for one of the cuffs that had circled his wrist, he held it up. "Where did you get all this stuff?"

"We have it at the spa. Sometimes we enjoy playing bondage games."

"You've done that?"

She kept her gaze steady. "Yes. Your mother must have told you we're taught to dominate men."

He laughed. "There's only so much a guy can discuss with his mother."

She flushed. "I guess that's right. There was never any barrier with my sisters. We talked about . . . everything. Our heritage. Our sexuality."

"The dangerous Minot," he put in.

She gave him a stern look. "They *are* dangerous. Most of them are like that guy who attacked me on the road."

"You can't be sure of that. What if it's all indoctrination?"

She shook her head. "You won't convince me of *that*. You have a background no one else has. But we're getting off the subject. We were talking about sexual information."

"Uh-huh."

"When we were younger, the older sisters taught sex education classes. When we got older and started experimenting, we discussed the men we'd had and what we did with them. Lysandra told me I would enjoy making a man my slave for a night." She raised one shoulder. "Maybe she thought I'd be too timid to try it."

"But you had to prove you could do it?"

"It's no big deal."

"But you thought it was a way to test me."

"I thought no Minot would agree. Or if he did—he was different from the others."

"I am. But now I hope we don't need anything artificial in our lovemaking. Unless we both agree on the game."

He was carefully not giving her an order. He was saying what he'd like.

She smiled at him. "That's fair, but maybe we should test the theory."

She wasn't sure of the future, but she was sure she trusted him now. And she knew what they had together was different from what she had ever experienced. She'd always enjoyed sex, but she'd never thought of it as sharing anything profound. She'd learned today that she'd been missing a lot.

Raising her mouth to his again, she nibbled at his lips as her hands roamed over his back and shoulders, feeling her arousal begin to build again.

"You've been missing a lot," he whispered, and she knew he'd picked that up from her mind. "And I have, too."

When she felt his erection against her thigh, she moved seductively against him.

Last time had been a frantic joining. This time she wanted a slow buildup, and he seemed to know exactly what she craved.

Once again, the intimacy was opening her to his thoughts, and she welcomed that, too.

His hand moved lazily over her, touching and caressing, and when he rolled her to her back and sucked one of her nipples into his mouth, she arched into the caress.

He used his teeth on her, then his tongue, his thumb and finger mirroring the caress on the other breast.

Up until now, everything she had felt and sensed was

confined to the cave, and she wanted to keep it that way. Just the two of them, before they had to go back to the real world and figure out what they were going to do.

But she became aware of something beyond the little refuge they had made for themselves.

And she knew from his sudden tension—and the jolt from his mind—that he felt it, too.

CHAPTER SIXTEEN

"YOU SENSE DANGER?" Sophia whispered.

"Yes. Someone sneaking up on us?" he asked.

"To me, it feels more like something's happened down at the spa. We need to go back."

"I know."

"The high priestess could have found out I'm missing. She could wonder if I'm with you. She could have sent my sisters out looking for us."

"You think she'll try to separate us?"

She didn't answer, but a zing of uneasiness traveled over her skin as she realized how little she'd thought this through.

"Maybe I should go down there alone, and you go back home."

"Not a chance," he answered. "I'm staying with you."

"You're trying to provoke a confrontation?"

"I'm not going to let you face her by yourself."

"You must."

He looked thunderstruck. "We forged a bond."

"But no one at the spa will believe it."

"We'll make them believe."

Was that possible? She'd been so sure the two of them belonged together. Now she was suddenly afraid.

They both stood and found their clothing. As they'd driven here, she'd thought about staking him down and cutting off his shirt and jeans. Now she was glad she hadn't destroyed his clothing. Or had she known deep down that they were going back to the spa together?

She gathered everything that she'd brought and stuffed it into the knapsack. When she started to hoist it over her shoulder, he stopped her.

"Wait. I want to check that nobody's outside."

She hadn't even considered that, but she stayed in the cave while he went out and inspected the area, walking a little way down the path and coming back.

For the first time, she knew what it was like for a man to protect his mate. A very unique experience for an Ionian.

"I think we're alone," he said as he reached for the knapsack.

"I can carry it," she protested.

"I know. But I think we'll get there faster if I'm the one with the pack."

He was right. She handed it over, and they left the cave, making their way as fast as they could down the steep trail that they had climbed earlier. Then she'd been worried about what would happen between the two of them. Now she had bigger worries, and she couldn't even say what they were.

It was late in the afternoon, and the shadows were longer. She realized that she hadn't worked out what she'd planned to do after she tested Jason. Would she have spent the night up here with him, or tried to come back in the dark when it was more dangerous?

And how would she have explained that?

By the time they reached the truck, the sun was a huge red ball in the west, and the sky was shot through with beautiful streaks of pink and purple. It was a glorious desert sunset, but neither of them had the leisure to enjoy it.

Sophia handed Jason the keys.

He climbed behind the wheel, then waited while she slid into the passenger seat. "You realize I'd like to just keep driving—somewhere else," he said as he started the engine.

"But you won't."

They headed cross-country toward the access road and joined it where they'd turned off.

Sophia watched the spa come into view.

"Stop here," she said when they were still out of sight of the gate.

He did as she asked, pulling off the road before turning to her. "Let me come with you."

"I'm sorry. I have to go back there alone now."

"I can't let you do that." He reached for her hand and held on tightly. "We should be able to rely on each other now. Don't you want that?"

"Of course I do. But I can't . . ."

"Can't what?"

"Just rearrange my thinking—and my life—so quickly. You've been planning this for a long time. I'm just adjusting to it."

"That's what it is? An adjustment?" he asked in a gritty voice.

"Don't."

"I'm sorry. I shouldn't push you. This won't work unless it's something you really want."

"I do!" she said, still not sure it was completely true. She didn't know what she wanted. Or maybe she was afraid to reach for something that had always been forbidden. "But I know there's a crisis at the spa. I have to join my sisters. I owe them that, don't you think?"

The way she asked the question must have convinced him, because he sat gripping the steering wheel as she climbed out.

But when she walked around to the back of the truck, she found him standing beside her.

He pulled her into his embrace, holding her close, his hands moving up and down her back, tangling in her hair. When he tipped her face up, she met his lips in a fierce kiss that brought her back to the intimacy of the cave.

Yet this was different. Was it good-bye?

She couldn't answer that question. She could only kiss him with a desperation that gathered in every cell of her body. Until she forced herself to ease away.

"I'll call you when I can," she said, knowing it wasn't what he wanted to hear, but it was the only thing she could say.

"Leave the knapsack," he said. "If someone looks inside, they'll wonder what you were doing with that stuff."

She nodded. "You're right. I'm not thinking straight."

Feeling like her heart was breaking, she turned and ran back toward the spa, fighting to keep the tears blurring her vision from welling over.

She could feel Jason's gaze on her. Would he stop her—the way a typical Minot would take matters into his own hands?

But he stayed where he was, and she knew he understood that the two of them would only work out if she gave herself freely to him.

She was out of breath when she reached the gate.

"What's wrong?" the guard asked when he saw her in the glow from the floodlights.

"I got sand in my eyes."

"They're looking for you."

"Thank you," she answered, as though he'd given her information she hadn't previously possessed.

She walked onto the spa grounds, which were strangely quiet. She knew the guests were gone, but she'd expected to see some of her sisters.

Where was everyone?

With a feeling of dread, she headed toward the lounge where the women usually gathered in the evenings.

Before she reached the building, she saw Cynthia striding toward her.

"Where were you?"

"Up in the hills."

Cynthia's gaze was piercing. "The guard said you left with Jason Tyron. Why? Where is he?"

"I don't know where he is. He gave me a ride into the desert. Then he left," she said. That was true, as far as it went, but she felt like she was digging herself into some kind of hole as she spouted the explanation.

"And what were you doing out there?"

"I went to a place of power that has served me before. Why are you asking so many questions? What's happened?"

Cynthia's eyes were fierce and sad.

"Tessa's missing. We thought you were missing, too."

"No!"

Sophia felt like she'd been hit by an adobe brick in the center of her chest. While she'd been out in the desert with Jason, something had happened to her sister.

She reached to steady herself against one of the garden walls.

"Missing?" she gasped. "How can that be?"

"Did you help her get away from the spa? Is that what you were doing?"

"Of course not. I didn't even know she was gone."

They stood facing each other.

When the high priestess reached to touch her, she took a step back, and Cynthia gave her an appraising look.

"Are you afraid I'll read your thoughts?"

"Yes." She swallowed. "I feel guilty. I should have considered that something like this could have happened."

"Why?"

"I've never seen Tessa doubt herself more. I think she

was worried that she was putting us all in danger by staying here. I should have seen that."

"Did she give you any idea where she might go?"

Sophia shook her head, wishing she'd paid more attention to her sister's mood before charging off into the desert with Jason.

CHAPTER SEVENTEEN

RAFE BENT TO the computer screen. His informant, one of the guards who covered the spa gate, had told him about the blue Ford truck leaving the Ionian compound—with Sophia and Jason Tyron, the vet.

Going where? He'd like to know.

But the guard had also given him a more tantalizing bit of information. Tessa had also left the spa.

Rafe could have gone looking for Tyron.

But not when he had a chance of capturing Tessa. He glanced up at the red mountains that stood out in the view framed by his window, picturing her alone and vulnerable.

Had she stayed in the area? It was possible, but not probable. Why would she leave and hang around where her sisters could find her?

She'd want to get away, and he knew from his current research that she hadn't rented a car.

She was probably taking a commercial flight, unless she'd been stupid enough to hitch a ride. Or could she have driven out of there in one of the vehicles the Ionians owned? His informant hadn't said. And Rafe couldn't exactly call him back and get a full account. The guy knew the Ionians were under siege. He'd lose his job—or worse—if they discovered he'd ratted out Tessa.

With a sound of frustration, he turned back to the computer.

He had a number of sophisticated search engines on his hard drive that could crack into proprietary databases. If she'd gotten on a commercial flight, he'd know where she'd gone.

Would the Ionians do the same thing—try to trace Tessa through the Web? He was pretty sure they wouldn't even think of it. They might pride themselves that they were keeping up with the modern world, but their feet were firmly planted in the ancient past.

And even if they thought of doing some kind of Web search, he was sure they wouldn't have access to the expensive databases at his disposal. They wouldn't think they needed them—not when they had psychic powers.

Hopefully when he found her, he'd have a head start on getting control of her.

Or was he making too many assumptions? The only way to find out was to go ahead with his plans.

IT was early in the morning when Tessa landed in New Orleans. She'd caught a ride to Sedona with a tourist group viewing the Red Rock Country, taken a bus into Phoenix, then gone straight to the airport to find a flight. Luckily, she'd only had to wait a few hours, because the whole time she'd been in Phoenix, she'd expected to look up and see a group of her sisters charging toward her, lips firm and eyes fierce.

But it looked as if she'd made a clean getaway.

On the plane, she'd thought she could hear them calling to her, and she imagined them in the temple, sending out their thoughts. Or maybe she was just making that up.

In any event, she closed her eyes and blocked the contact. She hadn't left the spa to keep her sisters apprised of where she was.

After getting off the airport shuttle at a hotel near the French Market, Tessa dragged in a breath of the humid air, so different from what she was used to at the spa. But New Orleans was the best place she could think of to go.

She'd been here once before, on a trip with several of her sisters. Eugenia had wanted them to have some experience of the outside world, and she'd picked New Orleans for one of their trips because of the wide-open atmosphere of the city. It was a freewheeling place where you could walk around on the street with an alcoholic drink in your hand. Listen to jazz drifting from the doorways of bars, see topless women dancing in the windows of strip joints, or buy condoms from a sex shop on Bourbon Street.

She looked around at the covered market where dealers were selling everything from local produce and bottles of hot sauce to T-shirts, feathered masks, and dried spices.

This was a place where ancient cultures mixed with modern values. There was an old voodoo tradition in the city. And also women who made their living reading Tarot cards, palms, and tea leaves. Eugenia had said some of them had real talent.

The palm reading had intrigued Tessa, and on her previous visit here, she'd bought herself a couple of books on how to do it and started working with her sisters.

She was pretty good at it. In fact, she often did readings for guests at the spa, and she could surely do that here, probably in Jackson Square.

But first she'd better find a place to stay so she wasn't walking around pulling a suitcase, which made her look like an easy mark for any of the scam artists she knew were also here.

But that was the least of her problems.

It was clear a Minot was after her, and if she was gone, he'd leave the rest of her sisters alone, wouldn't he?

She shivered, hoping she wasn't making the wrong assumptions.

Firming her lips, she walked into a bookstore at the upscale end of the market where tourist-oriented shops and restaurants were strung along a colonnade. After looking at several guides to the city, she purchased one and took it outside, where she sat down on a bench beside a fountain and turned to the section on accommodations. There were lots of places to stay here, from large hotel chains to bed-and-breakfasts. She'd find something inexpensive, and drop off her luggage before going down to Jackson Square.

BEFORE Sophia's return, the sisters had searched the spa to make sure Tessa wasn't hiding out somewhere. Then they'd gone into the temple, where Cynthia had called upon the ancient powers to help them. Because Sophia had been seen leaving with Jason Tyron and was presumed to still be in the area, they focused on Tessa and sent their thoughts out to her, but they got no response.

Sophia might have tried calling out to her sister on her own, but she suspected it wouldn't do any good. If Tessa had wanted to be found, she would have stayed here.

Perhaps this was her fault. What if she hadn't gone off with Jason? What if she'd tried to get Tessa to talk to her? But she hadn't done any of that.

And what about Julia and the other two women who had left?

She wanted to ask the senior women—Cynthia and Eugenia—if they knew about them. But then she'd have to explain where she'd gotten the information. It was true that

Tessa had been the one to tell her initially. But she'd discussed Jason's parents with him, and if she started talking about Julia, she might give that away.

Feeling trapped, she closed herself in her room, praying that Tessa would come back on her own.

CHAPTER EIGHTEEN

RAFE FELT A zing of elation when he found Tessa Thalia on the passenger list of a United flight from Phoenix to Houston and another from Houston to New Orleans. She'd left Phoenix quickly, and she'd only been in the Big Easy for a few hours. She'd probably picked it because an exotic woman like her would fit in. If he acted fast, he could pick her up before she got her bearings.

And bring her back here?

No. He'd only used this house to be close to the spa. It had served its purpose, and he wanted her in a location where it would be a lot harder to get away. Somewhere unfamiliar where she'd be off balance. His main residence, the estate in the hills above Santa Barbara, would be perfect. She'd be secure yet comfortable there.

It was a little like the Ionian compound in that it was surrounded by a fence and equipped with security cameras. But he had other protective devices in place in case any unwanted visitors showed up.

As soon as he made up his mind about the location, he called his housekeeper, Mrs. Vincent, who answered on the second ring.

"I'll be coming back home," he said. "Have my room ready." He hesitated. "And also prepare the guest room next to mine."

"Yes sir."

"I'll send you a list of foods to buy."

"Yes sir. When should we be expecting you?"

"This evening or early tomorrow."

"Very good, sir."

There was no protest about the short notice of his orders. He paid Mrs. Vincent and his other staff members well, and they knew that it was unwise to incur his disapproval.

Probably they'd all been sitting around on their asses while he'd been gone. Now they had work to do.

Rafe hung up the phone and called the number of the general aviation service he used. He wanted to travel on his own schedule, and when he took Tessa back to Santa Barbara, he wanted privacy.

JASON drove along the two-lane highway and past the access road to the spa. He wanted to turn in and head for the gate, but when he'd gotten home, he'd found a call from Ophelia on his answering machine. She'd told him that the spa was closed to guests until repairs were finished, and he wouldn't be needed at the stable unless there was an emergency with one of the horses.

He knew she wasn't telling him the whole truth. She hadn't barred him from the spa right after the fire. Something else had changed, but he couldn't call back and ask or go over there and talk to Sophia, no matter how much he wanted to.

There was still something crucial he hadn't told her, hadn't even dared think about while he was with her. It had to do with what he'd discovered about the Minot. When she found out, how was she going to react?

He'd made himself totally vulnerable to her, but he should have realized how much her bond with her sisters would color her decisions. She had lived with the Ionians all her life, and she couldn't simply rearrange her thinking.

Did that mean he had to win the trust of the rest of the order? Although he didn't know how that was possible, he wasn't going to give up.

AFTER booking a room at a bed-and-breakfast, Tessa walked along the side of Jackson Square, staying out of the landscaped interior with its equestrian statue of Andrew Jackson.

Behind it was a huge white structure with three black spires, two at the sides and a larger one in the middle. St. Louis Cathedral.

As soon as she saw the building, she stopped short. She had visited it on her previous trip to the city. But she had also encountered it more recently. When?

She tried the trick of not thinking about the thing she was trying to recall—and it popped into her head. She'd seen the cathedral in her vision—when she and Sophia had been trying to divine their future.

It had been burning. But then the spa had burned. So somehow the visions must have been mixed up.

Now she realized she'd seen the cathedral because she was coming to New Orleans. Only when she'd had the vision, she hadn't understood.

That was the way things worked. You could sometimes see the future, but you didn't necessarily know what it meant.

She relaxed a little, looking at the crowd around her. The area was full of tourists, which meant that there were also a lot of locals on the streets. Musicians playing jazz, artists doing quick sketches of people, jugglers, palm and Tarot card readers. The latter were mostly women, sitting at card tables, where their customers could join them in an extra chair or one of the iron benches. As she watched them, Tessa hoped there was room for one more practitioner.

"You look like you need to know your future," a plump, gray-haired woman in a bright red dress and fringed shawl called out to her. The sign in front of her card table said Madame Victoria.

Tessa stopped short. "Why?"

"I think you're in trouble."

"You see that on my face?" she asked in a quavering voice, hoping the woman was simply fishing for a customer.

"I see it all around you. Like a gray cloak."

That wasn't reassuring news. Tessa considered asking for more information. Perhaps this woman could help her. And do something that the Ionians had not? She dismissed that notion quickly.

After a polite, "No thank you," she moved off, wondering if she had made the wrong decision about coming here as she turned the corner and hurried past horse-drawn carriages waiting along the curb. When she saw a man striding purposefully toward her, she stopped short.

Dressed in jeans and a black T-shirt, he was young and good-looking, with dark hair and an arrogant posture that told her he was very sure of himself.

She was certain she had never met him before, but she was instantly certain who he was. The Minot who had stopped Sophia on the road. She had described him, but knowing who he was now had more to do with his attitude and posture than his looks.

Glancing wildly around for an escape route, she spotted the cathedral again and realized why she had seen it in her future.

She could take refuge there.

Before the man got within twenty yards of her, she turned and ran, dodging tourists and locals alike as she made for the church. If she could get inside, she'd be safe. He wouldn't dare do anything in a house of worship.

Or would he?

She pounded down the sidewalk, hearing him keep pace with her and wondered why. Probably he could catch her at any time, but he was letting her run.

Had he done that with Sophia?

Tessa had vowed not to tell her sisters where she was. Now, in desperation, her mind went out to Sophia. *He's found me. I'm in New Orleans. He's found me here. You've got to help me.*

She had no idea if the message got through. Probably not, because she was so far away.

But she had to try, because she realized she'd been a fool. She'd run away from the one place where she might have been safe.

He's found me. In New Orleans. Help me. Please help me, she repeated as she ran, her breath sawing in and out of her lungs.

She climbed the steps to the main door of the church and pulled. When the door didn't open, she cried out, dodged to the side, and went running down an alley along the side of the building.

"Hey," someone shouted behind her. "Leave the lady alone."

There was some kind of angry exchange. Maybe even a fight, but she didn't stop to find out what was going on. She just kept running. If she could get around the building, she could disappear, and he wouldn't find her. Then she'd leave her bag at the B and B and take the first plane home where she'd be safe. Or would he look for her at the airport? Maybe she should take a taxi out of town. It didn't matter how much it cost. She had the money.

How had he found her in New Orleans? She didn't know. She only knew she had to get away.

After turning the corner, she kept going along the back of the church, heading for the next street. Her side hurt now, her chest burned, and she didn't know how long she could keep running at this pace.

She thought she might have escaped until he came up behind her again, his hot breath rasping in her ears. Reaching out, he drew her to him, pressing the front of his body to the back of hers.

"It's all right. Everything's going to be all right," he said in a voice that sounded strangely normal.

"No. Please, let me go."

"It's not what you think. I'm not going to force anything on you. You'll like being with me."

He pressed something against her arm, and she realized he'd stuck a needle in her flesh. Then everything turned hazy, and she sagged against him.

Behind her, she could hear someone speaking.

"Is she all right? What's going on?"

"Everything's fine. She's not used to the big city and she had one of her panic attacks. Haven't you, darling?"

She tried to answer, tried to call out for help, but she knew her words were garbled.

"I'm going to take her back to our hotel, where she can relax."

She was too limp to fight him. He lifted her into his arms and carried her away, striding around the corner. She wanted to struggle, but she felt too warm and woozy.

"That's it, darling," he murmured. "Just let me take care of everything. You're going to be fine. I promise."

Would she?

They'd always told her that the Minot were dangerous. Could she have been mistaken?

No. He had drugged her. That was why she felt so weird. So confused.

SOMETHING jolted through Jason. He couldn't say what it was. Something that had zinged into his brain. Like when he and Sophia had been in the cave. He'd read her thoughts then. Now he sensed another mental message, but he couldn't make it come clear. All he knew was that she needed him, and he had to go to her.

He had driven past the spa a few minutes ago. Reversing directions, he headed back toward the access road, then continued toward the front gate.

The guard came out of his house and stopped him. "We're closed until further notice," he said.

"I know. I'm Dr. Jason Tyron, the veterinarian. There's an emergency down at the stables."

"I wasn't informed."

"They might not have called you, but you'd better let me through."

"I'm going to check on that."

With a silent curse, Jason waited tensely while the guard called up to the main building. Jason had told a stupid lie, but it was the first thing that had popped into his head. When the guard got off the phone, his expression was stony.

"There's no record of them having sent for you."

Jason balled his hands into fists. He could pound the man into the ground, then break through the wooden barrier and speed into the compound. And then what? Prove that he was the barbarian they thought he was.

"All right," he said, backing the truck up. He shot the man another glance and saw the guy was watching him carefully. Maybe getting ready to call the cops, and Jason wasn't going to be very effective if he was in jail.

Teeth gritted, he turned his vehicle around and drove back down the road, making it look like he was going away.

CHAPTER NINETEEN

SOMETHING BAD HAD happened. Sophia felt it in every fiber of her being. Tessa was in trouble, and she had tried to call out to her sister.

But she was far away. Sophia had gotten only the glimmer of a message. And at the same time, she had sensed the touch of Jason's mind. But how?

"Jason?"

He wasn't here. She'd sent him away. Maybe she'd only *wanted* to think she felt his presence.

She hurried back to her room and got out the candles and cloth that turned the table in her room into an altar. Then she knelt before it, eyes closed and hands clasped in supplications.

"Help me," she whispered, calling on the life force of the earth. "Help me know what has happened to my sister, Tessa."

JASON'S vision blurred. One moment he was driving his truck away from the spa, staring at the road ahead. In the next moment, he caught a vision of Sophia kneeling in front of an altar. In her bedroom, he thought.

He hadn't seen her since she'd left him yesterday on the road after their mind-blowing encounter in the cave, and he wanted to stop and marvel at his first view of her since they'd parted, but he knew this image wasn't coming to him for his enjoyment.

Before he ran off the road, he skidded to a stop. His heart pounded as he eased the truck onto the shoulder, cut the engine, and sat behind the wheel.

Eyes closed, he tried to open himself to Sophia, softly calling her name.

She didn't answer, not in words, but he sensed some of her thoughts. Something had happened to Tessa. He knew that much.

An image came to him. An image of the Minot he had encountered in the desert not far from here. He saw him with Tessa. Or was he just making that up?

He tried to ask Sophia, but the vision of her snapped off as quickly as it had zinged into his mind, leaving his head spinning and his chest heaving as he struggled to drag oxygen into his lungs.

For long moments, he sat in the truck; then he started driving again, heading off the road and into the open desert. He didn't have to go in by the front gate. There were other ways into the estate.

SOPHIA blinked, coming out of what felt like a trance. She had seen Tessa, with the same man from the road. She still didn't know who he was, but she could see his face more clearly this time. He was dark haired. Dark eyed. Aggressive.

In the background she saw a large white building that looked like a church and formal-looking palm trees. The scene was somewhere tropical, but she didn't know where.

And she had sensed Jason, too. He was nearby. Closer than she thought.

But not close enough.

Scrambling up, she stood on shaky legs. Then she automatically followed one of the rules she had learned from childhood, carefully putting away the altar objects before leaving her room.

Tradition and training still guided her as she hurried to Cynthia's office. When she found the high priestess at her desk, she breathed out a sigh of relief.

"I need to speak to you."

The high priestess looked up. She was sitting at her desk in front of her computer, and her expression turned sympathetic as she took in Sophia's anxious expression.

"You look distressed."

"He has Tessa," Sophia blurted.

"Who?"

"The same man who stopped me on the road."

Cynthia nodded. "You had a vision of her with him?"

"Yes! But it wasn't clear. I don't know where they are. Somewhere with palm trees and a big church. I think that was the building in the ceremony we shared. But it was mixed up."

Cynthia nodded.

"I was in contact with her. Then the connection broke. If the rest of us join me in the temple, I may be able to get more information."

She expected Cynthia to jump up, but the high priestess stayed where she was, sitting behind her desk.

"Aren't you going to call the others together?" she asked. "Like we did when I came back from being ambushed on the road?"

"No."

Shock reverberated through Sophia. Had she really heard that correctly?

"Why not? We have a chance to get Tessa back."

Cynthia sat up straighter in her seat. "And put all of us in jeopardy. If you're right . . ."

"I am!"

"Then he has what he wants. One of the Ionians. If he's taken her, then the rest of us are safe."

Sophia couldn't believe what she was hearing. "You're going to sacrifice her?"

"She wanted to leave. Maybe that's what she had in mind. Sometimes the sacrifice of one is necessary for the good of the order."

"You mean if I hadn't come back the other night, you would have just left me with him?"

"I would have thought carefully about the incident. And I would have tried to get more information. Before you came back, we didn't know what had happened. When you got to the spa, it was clear that you wanted to be with your sisters."

"Please, can't we ask the others what they think? Don't we get a vote? Like when we voted to close the spa."

"In that case, I wanted a consensus. But that was my choice. The order is not a democracy. In times of crisis, my word is final."

Sophia wanted to scream. Forcing her voice to an even timbre, she said, "Do you know about Julia or Chandra or Linda?"

She couldn't tell from Cynthia's face if she recognized the names or not. Did a high priestess pass on secrets to her successor, things that an ordinary Ionian didn't know?

When the other woman didn't speak, Sophia went on. "They all left the order and didn't come back."

"How do you know?"

"Tessa found the record of their names in the great book, but there was no mention of their deaths."

"If they left the order, then it's over. Whatever happened."

Sophia was aghast at the callous answer. At the same

time, she wondered what she had intended to say. That she'd met Julia's son, and maybe he could help get Tessa back?

Realizing that was the wrong tack, she pressed her lips together. If a previous high priestess could let one of the sisters go, Cynthia could do the same thing.

In the face of Cynthia's stony stare, she turned and walked out of the office, stiffening her legs to keep from toppling over.

She hurried down the hall, out of the building, and into the sunlight, surprised that it was so bright after the dark atmosphere of Cynthia's office.

For long moments, she stood under the desert sky, breathing hard, trying to figure out what had happened and what to do next.

A blast of insight made her stagger, and she reached to steady herself against the side of the building.

When she'd come back to the spa from her encounter with the two Minot on the road, she'd reached out to Cynthia with her mind. She'd found the high priestess in her bedroom with Layden, and she'd wondered if there would be any repercussions.

Was that what was going on? Cynthia was punishing her? And punishing Tessa?

Could the high priestess be that petty? It was hard to believe. Maybe she didn't even know what she was doing, although it seemed that she wasn't going to lift a finger to help Sophia's sister.

But Sophia wasn't going to simply cave in.

She'd made a mistake. She'd turned to Cynthia because that was what she had been trained to do all her life, rely on her sisters for strength and comfort. Instead she had a much better alternative. Someone who *wanted* to help her. How could she have been so stupid?

At a run, she headed for the fence at the back of the compound, stumbling through the gardens, not caring if she stepped on low-growing plants, then climbed over a waist-high wall.

The boundary fence was several hundred yards away. Through the chain links, she saw the figure of a man, pacing back and forth, looking like a wild animal confined to a cage and going crazy.

He raised his head and stared at her, and their gazes met across all that distance.

It was Jason, waiting for her.

As she watched, he backed up and came running forward, leaping high in the air to clear the barrier.

He sailed over like a pole-vaulter, landing in the red dirt on his hands and knees. After brushing himself off, he started running forward. They met in a scrubby patch of vegetation.

"Jason. Why are you here?" she asked, already sure she knew the answer.

"Something happened to Tessa. I knew you needed me."

"Yes. Tessa."

He hadn't guessed. He *knew* because he'd shared flashes of the same vision she'd experienced. Maybe what had happened in the cave had changed her. Maybe Jason was even the reason she'd be able to contact her sister. At least for a few moments.

They clung together, holding each other tightly, and she understood as she cleaved to him that she'd been so wrong to walk away from him.

"We've got to find her."

"We will."

"Step apart." The commanding voice came from Cynthia, who had apparently followed Sophia out of the building and into the gardens. But she wasn't alone: a whole host of Ionians had come with her, making a circle around Sophia and Jason as they held each other.

She looked pleadingly at them. Ophelia, Denada, Adona,

Vanessa, Rhoda, Lysandra. They were all staring at her with a kind of horrible fascination.

She had broken their rules, and they were prepared to punish her.

Without considering the consequences, she blurted, “Jason can help me find Tessa.”

“I think not. Step away from him,” Cynthia ordered, “before you and your clandestine lover get hurt.”

CHAPTER TWENTY

THEY WERE ON a plane, Tessa thought. She remembered the man taking her to a car that was waiting on a narrow street in the French Quarter. He'd climbed into the backseat, cradling her gently in his arms as someone drove them out of the city. Then he'd carried her up some steps, settled her in a seat, and buckled her in before the plane had taken off.

Now they were in the air. Or maybe she was simply drifting through time and space on her own power.

When her eyes blinked open, the world still looked fuzzy, but she saw the man leaning over her.

He stroked damp strands of hair back from her face, then held a cup to her lips.

"What is it?"

"Water. You must be thirsty."

"Is it drugged?"

"No."

She took a small sip, then another, trying to quench her sudden thirst.

"Better?"

Instead of answering, she asked, "Who are you? What do you want with me?"

"My name is Rafe Garrison. I'm not going to hurt you. I want to show you new possibilities for your life."

"I want . . . my sisters."

"Because they're familiar. You've lived with them your whole life, but you might find you like being on your own better. That's why you left the spa, isn't it?"

His voice was reassuring and tender, but his demeanor could just be an act.

"You're a Minot," she accused.

"Yes. But I'm not like the others."

"How do I know that?"

"I'll prove it to you."

"You're the man who stopped Sophia on the road."

"Yes."

"You . . . frightened her. You frightened me."

"I'm sorry. I knew none of you would come with me willingly. I had to get you alone so I could make you understand what the two of us can mean to each other."

He bent down, stroked his lips against her cheek. She wanted to yank herself away from him, but she didn't have the strength. He caressed the line of her jaw, her neck, her shoulder, her arm, then trailed his hand inward, barely touching the side of her breast, yet she felt arousal leaping inside her.

From the drug, she told herself.

He had done the same thing to Sophia, drugged her so that she would respond to him.

"The two of us are going to be very good together," he murmured.

"No."

"I'll never force myself on you. I'll wait until you're ready to admit that you want me."

He raised his hand to her face again, stroking between her eyes. "Sleep. We'll be home soon, and we'll talk more."

"My home is the spa."

"You'll like my house. It's very comfortable. Very luxurious. My staff will take care of you. You'll never have to do work you hate, like being a clerk in the gift shop."

She sucked in a breath. "How do you know about that?"

"I know you have a free spirit that longs to be what you could never become at the spa."

Was that true? Or was he making up a scenario from his own imagination?

She fought to stay awake. When the plane landed, maybe she could get away, but her eyelids blinked closed and she drifted off to sleep again.

RAFE watched Tessa sleeping, all his tender emotions—and his needs—welling to the surface.

She was his now. He had cut her out of the herd, and he wanted her so much that he could hardly bear to let go of her. He glanced toward the curtain at the front of the plane that blocked off the section where the pilots were sitting.

He'd settled Tessa way in the back, where they'd have the most privacy. He could wake her up and make love to her right here, and nobody would interrupt them.

As that thought surfaced, he couldn't stop himself from touching her. Gently he cupped her breast, circling his hand until her nipple stabbed into his palm, making his cock so hard that he thought it might explode through the front of his pants.

Taking a deep breath, he pulled away.

He could do it here, but that wasn't what he wanted for the first time he made love with her.

It must be right. She must think that she had a choice in what happened next.

He'd studied the Ionians. Not just the modern Sisterhood—he knew about their ancient past, too. And he knew that they had used drugs in their ceremonies. They were vulnerable to certain compounds, and he had used that knowledge to help him subdue Sophia, then Tessa.

For now he would let her sleep. In fact, he would give her another dose before they got off the plane so that it would be easy to transport her to his estate. Once he'd gotten her there, he could go into full seduction mode. After he'd made her his, he'd go on to the next phase. The phase where he consolidated his power.

SOPHIA stepped away from Jason, her gaze going to the circle of women around them.

"You don't understand," she said.

"It is you who doesn't understand. Jason Tyron is obviously a Minot who came here under false pretenses, then seduced you. You're not thinking rationally."

"But he's different." She glanced at him, then back to Cynthia. "How did he get in here if he's just a Minot?"

"Somehow he circumvented our defenses."

Beside her, she sensed tension bursting through Jason. He wanted to speak, but she knew it would be better if she did it. With a small shake of her head and a mental warning, she asked him to remain silent.

When he gave a little nod, she knew he understood.

"He didn't use trickery to get in here," she said. "Our defenses didn't stop him because he's the son of Julia, one of the Ionians I told you about. A sister who left the order in the sixties."

She heard gasps from the women around her.

"You mean a Minot raped her," Ophelia said in a flat voice.

"No. I mean the two of them had a good marriage. Julia raised Jason to have our values. That's why he came here."

Denada ignored the last part. "Why didn't she come back to us?"

Sophia's gaze swung to Cynthia. "Because the high priestess wouldn't take her back."

"An Ionian's loyalty is to her sisters. Not to any man," Cynthia answered. "She made the wrong choice. Her sisters would have welcomed her back. Gladly."

There were murmurs of agreement around the circle.

"If she'd given up her lover," Sophia said, her gaze on Cynthia. For a long moment, the two women stared at each other, and Sophia realized she was treading on dangerous ground.

Swallowing, she brought the conversation back to Jason. "He's different. He didn't take me away."

"They're all the same."

"Let him prove what he is," she begged, then turned to him. "Will you open your mind to my sisters, so they can see what I've seen?"

She felt emotions warring inside him. He had submitted to her in the most intimate way. They'd know that if they probed his mind. But he was in a terrible position no matter what decision he made.

After a long moment, he nodded.

"You must be the link," Cynthia said.

"Can we do it?" she murmured to Jason.

When he answered, "Maybe," she felt her chest tighten painfully, but she walked to him and put her hands on either side of his head, the way Cynthia had done with her in the temple.

"Don't block me. Let me into your mind."

He looked defiantly at the women who stood in a circle around him.

Sophia felt their skepticism and their hostility toward the Minot they had captured. She knew Jason must feel it, too.

"Close your eyes," she whispered, hoping that would help.

Against all expectations, she had made a connection with

him that was stronger than she had made with any of her sisters. She could do it again.

But when she tried, nothing happened. She might have been grasping a tree or a stone pillar.

Don't panic. Let it happen, she ordered herself. And him, because this wasn't going to work unless he could open himself up in a way no Minot ever had. This wasn't just a private encounter with her. This was with the whole Sisterhood.

And they both knew that his resistance was part of the problem.

Her heart pounded as she stood with her hands on Jason's face, sensing the intense scrutiny of all her sisters. She felt vulnerable. More vulnerable than she ever had in her life. Even in the temple. There she'd known the group wished her well. Here she knew that life and death hung in the balance.

As she started to tremble, she felt Jason's hand on her waist. When she focused on his touch, a door seemed to open, and she slipped into his mind, reading the surface thoughts.

She sighed in relief. They had made the contact. The relief lasted until she caught what was in his mind.

He was struggling for calm, but it wasn't coming through. And she knew he felt defiant. Angry. Trapped.

Don't.

Her warning had no effect. Scenes leaped out at her. Jason making long-range plans to invade the spa. Jason stalking them. Jason running out of the desert and fighting with the other Minot who had tried to take her captive.

Show them what I've seen in your mind.

She wanted to say more, but she couldn't because her sisters would hear, and he wasn't listening.

Was all the bad stuff coming from Jason, or was Cynthia somehow helping along his anger and his frustration?

Sophia couldn't answer that question. She only knew that the images were being transmitted to her sisters with awful clarity. And they didn't accurately represent the man who had held her in his arms.

Was she wrong about him? Had everything that had happened between them been a lie?

She didn't want to believe that, yet her faith in him was being drained away.

She felt a shudder go through him, and he fell to the ground in front of her.

When she tried to go down on her knees beside him, two of her sisters grabbed her arms, holding her erect.

TESSA'S eyes blinked open. She was in the backseat of a stretch limo, leaning back against the soft leather seat.

A very good-looking man was beside her, and it took a moment for her to remember who he was. His expression was concerned.

"You're awake."

"You're Rafe Garrison," she whispered.

"Yes, that's my name."

"Let me go."

He patted her hand. "I can't do that. Not now. I want to give you a chance to get to know me. That's only fair."

"I just want to go back to my sisters."

"You can later. If that's what you decide. But you have to be fair to me, too. Now that we're together, you have to let me show you how much I can give you. Everything you've always longed for and more."

The determination in his voice made her close her eyes. She wasn't going to persuade him simply with talk. Perhaps she couldn't persuade him at all. Which meant that she'd have to figure out how to get away from him.

She swallowed, urging herself to a semblance of calm before she opened her eyes again and looked out the window at dry brown hills dotted with low vegetation. Some of it reminded her of the plants she would have seen in the desert around the spa, but this wasn't desert country. Even if the grass was brown, there was too much of it to be the Arizona landscape.

"Where are we?" she asked.

"On the way to my estate. It's in Southern California, just above Santa Barbara."

She took that in, then said, "We were on a plane. It wasn't a commercial flight."

"That's right."

"I was in New Orleans. How did you find me there?"

"I checked the airline schedules."

That sounded reasonable. At least he hadn't used some kind of magic. Or had he? She couldn't be sure what skills he'd acquired.

"Why did you take me . . . away? Without asking me first."

He stroked her arm. She should be afraid of his touch, she knew, yet it was strangely reassuring.

"There's a lot of crime in New Orleans. It was a dangerous place for you to be on your own. I couldn't leave you there—unprotected."

"I wasn't in danger!"

"Of course you were. You don't have much experience away from the Seven Sisters Spa. A lot of things could have happened to you."

And one of them had, she thought, but she didn't say it aloud.

"You've lived with your sisters all your life. They had a lot of rules, didn't they?"

She answered with a small nod.

He covered her hand with his, stroking his fingers against her, sending a little shiver over her skin.

"You were allowed to make love with men, but you weren't allowed to have a real relationship."

When she didn't answer, he continued. "Your high priestess, Cynthia, has a man who's more than just a lover."

"How do you know about that?"

"I make it my business to evaluate a situation from every angle. I know that Cynthia has forbidden you something that she enjoys herself."

That was true, but she wouldn't acknowledge it. Not to Rafe Garrison.

"I'm giving you a chance at the same privileges she has."

"She's the high priestess," Tessa whispered.

"And you are no less worthy."

The limo stopped at a gate, and she could see an electronic keypad. The driver reached out and pressed a sequence of buttons. When the gate opened, he drove through. She looked behind her, seeing the barrier close and wondering how she was going to escape from this place. Or did she want to escape?

She'd never been sure of herself at the spa. She'd never thought that she was living up to the traditions of the Ionians. Then she'd found out about the three missing Ionians, and she'd wondered if everything they'd told her at the compound was a lie.

Well, not *everything*. Some of it had to be true, but maybe they had a prejudice about the Minot that everyone had taken for granted for hundreds of years. And maybe she had a chance to prove that it was a bunch of baloney.

What if she stayed with this man for a while and found out what he was really like? Then she could go back to her sisters and report on what she'd learned.

The thought calmed her, but was she making the right decision?

Well, she had time to figure that out. Rafe Garrison was giving her time, in a safe environment. And even if she was wrong, playing along with him now was her best strategy.

CHAPTER TWENTY-ONE

WHEN JASON FELL to the ground, Sophia's contact with him snapped off as though someone had severed an artery with a knife. Only blood didn't spurt.

Her gaze shot to Cynthia. "What have you done?" she gasped.

"I've only put him to sleep," the high priestess answered. "I've seen enough. It's obvious that he doesn't have your best interests at heart."

"You don't know that. You didn't give him a chance to show us anything but the . . . bad parts."

"Interesting that's what came out. I know what I saw in his mind—unfiltered by you."

"Because he was intimidated. You really expected him to just open himself to you—all at once?"

Eugenia stepped forward and took her arm. "We will leave him here while we discuss what we're going to do."

Sophia wanted to protest, but she knew she wasn't in

control of the situation. Better to go along with her sisters for the moment.

Cynthia knelt and made a chalk circle on the ground. "This will bind him until we decide his fate."

Sophia wanted to wrench out of her sisters' grasp, but that wouldn't do Jason any good. She must stay with the others, because if she simply let them debate his fate, he would have no advocate.

She wanted to scream. Or rush at Cynthia and pound her with her fists. The violence shocked her. Struggling to get a grip on her emotions, she let herself be led away.

In the private lounge, Sophia felt the tension around the room, much of it directed at her. Ophelia and some of the others kept giving her disapproving glances, and she felt like she was the one being tried.

Did they think she'd betrayed them by going off with Jason to the cave of power? That hadn't been her intent. At least she didn't think it was, yet she knew she had been feeling restless in the past few weeks. And perhaps deep down she'd been looking for another way of life.

Cynthia spoke again. "You have let yourself come under his spell."

"No."

"What do you think happened?"

"I connected with him on a very deep level. Otherwise, I couldn't have showed you—" She started to say "what was in his mind" but stopped short.

"Right. It wasn't very pleasant," Cynthia said in a dry voice.

"He was defiant. And nervous," she answered. "How would you react to such an ordeal?"

"I'd try to show what was good about me."

"He couldn't. Not like that, but he's a good man."

"It was to his advantage to let us see that, but he didn't do it," Eugenia said.

Sophia gave her a pleading look. She had hoped Eugenia

would be on her side, but she seemed to be with the others.

"He came here to help me. When he knew something had happened."

"So he said. Perhaps he's working with the other one, after all."

"Of course not!" Sophia protested. It was the only answer she could give.

"We must make sure he is no longer a threat to us," Cynthia said.

Sophia's head jerked toward her. "How? What are you going to do, kill him?"

"We could kill him, of course," Cynthia said in a mild voice. "But there is another way. I propose that we operate psychically on his brain. Like the other Minot, he has heroic powers. I believe we can take them away from him. That will make him much less effective. He will be weakened in body and spirit."

Others were voicing their approval. Sophia repressed a gasp. "Let me prove his good intentions," she said.

"How?"

"There's something in my room I need to show you."

"What?"

"I can't tell you. I must bring it to you."

She stood. Before anyone could stop her, she left the lounge and hurried down the hall toward her room.

Once she was inside, she shut the door and locked it. There was nothing she could show them. She didn't have anything Jason had given her, or any kind of proof. She'd said it because it was the only way she could think of to get out of the room and back to Jason.

Grabbing a chair, she rushed toward the window, stood on it, and unlocked the sliding panel. When it was wide enough for her to climb out, she threw a leg over the sill and shifted her weight so that her body was on the outside. Then she lowered herself to the ground.

As she landed, she heard someone knock on her door. "Sophia? What are you doing in there, Sophia? Let me in."

It was Ophelia, and she knew that Cynthia had sent her.

"This has given me a horrible stomachache. I have to go to the bathroom first," she called out. Then she took off through the garden, running as fast as she could, heading back to Jason. She had to get to him before the others, because she couldn't allow Cynthia to do what she'd said. It would be fatal to him. He'd never be able to live if she took away his powers. They were too much a part of who he was.

She made it to the spot where they'd left him and saw that he was still lying on the ground.

When she tried to step across the circle, the chalk line stopped her, and she bounced back against an invisible barrier. Not only was it keeping him in. It was keeping her out.

"Jason," she called out. "Jason, wake up. You've got to help me."

She looked over her shoulder, and she didn't see her sisters following, but she knew that when she failed to come back, they would guess where she had gone.

When he remained inert, her desperation rose. "Jason," she called again. This time she sent him a strong mental jolt, as well. When his body jerked, she was heartened. She did it again, and again, using every ounce of power she possessed.

After an eternity, his eyes blinked open, and he looked around as though he had no idea where he was.

"Jason," she cried. "They're going to do something awful. We've got to get out of here."

He pushed himself to a sitting position and ran a shaky hand through his hair. "What happened to me?"

"Cynthia did something . . ."

"Oh yeah." Anger flared in his eyes.

"Stop it! Getting mad about it doesn't do you any good. That's how you got into this mess."

"I got into it because I was trying to help you," he said, punching out the words.

"Please, don't start an argument," she begged. "We have to get you out of here, and I can't get through the barrier."

"What barrier?" He stood up and tried to walk toward her, but when he reached the chalk line on the ground, he couldn't get any farther. Backing up, he took several deep breaths, then ran toward her, but still he couldn't get past the wards.

"It looks like I'm trapped," he said in a hollow voice.

"I think we can get you out. If we work together."

"How?"

She raised her hand, palm outward, pressing it against the transparent barrier. "Put your hand against mine. We can't touch, but I think we can make a hole in the field."

He did as she asked. It looked like he was pressing his hand to hers, but she couldn't feel his skin, only a tingling where their flesh should have met.

"Open your mind to me," she murmured.

He stared at her, and she felt something stirring between them. She knew he was trying to drop his mental barriers again, but this time the process was more difficult. Whatever Cynthia had done to him had affected his brain. He wasn't thinking as clearly or as swiftly, and probably the barrier was affecting their ability to communicate.

She knew he sensed her reaction, and his face contorted.

"It's okay," she whispered. "You'll be okay when we get out of here."

She hoped that was true, and she knew he caught the doubt in her mind. Opening yourself mentally to another person wasn't always as convenient as she'd like.

"We have to focus on freeing you."

"I know."

She felt him struggle to concentrate and work with her. Together they focused on the barrier, using the silent communication that they'd forged before. For a long moment, nothing happened, and she was afraid that they'd lost the mental power that they'd developed together. Then, where their hands were pressed against the invisible force field, she felt something change. Molecule by molecule, it began to thin so that gradually she felt the skin of Jason's hand.

"Thank the great spirit of the universe," she whispered as his palm finally pressed against hers. Yet it was only a small hole, not nearly large enough for him to get out of.

"What should we do?" he asked.

"Move your hand with mine."

She began to sweep her hand in a circle, in a motion she might have used to rub soot from a windowpane, and he kept pace with her.

Gradually she enlarged the opening, until it was finally large enough for him to step through.

She pulled him into her arms, and they clung together. She wanted to keep holding him, but there would be time for that later.

"We have to get out of here."

"I think it's too late," he answered in a gritty voice.

When she raised her head, she gasped. While she'd been focused on Jason, the Ionians had been moving into position. Now they formed a circle around the two of them.

CHAPTER TWENTY-TWO

WHEN RAFE HELPED Tessa out of the limousine, she focused on her surroundings. They were under a large portico that led to a wide doorway.

"Come into my house and make yourself comfortable," Rafe said.

As she studied the property, she struggled to remember as many details as possible. The entrance to the house was beautifully landscaped with bright flowers and fruit trees: lemons hung nearby. Also oranges and plums. Beyond the trees, a cheerful fountain bubbled.

This was no small estate. It was a luxury enclave that only a very rich man could afford.

"Come in," he said again, gesturing for her to go inside. Beyond the doorway, a woman in a black dress and a formally attired man waited. Both looked to be in their fifties, with salt-and-pepper hair. The man was lean and tall. The woman was short and plump.

"This is Tessa Thalia," he said to them. "Please make sure she has everything she needs."

"Yes sir."

"Tessa, these are Mr. and Mrs. Vincent."

"Nice to meet you," Tessa said politely.

"They take care of the house for me."

"Um." She smiled at the couple, and they smiled back. Were they being friendly? Or were they just doing what their master commanded? She couldn't tell, and she didn't have a chance to study them further.

"We'll be on the patio. Please bring us some refreshments." He looked at Tessa. "What would you like?"

She thought for a moment and dredged up something. "Iced tea."

"And some of those wonderful sandwiches that cook makes," Rafe added.

They walked through the large entrance hall. Off to the side Tessa saw a formal living room and dining room. He led the way to a large airy space that was set up like a Spanish courtyard with another fountain, pots of flowers, and comfortable wicker furniture.

He gestured to a small sofa under a wide awning, and she sat down, trying to take it all in.

Perhaps Rafe had called ahead, because the food and drink came almost immediately. Then the servants withdrew, leaving them alone.

She took a sip of tea, which was excellent, then picked up a sandwich quarter and nibbled. It was chicken salad. Also very good.

"You will be very comfortable here," Rafe said.

He didn't eat or drink—only watched her until she put down the glass with a shaky hand.

He stroked her arm. "Don't be afraid of me."

She swallowed. "You're not what I expected."

"Of course not. For almost two thousand years, the Ionians have been . . . prejudiced against the Minot. They wanted you to think I was dangerous. But it's not true."

"Then why did you have to kidnap me?"

"I explained that. It was the only way to get you alone, so we could get to know each other. You don't think your sisters would have allowed me access to you at the spa, do you?"

"I guess that's right."

"Since we're free to do what we want, let me show you what we can mean to each other."

She should refuse, but when he reached for her, she let him pull her close.

She'd been deathly afraid of him. At this moment she felt safe in his strong arms. She'd had lovers, of course, but her loyalty had always been to her sisters. Suddenly, everything had shifted, as though she was in a speeding vehicle that had unaccountably changed directions.

When she eased back and tipped her face up, she found that her mouth was only inches from his. He looked down at her with an intensity that made her blood heat to boiling point, yet she told herself it wasn't too late to pull away. Somewhere in her mind she knew she *should* pull away, but she stayed where she was for a breathless second and then another.

"Tessa." He said her name with aching tenderness as he covered her mouth with his and moved his lips over hers. The kiss carried so many emotions. He was comforting and needy and, at the same time, sexy.

She closed her eyes, shutting out the world so that she could focus on the man who was weaving a magic spell around her.

Perhaps he was doing something to her mind as he brushed his mouth against her, angling his head and deepening the kiss. But no mind game could account for the seductive taste of him. The soft velvet of his lips. The heat radiating from his body.

She loved all that. Did she love the man as well?

Maybe not, but did that matter? In a gesture of surrender, she lifted her arms, circling his neck.

She felt him smile against her lips as they kissed. His hands came around her waist, gathering her closer as he turned his head first one way and then the other to change the angle of the kiss, then change it again.

Somewhere in her mind, doubt flickered. Everything she had been taught from childhood told her this was wrong. She shouldn't be in his arms. She shouldn't be kissing him. But it was impossible to hold on to that conviction when it felt like the most natural thing in the world to be close to him like this. As she nestled in his embrace, she could imagine what it would be like to share more than this kiss with him.

She made a small sound deep in her throat, telling him she liked what he was doing. When his tongue dipped further into her mouth, she felt hot, needy sensations swirling through her body.

His hands stroked up and down her ribs, against the sides of her breasts, and she wanted to beg for more. She'd forgotten where they were. Forgotten why she shouldn't allow this man—above all others—such liberties.

SOPHIA felt a terrible pressure bearing down on her as though she were deep under the sea with tons of water squeezing the life from every cell of her body.

She gasped, sagging against Jason, who kept his arms around her, holding her up.

"You have betrayed us," Cynthia said. "You are no better than he is."

Jason raised his head, and she knew he was making a tremendous effort to speak. "Let her go. She only wanted to help me get away."

"She made her own choices and sealed her own fate."

Sophia clung to Jason to stay on her feet. Fighting the

force around her with every ounce of power she possessed, she spoke to her sisters.

"This happened because I came to Cynthia about Tessa, but she refused to help me find my sister. I pleaded with her to discuss it with everyone, but she said that the Ionians were not a democracy and the decision was hers alone." She paused to drag in a breath and let it out. "But I can't just let Tessa go. Cynthia says she's lost to us. How can any of you accept that? And how can you deny me the chance to find her—with Jason's help."

She heard voices babbling around her as the sisters all began to speak at once.

"Silence," someone called out.

It wasn't Cynthia. It was Eugenia.

In the sudden quiet, she addressed the high priestess. "Is that true?"

Cynthia gave her an angry look. "Yes."

"Abandoning Tessa is not your decision alone."

Cynthia raised her chin. "I am the high priestess, and I think it is. She left the spa on her own. Nobody kidnapped her."

"We must not act so hastily," Eugenia answered. "We are few in numbers, and every one of us is precious to the order. We have fewer daughters now than when Tessa was born."

Suddenly, Sophia felt some of the pressure on her body ease, and she dragged in a grateful breath. "Thank you, Eugenia," she whispered.

"What else can you tell us?" the older woman asked.

"Cynthia said that because the Minot had what he wanted, the rest of us were safe. But we don't even know if that's true," Sophia protested.

"There's something else you need to understand," Jason said in a strong voice that had them all switching their attention to him. "Something important you don't know about the Minot."

Sophia heard more than his words. She caught what was in his mind, and it jolted her.

You wanted to get close to me to lift a curse?

Not just that!

Had he spoken aloud? She wasn't sure above the roaring in her ears.

The betrayal slammed into her. The shock was too much for her system, and she would have fallen, but Jason caught her in his strong arms and cradled her against his body.

"Sophia! No."

He was too strong for her to break from his grasp. But she had to get away from him, and her only refuge was unconsciousness.

CHAPTER TWENTY-THREE

JASON CRADLED SOPHIA in his arms.

"What have you done to her?" the one named Eugenia asked. Like the rest of the Ionians, she looked young, but he sensed that she was much older than Sophia.

"Nothing," he answered.

"Don't tell me 'nothing.'"

"She was hearing my thoughts. She thinks that I got close to her to lift a curse."

"Did you?"

He swallowed. "That was part of it."

The woman made a rough sound. "So much for your integrity."

"I think you'll want to hear my explanation. Where can I lay her down?"

After a short hesitation, she answered, "The guest lounge."

He walked along with the women, carrying Sophia, feeling strange to be surrounded by her sisters.

But they weren't his focus. Sophia was his main concern.

As he cradled her in his arms, he spoke silently to her.

It's not what you think. The curse is only part of it. I wanted to bond with you, the way my parents bonded. I wanted the joy they created together. I knew I could only find that with an Ionian. And from the first moment we met, I knew that was you.

He kept speaking to her urgently, saying the same thing over and over. Praying that he was getting through to her.

Did she stir?

"Sophia?"

She didn't open her eyes, didn't speak to him or reach for his hand.

When he saw the others watching them, he stared straight ahead, wishing he and Sophia could be alone.

He had said he would lay her down, but he simply couldn't turn her loose. As he cradled her in his lap, she opened her eyes and stared at him, and he felt the breath freeze in his chest.

TESSA pressed her hands against Rafe's chest, pushing him away.

A moment ago she'd been under his spell. Then a bolt of strong sensation had made her realize she was walking down a dangerous path.

Well, not just a bolt from the blue. She was sure it had something to do with Sophia—calling out a warning across the miles that separated them. A warning about this man? Or all Minot?

She didn't know. But it had jolted her from her sensual fog.

She opened her eyes to see Rafe Garrison looking at her questioningly.

"What's wrong?" he asked urgently.

"I don't know." She blinked at him. "We shouldn't be . . . making love."

He gave her a regretful look. "Of course. I don't mean to push you too fast. You need to rest. Let me show you to your room."

To her relief, he stood up.

She also got to her feet and swayed for a moment on shaky legs. He reached out to steady her, then dropped his hand when she made a little motion to warn him away.

He looked at her with concern and pressed his lips together. When she was standing more firmly, he said, "This way."

He led her back into the main part of the house, then down another hallway to what must be the bedroom wing. When he opened a door and gestured for her to step inside, she found herself in a room that was like something out of a seventeenth-century French château, with white and gold furniture, an heirloom Oriental rug, and a painting of cherubs and clouds on the ceiling. The bed was wide, with a brocade spread that matched the padded headboard and the drapes.

He crossed the patterned rug and opened another door, revealing a large dressing area with women's clothing hanging on either side and a luxurious bath beyond.

As she eyed the wardrobe, he smiled. "I knew your size—and taste."

"Oh," she managed to say, wondering exactly how he had gotten the information and when he had done the ordering.

He stepped back into the bedroom and neatly folded down the spread. "You should lie down and rest. I'll be in my office when you get up. It's right down the hall from my bedroom, which is the next room over."

Before she could comment, he left her alone, quietly closing the door.

She rushed over and made sure it wasn't locked from the

outside. Then she turned the knob on the inside, before walking to one of the windows and raising the sash, sighing with relief when she determined that she could easily get out of the room and that it was only a short drop to the ground.

But then what? In the car, she'd traveled through mile upon mile of brown hills with no sign of habitation. Where would she go if she could get off the estate?

RAFE stood outside the bedroom door burning for the woman beyond the barrier. He'd heard her lock the door, but a flimsy lock wouldn't stop him if he wanted to get inside.

If he went in, he was sure he could persuade her to continue where they'd left off.

Too bad he knew in his heart that it was still the wrong course of action. He had to let her regain her strength, then make her think she was reaching out to him.

But it didn't have to be entirely real. He knew how to make that happen.

Meanwhile, he could have the pleasure of crowing about his progress. Down the hall in his office, he picked up the phone, and dialed a familiar number.

"Hello," a voice said on the other end of the line. The man was another Minot. Although Minot rarely worked together in the modern world, Rafe had decided he needed an ally if he was going to bring his plans to fruition. After checking out scores of his brethren, he'd decided that this guy was his best bet. He was older than Rafe, experienced in the ways of the world and also a sworn enemy of the Ionians because he believed they had ruined his life.

"It's Rafe Garrison."

"Why are you calling?" came the sharp retort.

Rafe ignored the annoyance in the other man's voice. "As I told you I would, I have captured one of the Ionians."

"Okay. You've managed that much."

Although Rafe wanted this man's help, he couldn't stop himself from saying, "You don't sound too impressed."

There was only silence on the other end of the line.

Rafe tried another approach. "You want to get even with them—for what they did to you."

The response was instantaneous. "Yes."

"Then come to my estate. I'm sure we can work out a plan to make the rest of them wish they'd never screwed with you."

"I've stayed away from them for years. Why do you want to help me now?"

"Because I have a plan that will interest you."

"What do you have in mind?"

"We can't discuss it over the phone."

"You really think you can just walk into their compound and do anything you want? They have safeguards you haven't even thought about."

"I got a man in there."

"And the fire put them on guard."

"You know about that?"

"Of course."

"So you're keeping track of them."

"I don't have to talk to you about my activities."

Rafe sensed he was losing control of the conversation and felt his composure slipping. He'd better get off the phone before he said something he regretted. "Just give it some consideration and get back to me."

"TELL us what you've been hiding about yourself," Sophia said in a hard voice.

Jason had already tried to tell her silently as he'd carried her inside. Hadn't she heard any of it? He'd have to say it all over again. In front of her sisters.

It wasn't the way he wanted to have this conversation with her, but he knew he had no options.

When she moved off his lap, he clenched his fist. But she stayed on the couch near him.

Tension coursed through him, and not just because everybody in the room was watching them. He'd boldly said he would tell them about the curse, but now his mouth had turned dry.

He looked at the women staring at him. This was it. Either they believed what he had to say, or . . .

He didn't want to examine the alternative, so he said, "You've forgotten a lot of things about us. And we've forgotten the same things about ourselves."

"Are you implying you alone know something the rest of them don't?" Eugenia asked.

"Yes."

"How?"

"Because my parents dared to explore their heritage. Working together, they were able to uncover secrets that no one remembered. An Ionian and a Minot who can join forces have more power than either of them has alone."

"Or you think they have," Cynthia snapped.

Knowing he had to give them more information, Jason began to speak again. "The reason the Minot are so focused on the Ionians isn't because they're the descendants of the ancient warriors. They *are* the ancient warriors."

As he'd expected, there were reactions of surprise and disbelief around the room. He was introducing a completely new idea, and one that had vast implications for the relationship between the Minot and the Ionians.

"Explain that," Cynthia demanded.

"They were fierce warriors, but they became overconfident and got into trouble when they invaded Scythia. They thought they were going after a primitive people, but the Scythians were very advanced in the mental arts. They cursed the Minot."

Cynthia glared at him. "Go on."

"The curse was that they would be doomed to be

reincarnated over and over with no hope of a satisfying life. Sometimes it would seem as though things were going to work out for them. But no matter how successful they were, it would always end in disaster. Then they'd be forced to start the cycle over again."

"And the others don't know this?" Cynthia asked in an even voice.

"No. They may have glimpses of their past lives—usually in dreams—but they don't know what it all means. Not really." He paused again. "I've dreamed of my former failures. It would be nice to think I made up those episodes, but I know that they're my true history."

"Like what?" Ophelia challenged.

"Like I was a knight in thirteenth-century France who became a lord with great wealth." He dragged in a breath and let it out, wishing that he didn't have to bare his soul to these haughty women, but he saw no alternative, so he kept speaking. "Just as I was about to marry the woman I loved, she died of the plague. Then I did, too. Another time I was a wealthy English industrialist. I'd done so well for myself, that I was expanding my business interests into America. I set sail on a grand new ocean liner—the *Titanic*. Unfortunately, I ended up going down with the ship.

"In the seventeen hundreds, I was a fur trapper in what would now be Michigan. I was doing well until I was caught by a Native American tribe who thought I was poaching on their land. They roasted me alive over a fire." He winced, remembering the pain. "I could go on, but you get the idea. No matter how hard we try, it never works out for us. And almost none of us knows why."

He paused and looked around the room. "My parents thought they could break the cycle."

"Why? The Minot didn't even know the Ionians when they were cursed."

"But the Ionians asked the Minot for help long ago, and when they did, a bond was formed between them."

"It didn't work out!" Cynthia snapped. "The Minot only wanted to dominate us."

"No. Not just that. Neither group knew how to deal with it. The Minot are too proud to beg for help, and the Ionians are too sure their way is the only way. They aren't willing to try anything that hasn't been tested for centuries. So they each go on repeating the same mistakes over and over."

"You're fabricating this—to get yourself out of trouble. I notice it didn't work out for your parents either," Eugenia pointed out. "They're both dead."

He wanted to raise his voice as though he were talking to a child who refused to understand basic truths. Instead, he kept his tone even.

"Because the Ionians wouldn't accept their relationship, and my mother couldn't deal with the loss of her sisters. It finally killed her."

"We only have your word for that."

"I'm hoping I can change your thinking." He looked around the room. "And it did work out for my parents, I believe. They're both dead, and I'm sure their love broke the cycle of failure for my father. They're together in the next life. And he's finally at peace."

Cynthia gave him a doubtful look. "Or you've made this whole thing up."

"I could say, 'believe what you want,' but this is too important to let you simply dismiss it."

CHAPTER TWENTY-FOUR

OVER THE PAST few hours, Rafe had checked the monitor that gave a view of Tessa's room. She seemed to be sleeping peacefully.

With a sense of tingling anticipation, he went into the locked closet in the dressing room that shared a wall with her bedroom.

In it was a tank of gas, a special mixture that he'd had made up, using an ancient formula that few people would recognize today. But he knew it was significant to the Ionians. When he'd researched the order, he'd found out that there was a crevice in the ground inside their temple. The high priestess or one of the others who was giving a prophecy would sit in a chair over that crack, breathing the vapors that wafted upward from deep in the earth.

The vapors had loosened the inhibitions of the priestess, allowing her to let her mind spin out into the universe and gather what it might. Maybe she saw the future, or maybe not. But the gas had an effect on her senses and her behavior, and he was sure it would have the effect he wanted on Tessa. He'd used something similar on Sophia in the desert, and it had made her respond to him.

He wasn't going to drug Tessa into submission, the way he'd tried to do with Sophia on the road, but the gas would put her in a compliant mood so that she would accept him.

He listened to the almost undetectable hiss at the tank valve, then turned back to the monitor. Tessa had been lying still. As the drug took effect, she began to move around on the bed, stirring his senses as the covers slipped below her waist and he saw her breasts through the modest T-shirt she was wearing. The nipples were beaded, poking against the fabric, riveting his gaze.

He couldn't take his eyes off her. He'd tried the gas himself; it had a very pleasant, very freeing effect. Instead of pumping it out of the room, he simply turned off the gas jet, then took off his shirt, shoes, and socks.

He left on his jeans as he walked to the bedroom door, unlocked it with a quick twist of the knob, then closed the door behind him and walked to the bed.

Tessa must have sensed him standing there, because her eyes blinked open, and she looked at him with a mixture of emotions. Sleepy disorientation. Arousal. And uncertainty.

"I won't hurt you," he said as he sat down on the side of the bed, stroked back the blond hair that had fallen across her forehead, and kissed her gently there.

Her tongue flicked out and licked her lips. "I feel strange," she whispered.

"Because you're finally admitting that we belong together."

"Did I? Or is this wrong? Am I making the worst mistake of my life?"

Her aching candor made his throat constrict.

"Last time you kissed me, I felt . . . a warning."

"Do you hear warnings now?"

She shook her head.

He managed to speak in a soothing voice. "That's good. Nothing is wrong that happens between two people—if they both want it. We're halfway there. See how much I want you."

Because he knew that Ionians wanted to take the lead in sexual encounters, he picked up her hand and pressed it against his chest so that she could feel the wild beating of his heart. Then he turned her hand loose and let his arm drop back to his side.

Although she broke eye contact, she kept her hand where it was, then flattened her palm against him, her touch like a brand on his flesh.

When she began to stroke his smooth chest, heating his skin, his nipples instantly turned hard.

He made a low sound, letting her know how vulnerable he was to her.

The white T-shirt she was wearing shouldn't be provocative, but the outline of her breasts through the knit fabric was the sexiest thing he had ever seen.

He unbuttoned his jeans, then unzipped them and kicked them onto the floor. After a moment's hesitation, he kept on his briefs when he climbed under the covers with her and gathered her close.

She went rigid as he took her in his arms, but she began to relax as he gently stroked her back and hair, knowing this must be right for her.

And right for him. As he held her close, a vision of the future came to him. Having this woman at his side could be the most wonderful experience of his life. Of any life he had led. It could change him forever.

Any life?

Was he admitting that his disturbing dreams were real? He didn't want to entertain that notion, and he thrust it out of his head as he began to tenderly nibble his lips over Tessa's forehead, her cheeks, her throat.

"I worship at the altar of your beauty," he murmured, amazed that he had conjured up those words. Yet they were true, at least at this moment. He had worshiped her from afar. Now he had the chance to make her his own.

As he kissed her, he stroked his hands over her shoulders, her back, her hair, then slowly made his attentions more intimate as he brought his mouth to hers.

It was the sweetest kiss he had ever shared. Could ever imagine, and he savored it. Not just for his own pleasure but because he wanted to please her more than he had ever wanted to please any other woman.

When he felt her responding to him, joy leaped inside him. And again he had the sense that making love to Tessa could bring him something he had searched for through a thousand lifetimes.

With a shaky breath, he put her into those lives, remembering women he had conquered before. He couldn't make himself believe any of them was her.

This was different from anything he had ever imagined, ever experienced.

He wanted to simply surrender himself to the joy building between them, but he couldn't let go. Not completely. He had worked too hard for this moment, and he was too close to his goal to drop his guard.

So he let the joy simmer inside him as he stoked her pleasure and his own, allowing her to push him to his back so she could kiss his chest, and slide her lips over his abdomen and lower, until she encountered the waistband of his briefs.

"Are you modest?" she asked with a soft laugh.

"I'm trying to be. With you."

"Let's see what you're hiding in there."

She giggled and tugged at his underwear. He helped her by raising his hips so that she could drag the shorts down his legs and throw them to the floor.

When she stared down at his cock, he held his breath.

"You don't want to hide something as nice as that."

With one extended finger, she stroked delicately up and down his length, making him want to beg for a firmer touch.

Finally she grasped him in her fist, squeezing him before replacing her hand with her mouth, sucking on him as though he was the most delicious thing anyone had ever offered her.

"Enough," he growled. "I want to finish inside you."

"Oh yes."

She raised her head, staring down at him, then straddled him, slowly, teasingly lowering herself. He wanted to grasp her hips and pull her all the way down. Instead he clenched his fists as she finally touched the head of his cock with her body, then brought him inside in one swift motion.

For a long moment, she went perfectly still, and their gazes locked. He could feel something between them now, something he hadn't expected at all. At the edge of his consciousness, he sensed her thoughts.

He didn't just imagine her wonder, he experienced it.

Rafe?

Yes.

Oh my. What's happening?

Something . . .

The physical sensations overwhelmed the mental connection and it faded to the background, although it didn't entirely disappear.

He'd started out to conquer, and she had taken over. As she began to move, he thought of what the two of them could have together. It was a perfect match. An Ionian and a Minot. He knew of only one other couple who had bridged the gap between the two sets of rivals, and he knew how that had ended because he'd made it his business to know everything that had happened to the Ionians in his lifetime. And before.

Rafe. She said his name again in her mind as she smiled down at him. Moving above him, driving them both to ecstasy as her hips rose and fell. When she plunged over the edge and took him with her, he forgot to hang on to his resolve.

She was fantastic, and he was so lucky that he had found her. At last—after all this time.

When the storm of his climax subsided, he gathered her to him, holding her tenderly in his arms.

"That was incredible," he murmured.

"Mmm. I wonder why I was ever afraid of you."

The words reminded him why she should be afraid, and why he must stick to his resolve. Sex with her had been beyond his imagining, but that didn't mean he was going to give up the plan that he'd been working toward for years.

"We're very good together," he said, gathering her to him.

She nodded against his chest.

"Something happened. Something I never expected."

"Nor I," he agreed. That at least was true. The difference was that she wanted to embrace the newfound closeness, and he wanted to keep part of himself private. Very private.

"Did you feel like you touched my mind?" she murmured.

"Yes."

"That was wonderful. I want to explore that. I can do it with my sisters sometimes. It's never happened with a man. That must mean something important."

"We'll see where it takes us," he said, knowing that he couldn't allow her complete access to his thoughts because they would drive her from him.

But the experience had made her drop her guard, and he could feel her drifting off to sleep, probably because of the drug that he'd made her breathe.

Maybe next time he wouldn't use it. Or maybe it was what he needed to keep her in line.

Had the gas triggered the amazing mental connection? Or was that something that happened when a Minot took an Ionian? Not by force, but by mutual consent.

Or at least she thought it had been mutual consent. She didn't know he had helped her feelings along.

However it had happened, he was sure the equation had changed. Until now, her loyalty had been only to her sisters. She'd admitted that he had opened up possibilities she hadn't imagined. Which meant he had all the time he needed to master her and then get on with the most important part of his plan.

Or was his plan the right course? Was he giving up something spectacular out of fear? What if everything he had always known turned out to be wrong?

He quickly canceled the thought. He had worked too hard for this moment to throw away his plans. Nothing fundamental had changed.

CHAPTER
TWENTY-FIVE

SOPHIA WASN'T SURE what Jason's revelations had meant to her sisters. But his honesty had affected her deeply. She wanted to be alone with him now, but they couldn't. Not yet.

She cleared her throat. "If you're arguing about what Jason's told you, you're picking the wrong fight." She looked around the room, then swung her gaze back to Cynthia. "The real issue is that you told me it was your decision not to try and find Tessa."

She could hardly believe she'd been so bold, and the statement drew reactions from her sisters, as she'd known it would.

When Jason pulled her a little closer, she looked gratefully at him. She'd always accepted the leadership of the high priestess, but perhaps she didn't have to.

"I'd like to know if the rest of my sisters want to abandon Tessa to some awful fate. You all know her, but maybe not as well as I do because I grew up with her, and we shared a special closeness. She's been an important part of my life since I was two years old. When our mother was killed, we turned to each other." She looked at Eugenia. "And we had you. Do you want to give up on her?"

Sophia knew she might have stepped over the edge with that last question. For years Eugenia had quietly challenged Cynthia's authority. Today Sophia was putting them into direct conflict, but so be it. She'd do anything to get her sister back. Even cause dissension in the order.

Everyone turned expectantly to Eugenia.

She waited for a long moment before answering, "I'd try to get Tessa back, if we can."

"I would, too," Ophelia said, surprising Sophia with the comment. She'd thought Ophelia would be on Cynthia's side. Maybe she had more allies than she'd imagined.

Everyone was talking at once now.

When Sophia looked at Cynthia, she was scowling. Obviously she didn't like having her judgment called into question or her authority challenged, which could be a serious problem for Sophia later. But she'd chance that and deal with it—after Tessa was safely home.

"You don't even know who captured Tessa," the high priestess said.

"Maybe Jason and I can find out."

"How?"

"We established a psychic bond."

"When you were . . . having sex?" Cynthia asked.

She hated the way that sounded, but she raised her chin. "Yes. Maybe we can use that bond to locate Tessa."

Cynthia made a scoffing sound. "You mean sex magic?"

"If that's what you want to call it."

"You're saying it's stronger than the mental energy the order calls up in the temple?"

"I don't know. A while ago, I fainted. I thought it was

from the shock of what Jason had said, but I think there was more. I think it was because I knew something bad was happening to Tessa. She's a long distance away, and I believe I connected with her for a moment because Jason was holding me. I'd like to find out what else we can do."

Cynthia's eyes narrowed. "All right. You have twenty-four hours. And if you don't succeed, we'll conclude that Jason is of no use to us—and we can go ahead with our original plans for him."

Without waiting for an answer, she stood up and swept out of the room, leaving Sophia feeling like she'd been shaken by a whirlwind.

Eugenia also stood up and looked at them. "Perhaps you had better get busy."

Sophia swallowed. "Last time, we were in the cave of power out in the desert."

"You can't go there now. Jason might escape."

He spoke up. "I won't."

Eugenia had seemed to be on their side. Now she made a dismissive sound. "You expect us to take the word of a Minot?"

"The word of the man who rescued Sophia on the road. If that counts for anything," he said.

Eugenia thought for a moment, then turned to Sophia again. "You vouch for him?"

"Yes."

"I may be making a mistake, but I'll trust you."

"You won't be disappointed," Sophia answered, wondering if she could deliver what she'd promised.

TESSA woke alone in an unfamiliar bedroom. When she remembered where she was and what had happened here, she went very still. She'd made love with Rafe Garrison, and it had been good. More than good. Their thoughts had merged, just for a few moments.

Perhaps she'd misjudged him all along. Or perhaps he wanted her to trust him—and he'd made her believe he was different from what she'd assumed.

She couldn't work that out now because her head felt a bit muzzy. Like she'd had too much to drink, but she didn't remember having any wine.

She climbed out of bed, steadying herself against the bedpost, then went into the opulent bathroom where she showered, dried her hair, and put on a little makeup. From the clothing in the closet, she selected a pair of white slacks and a long tunic with fuchsia and peach flowers.

Still wondering how much freedom she had, she left the bedroom and walked into the public part of the house. In the kitchen, a woman in a maid's uniform smiled at her. She looked anxious to please. Would she get into trouble if this encounter didn't go well?

"My name is Anna. I hope you're feeling refreshed."

"Yes. Nice to meet you. I'm Tessa," she answered.

"I know it's not morning, but you don't have to pay attention to the time. You probably want a light meal. Should it be breakfast food? Or would you rather have dinner?"

She considered the choices. "Breakfast, thank you."

"We have anything you want. Fruit. Juice. Eggs. Pancakes. Just tell me what you prefer."

"Scrambled eggs. Orange juice."

"Toast?"

"Yes."

"Coffee or tea?"

"Coffee, please."

It was such a normal conversation, in such abnormal circumstances. But she realized it helped her relax. This wasn't a jail. It was a civilized household.

She was sitting at a table in the sun-filled breakfast room when Rafe came in.

He stopped and smiled at her, then walked to the counter

and poured two mugs of coffee, which he brought to the table, along with cream and sugar.

As she added them to her mug and stirred, he sat down and took a sip of black coffee.

"You're looking well," he said. "How are you feeling?"

"Pretty good."

"I'd love to show you around after you get something to eat. I've got a fully equipped gym that you're welcome to use. And a screening room. Swimming. A putting green. Tennis."

"And what if I want to leave?" she couldn't stop herself from asking.

"Let's not deal with that yet," he said easily.

She nodded, sipping her coffee. When the maid brought her breakfast, she tasted some eggs.

She ate only a little of the meal, before setting down her fork. "This is very good, but I'm not all that hungry."

"You'll probably feel more like eating later. Why don't we walk around a bit. I'd like you to be entirely comfortable here."

They got up and went outside, where he showed her the beautifully situated swimming pool, obviously very proud of the landscaping and the workmanship.

"Do you like it?"

"It's beautiful."

"Thank you. And we're very good together, don't you think?"

"It seems so."

He was about to draw her into his arms when a servant came hurrying up.

"I'm sorry to interrupt, but you have a video transmission," he said to Rafe.

"I'm busy now," he answered with an edge in his voice.

"He says you'll want to talk to him."

Rafe hesitated. "All right."

She followed him to a wood-paneled library where he pressed a button on a remote. A section of the wall slid aside revealing a large, flat screen. When he pressed another button, the screen sprang to life and Tessa saw a man's face.

She stared at him. He looked familiar. Had she met him before? Or maybe it was the distortion of the TV screen.

He was almost surely a Minot. Probably he reminded her of Rafe—and Jason, for that matter. Although he looked like he was in his forties, she guessed that he might be older.

Rafe looked back at her. "Would you excuse me please? I need to take this call."

It was a polite request, but she could hear the tension in his voice.

She stepped out of the library but remained standing just out of sight in the hallway.

"You didn't tell me you were going to call," Rafe said.

"I don't like to announce my plans. I've discovered over the years that it's better to be spontaneous. Then find out what happens next."

Rafe lowered his voice. "Are you calling to discuss my proposal?"

"I want to hear more about it. I think you're suggesting a drastic step."

"Perceptive of you."

"The Ionian. I hope you're treating her well."

"Of course," he answered. But it was obvious that he was being cautious in his responses. "We should wait until we have some privacy to talk more. If you come here, I'll drop my Minot defenses around the property. But you'll have to let me know you're coming. And I want you checked for weapons before you come into the house."

"Understood."

Before Rafe could exit the room and find her eavesdropping, Tessa hurried down the hall. If she ran, she might make it to her room. Instead she took a chance and stepped into a powder room. If he found her here, she could always say she'd needed to use the facilities.

As she stood in the darkness, she thought about the

conversation. Rafe hadn't said much, but the implications had disturbed her.

He was planning something that involved her. Could it also involve the order?

Or was she just reading too much into his tone and the way he'd cut off the conversation?

CHAPTER TWENTY-SIX

WITH A SENSE of urgency, Sophia stood up and turned to Jason. "We can't waste any time."

When he nodded and followed her out of the room, she knew the eyes of all the Ionians were on the two of them. Her relationship with Jason had challenged everything they had assumed about the Minot and about themselves over centuries. Some probably thought she was making a fatal mistake by trusting him. Others might envy her. If she and Jason succeeded, would that change the whole Ionian order?

She couldn't think about the future now. The important thing was finding Tessa.

When they had stepped into the hallway, he said, "You think we can only connect on a deep level in the cave?"

She hesitated. "I don't know."

"In the barn—I started to hear your thoughts. And when I was carrying you to the lounge, I was speaking to you. Did you hear me?"

"Maybe."

"You acted like you didn't."

"I was upset."

He nodded and glanced back at the women who trailed after them.

Sophia followed his gaze. "We can't talk here. The cave gives us some privacy, and we can call on the power the place generates."

He took her arm and led her outside into the sunlight, causing her to blink rapidly. It felt like hours since the women had surrounded them, but it hadn't been all that long.

They hurried to the parking lot and climbed into one of the four-wheel-drive vehicles the spa owned. When they'd both closed their doors and she'd started the engine, he said, "Come to my ranch instead."

"That wasn't our agreement with Eugenia. She's trusting you not to run away."

"I won't. But it will give us more freedom."

"You didn't mention it while we were with the others."

He shrugged. "Do you think that would have been a good idea?"

"Is this some kind of test?"

"No. But if you want to spend time hiking into the desert, we can."

She thought about how long they had to get some information about Tessa and of her confidence in her ability to connect with Jason again. If they went to the vortex, they would be using up precious time, but if they couldn't merge their minds deeply away from that place, they'd have to go into the desert anyway.

Tension made his body rigid as he waited for her to answer.

"All right," she said.

"Thank you for trusting me."

"I have to."

"I think we have to trust each other."

They drove out of the compound, headed toward town, but he soon directed her onto a gravel road that led into the desert.

They bounced along until a low house came into view. It was earth-colored adobe, in the style that was popular in the area.

The place wasn't designed to impress anyone, but she saw that he'd landscaped the yard with succulents, cactus, and other desert vegetation. And in one corner was a bed of river rocks with a pedestal fountain in the center. As she watched, a goldfinch landed, drank, and flitted away.

"I don't need anything fancy," he said as they climbed out of the car. "But I built a meditation labyrinth out back."

"I take it you're referring to rock-lined paths leading in a circular pattern to the center? Not something underground like on Crete where the Minotaur lived?"

He laughed. "I'm not *that* ambitious."

"You use it?"

"Yes. It's got a calming effect on me. And building it was good occupational therapy."

"You needed therapy?"

He laughed. "Probably all Minot do."

"Why?"

"We have a lot of baggage to deal with." He turned toward the house. "Maybe Ionians do, too."

"We weren't doomed to repeat our lives!"

"You have trouble dealing with change. You stick to ancient rituals that don't necessarily work in the modern world."

"That's not fair."

He sighed. "We've got more important things to do than argue about our heritages."

She nodded. "Yes. Sorry."

Curious to see what he'd done to the interior, she followed

him inside and found he'd stuck with the southwest theme. The floor was made of large terra-cotta tiles, with a few Native American rugs. The furniture was leather. Bookshelves lined one wall. When she walked closer, she saw everything from popular novels to veterinary textbooks—interspersed with ornaments. Some were pottery. Others glass, metal, wood, or stone, and all were animals. Wolves lying down or howling. A pair of white monkeys. Rabbits sniffing the air. Horses, mountain lions, sea lions, dolphins, and other creatures.

She walked over and picked up a panther carved of what must be onyx and weighed it in her hand before putting it down again. She longed to examine all the objects that he'd selected for his own pleasure, but she knew she was only stalling. They had work to do, and she didn't know if they could do it.

"You've made the place comfortable," she said. "And unique."

"It was more occupational therapy—while I was waiting to get the job at the spa."

"You were sure you'd get it."

"I was the most qualified."

"You checked on the others?"

"Of course."

"Who are your other clients?"

He looked slightly embarrassed. "Nobody. I came here to connect with the Ionians."

She tipped her head to the side, studying the wry expression on his face.

"Lucky I didn't check your local references."

"I'm just getting started here, remember."

"What are you living on?"

"That's not a problem. My father left me a fortune. And I've made investments that have paid off." He took her hand. "Why are you stalling? We should get to work."

"We promised a lot. I'm wondering if we can deliver."

* * *

TESSA flushed the toilet, washed her hands, and came back to the breakfast room to find Rafe standing there.

"Where were you?" he asked, a sharp edge in his voice.

She flapped her hand. "In the bathroom. My stomach's a little upset."

"I'm sorry."

"It's nothing serious."

"Maybe eggs aren't the best breakfast."

"Right. Do you have any bananas? And maybe some crackers."

"Of course." He turned toward the kitchen, and she heard him giving orders to the cook.

SOPHIA had been holding herself away from Jason, postponing the moment when they came together, but when he gave a small tug on her hand, she walked into his embrace, and he wrapped his arms tightly around her.

They both sighed. Partly in relief and partly in anticipation. Could they join their minds on a deep level and reach out to Tessa? Away from the vortex?

Feeling a buzzing to her brain, she prayed that it was the start of something they could use.

He stroked his hands up and down her back, sensitizing her to himself.

She didn't have to ask if he felt the buzzing, too. Closing her eyes, she leaned into him, a host of emotions swirling through her. They had been apart less than a day, yet she had the sensation of missing him terribly and joyfully coming back to him.

They swayed together, touching and stroking. When she lifted her head, he brought his mouth down to hers for a kiss that was as much a homecoming as a promise.

"How should we do this?" she whispered when they broke apart for air.

He laughed again. "I recall that last time we were together, you tortured me."

She gave a little gulp. "You figure turnabout is fair play?"

"Not exactly. I think this time we have to torture each other. I mean," he clarified, "we have to bring each other to a knife edge of need—and stay there until we accomplish our mission."

She swallowed. "Or go insane."

"Yeah."

She wanted him so badly at this moment that she couldn't imagine jacking up the level. But she understood the suggestion.

"Are we allowed to be comfortable?" she asked.

"I think it's better that way." With his arm around her, he turned them toward a short hallway that led to the back of the house. His bedroom was in the same style as what she'd already seen, with a squared-off wooden bed and matching dresser and a masculine spread of brown microfiber.

They turned down the spread together, each of them standing on an opposite side of the mattress. Just the act of getting the bed ready made her blood run hotly through her veins. When he came around to her side and slipped his hands under the back of her T-shirt, she felt like she was going to explode.

They undressed each other, moving slowly, drawing out the anticipation until they were both naked, standing facing each other. Reaching out, she touched his shoulder, his chest, then stroked down to his belly where his erection stood out hard and firm.

His face was a study in need as he touched her, playing his fingers over her breasts, then lifting them in his palms and stroking his fingers over her nipples.

When he did, she caught the first sense of something far

away. She knew he was aware of it, too, because he looked at her questioningly.

"We'd better lie down before we fall down," she murmured.

They eased onto the bed together, and he rolled to his side, gathering her close. Reaching down, she grasped his cock, guiding him into her.

They both sighed at the joining.

When the Ionians had captured him, she had been afraid that they would never make love again. Now they locked intimately together.

He nuzzled his face against her forehead, stroked his hands gently over her back.

"We're here now," he said, and she knew he was following her thoughts.

She turned her head, kissing his cheek, his jaw. She wanted to enjoy this moment with him. She wanted to move her hips, but he caught that thought, too, and pressed his hands against her bottom, holding her still and reminding her what they had to do.

"We can't."

"I don't think I can manage this."

"You have to."

She massaged the muscles of his arms, marveling at his willpower. Given this opportunity, any other man would take his pleasure. This one was postponing gratification—to help her find her sister.

But it was more than that: their own future hung in the balance. He'd seen what his parents had together. He wanted that for the two of them.

He had made her want it, too, more than anything, even when she didn't completely understand it. Or maybe she didn't have the same commitment because she'd always relied on her sisters for emotional fulfillment. Even when she was enjoying a physical relationship with a man.

What if the order cast her out now? She had broken their

rules by wanting more with Jason than sex. But wasn't Cynthia doing the same thing? Was it all right for the high priestess to do as she pleased and not with an ordinary Ionian?

She knew Jason was following some of that reasoning, because he answered her.

We have to get through the present before we can think about the future.

How can you be so calm?

I knew that the Minot lacked discipline, so I focused on giving myself that advantage.

She had known he was extraordinary. Now she understood that she was just delving into his depths.

He tried to soothe her with calming thoughts, but it didn't help. Without warning, she was seized by a desperation that she couldn't control.

"I need you."

"You have me."

"I can't deal with this!"

When she began to move, he tried to resist—for the two of them.

"Don't."

But she swept him along, catching him in her urgency.

They moved together, frantic to give and take what they both wanted. A blinding climax overtook them. It should have shut out everything else in the world, but just as she drifted back to earth, she heard something from far away.

Tessa calling out to her with an urgency that made her go still.

Jason heard it, too, and he tightened his arms around her as she screamed in shame and frustration.

"I forgot what I was supposed to be doing," she gasped.

"Nobody said this was going to be easy."

Once again he was the voice of reason as he cradled her in his arms, stroking her.

"I messed that up," she whispered.

"No. It was when we climaxed that you heard her."

"She's in danger. We have to focus on finding her."

"We'll do that now."

His reassurance was interrupted by a blast of psychic communication.

Not from Tessa. From Eugenia.

You'd better get out of there. Cynthia found out you're not at the cave, and she's coming to bring you back.

CHAPTER TWENTY-SEVEN

SOPHIA GASPED. *WHY?*

She says that Jason has you under his control, and she's persuaded some of the others.

Doe she really believe that?

What does it matter? Hurry and get out of there. You don't have much time.

Before Sophia could ask another question, the communication snapped off.

Jason stood up and started looking for the clothing they'd discarded. "Nice of her to warn us. Get dressed."

She pushed herself off the bed, trying to take it all in. Her words came out in a stammer. "If . . . if . . . I run away, I . . . may never get back to the order."

"And if you stay here and let them take you captive, you will probably never see me again. Or your sister."

"But Cynthia gave us twenty-four hours."

"We don't know what happened back there, or who talked

to her. I'm sorry. She could be using the excuse that we came to my house. All I know for sure is that Cynthia must be too unsure of her own power to give up control of the situation."

The harsh words landed against her like stones—because they were both frightening and true.

Still, she couldn't stop herself from saying. "Are you asking me to choose between you and the Sisterhood?"

He kept his gaze fixed on her. "I'm not asking anything. I'm laying out your choices." As he spoke, he pulled on his clothing, then strode out of the room.

Panic was like a thick cloud, choking off her breath and her thoughts.

She reached for the clothing she'd so carelessly thrown off. A few minutes ago, she'd thought she and Jason had time to find Tessa. Time to work out their relationship. Suddenly she didn't have either luxury.

She stumbled out of the bedroom to find Jason standing rigid as he stared out the window at a cloud of dust advancing toward the house.

He looked back at her. "Too bad I don't live farther from the spa."

She nodded.

"I'm getting the hell away before she carries out her threat to operate on my mind."

"You said you wouldn't run away."

"That was before she changed the rules. Do you want to come with me—or stay here and wait for Cynthia?" he asked in a voice that made her chest tighten painfully.

"I want to go with you."

"Then we'd better make tracks."

She looked at the dust cloud. "They'll see where we've gone if we take my SUV."

"Yeah."

He paused for a moment. "I could leave a nasty surprise for them."

"Like what?"

"I could blow up the house the moment someone opens the door."

"No!"

"All right. Your call. Come on." He strode to the closet and picked up a backpack, which he hooked over his shoulder with one strap. Then he hurried to the rear door, and she followed. Shielded from view by the house, he scooped her up and slung her over his shoulder so that her head rested on the top of the pack.

"This won't be the most comfortable ride you ever had," he said, as he clamped his arms over her back and legs.

She gasped as he began to run away from the house, into the desert. No ordinary man could have carried her like this and run in the heat of the Arizona sun. Not for long. But he was no ordinary man.

As he moved between the cactus plants and the low trees, putting distance between himself and the house, she realized he must have been prepared to get away in a hurry. Maybe not from the Ionians but from the man they had met in the desert. The man who had abducted Tessa.

The hot air rushed past her, stinging her eyes. The bright sun beat down on her head and shoulders as Jason ran into the wilderness.

How long could he keep up this pace?

She raised her head and looked back toward the house. He'd said he could make it blow up. And he'd said he wouldn't do it. Was he telling the truth, or telling her what she wanted to hear?

PULLING to a halt, Cynthia climbed quickly out of the car and stood with her hands on her hips, looking around the property that Jason Tyron had bought.

It hadn't been difficult to locate this place, once she'd

known the name Jason Tyron. And once Eugenia had admitted they'd gone to his house instead of the cave.

From the outside, it appeared to be a modest abode, not what she'd expect from a Minot. Was he really different from the rest of them, or was he just trying to make sure they thought so?

Ophelia, Vanessa, Rhoda, and Lysandra joined her in the yard. She'd asked for volunteers to come here with her, and they'd agreed. They had always been loyal, sisters she could count on in a crisis.

Ophelia pointed to the SUV. "They're still here."

"Maybe." Cynthia looked toward the house, wondering if Jason or Sophia would rush out. She directed the women to circle the building, assigning each of them a position. When she judged everyone was in place, she knocked firmly on the door. There was no answer.

"Come out," she called in a confident voice. "We have you surrounded."

Again, nobody answered.

She took a deep breath, wondering what she'd find inside. When she reached for the knob, it turned easily. Was this a trap?

She wasn't going to let the others know that she was worried about that. Or anything else. Like the conversation she'd had with Sophia about the missing Ionians. She'd known about them, of course. It was written down in the secret notes that one high priestess passed to another.

As far as she was concerned, all three women had fared badly. But she wasn't prepared to discuss their fates with anyone.

Switching her attention to the present problem, she looked around the house. The living room was empty, and she took in details. He was an orderly man. And he'd made himself comfortable here.

"Hello?"

No answer.

With a growing feeling of disquiet, she hurried through the house. She could see that Sophia and Jason had been in bed together. The bedding was in disarray and the room smelled like sex.

But they were gone.

She ran to the back door, and threw it open, startling Vanessa.

"They're not inside?"

"No."

Shading her eyes, she scanned the desert. Far away she thought she saw a dust trail. Too small to be made by a vehicle.

Vanessa came up beside her, following her gaze.

"That must be him. On foot. Did he take Sophia with him?"

"She'd never keep up."

"He could carry her."

"And run at full speed?" Too bad they hadn't taken his powers away.

"Or is she hiding around here?"

Anger bubbled inside Cynthia. Anger that Jason Tyron, and probably Sophia, had gotten the better of her. Had one of her sisters warned them?

Contemplating the act of disloyalty made her hands clench. If someone had aided them, she'd find out who it was and punish her.

Could it have been Eugenia?

The notion that a sister of Eugenia's status would do such a thing made Cynthia want to scream, but she controlled the show of emotion. This was no time to fall apart. She had to solve the problem.

Struggling to speak normally, she said, "We'd better find out if she's here. And we'd better not take too long. I want to discover where he went. If we don't find Sophia, we will join our minds in a wider search."

* * *

LOOKING back, Sophia saw that Jason was making a trail in the red dirt. Someone could follow, but not in a vehicle, because the route he was taking wound around the red rocks, into gullies, and up the other side.

He rounded an outcropping of rock and stopped, dragging in lungfuls of air as he set her down, then looked back the way they'd come.

"No cloud of dust behind us. It looks like we got away—for the moment."

"You can't keep this up."

"We're almost there." Taking the pack from his shoulder, he pulled out two bottles of water and handed her one. They both drank thirstily.

He rested for a few minutes, then held out his arms. She knew he was planning to pick her up again. Instead, she clasped him tightly to herself, hanging on with every ounce of strength she possessed. She had abandoned her sisters and come with him, and she needed reassurances that it was the right thing to do.

When she raised her face, he lowered his and their lips met in a frantic kiss. As they broke apart, he said, "I know this is hard for you."

She nodded wordlessly, still trying to come to grips with what had happened.

"We have to trust each other," he said, and she knew it was true. Certainly, he had to trust her, because she could reach out toward her sisters at any time.

When he picked her up again, she could feel that he had less energy than before, but he started off at a brisk pace, changing direction, angling off to the right. After another fifteen minutes, they came to a small grove of cedar trees, where he set her down.

Moving into the trees, he pulled away loose branches he'd stuck in among the limbs to reveal a jeep.

"Your getaway car?"

"Yeah."

They climbed in, and he tossed the pack in back, then started off across country again. But now the route was manageable by a four-wheel-drive vehicle.

Ahead of them she saw a lot of green vegetation that told her they were coming to a creek. They forded it and kept driving, along the riverbank until they pulled up beside a low log cabin nestled under sycamore trees.

"This is yours, too?"

"Uh-huh. While I was looking for a home base, I was also scouting around for a good place to lie low."

He drove around back to a shelter where he could park the jeep.

She followed him to the cabin door and then into a room about fifteen feet square with a bed, two chairs, a desk, a stone fireplace, and a small kitchen unit along one wall. "Sorry, the bathroom's behind the carport," he said.

"I can handle that," she allowed, looking around at the minimal accommodations. They were rough but comfortable enough.

Crossing to the kitchen area, she opened a cabinet and found it stocked with the kind of dehydrated food someone might pack on a camping expedition.

Without turning around, she asked, "You think we're safe here?"

She wanted reassurance, but he wasn't going to simply relieve her anxiety.

"I hope so. But there are several problems. I'm going to assume that the Ionians are using every method they can to find us. Which includes their mental powers. If we try to send our minds out toward Tessa, one of your sisters may pick that up."

"Then we should get out of here. I mean out of the area. The farther away we are, the harder it will be to find us that way."

"We can't. Where do you suggest we go? South? East? North? West? Any direction may take us farther from Tessa and make it harder for us to find her."

She made a moaning sound. "You're right, but you're not making me feel any better."

"I'm trying to be realistic. As soon as we pick up some clue about where to find Tessa, we'll leave here. Okay?"

She nodded, because he'd proposed the only option that made sense.

"Did you buy this place the way you did the other property? I mean, could they find it through the property records, if that's how they found your house?"

"No. I'm actually renting it. A private transaction."

"I hope that helps."

"Can you set up some kind of mental shield?" he asked.

"The two of us might do it. But that would make it harder for us to find Tessa."

He nodded, looking resigned. "We should try to connect with her as quickly as possible."

"Can we do that without making love?" she asked.

"You're tired of me already?"

She laughed. "No. You're too much of a temptation."

He reached for her, gathering her close. "I know what you mean."

They held on to each other for a long moment, then he led her to the narrow bed, and they lay down together.

Last time they'd been frantic, and too needy to keep from pushing each other toward orgasm. This time she hoped they could control themselves. They'd gotten a flash of communication from Tessa during climax, but they needed a longer period to establish real contact.

He slipped his hands under her T-shirt and stroked her back, then brought his hands around to the front, touching and caressing her through her bra.

"When you were a teenager, did you do stuff with boys?" he asked, and she knew he was trying to lighten their mood.

"What kind of stuff?"

"Everything but go all the way."

She laughed. "Yes. The order is strict about some things but it's always been very permissive about sexual experimenting."

"So we'll make a pact now. At least for this afternoon. Nobody's pants come off."

"You're trying to make me crazy, right?"

"I'm trying to get us to a level where we can search for your sister without going over the edge."

She nodded, drawing in a quick breath when his fingers dipped into the front of her bra and inched down toward her nipple.

"You're trying to imitate a teenage boy stealing a feel?"

"Uh-huh."

"I'll make it easy for you."

She sat up and pulled her shirt over her head, then unhooked her bra.

When he drew in a quick breath, she grinned. "I'm taking you at your word. No nudity below the waist."

"A lot of good that's doing me," he said, capturing her hand and carrying it to the front of his pants so she could feel the erection straining against the fabric.

He closed his eyes as she pressed her hand against him, then cupped her breasts in both hands, tugging at the nipples before sucking one into his mouth.

"The trouble is, teenage boys didn't have your level of skill."

He moved his mouth far enough away to say, "I'll take that as a compliment." Then he blew on her hardened nipple, sending a shiver of heat over her body.

Feeling dizzy, she reached to pull at his shirt. He helped her get it off, and they fell into each other's arms again, stroking hands eagerly over naked skin.

She wanted more, but she knew he was right. They had to keep the temptation to a manageable level.

Both naked to the waist, they lay down again, holding each other. Touching. Exciting.

Almost unbearable heat built between them, but this time they had an unspoken pact to keep it under control.

She let the intensity of the contact fuse their minds. For long moments, her total focus was on him. Then she caught a glimmer of something else.

When she felt the sudden tension in his arms, she knew he felt the outside mind, too.

Hoping it wasn't Cynthia, she strove to send her thoughts outward. At first, she couldn't get anything more. Then she heard Tessa's voice inside her head.

Sophia?

Yes!

Thank the universe you found me. You've got to help me.

Where are you?

In . . .

Suddenly, she stopped speaking.

Tessa?

She heard her sister gasp. *You're with him?*

Yes.

You can't trust him.

As though the connection had never existed, it clicked off.

CHAPTER TWENTY-EIGHT

JASON FELT HIS insides clench as Sophia focused on him.

"Does she know something I don't?" she asked in a strained voice.

He kept his own gaze steady. "No."

"Then how do you explain that warning?"

He struggled not to shout his answer. "I can't. She knows I'm a Minot. I guess she assumes a Minot can't be trusted."

Sophia took her bottom lip between her teeth, and he knew that she was wavering. He wanted to grab her and shake some sense into her, but that would only prove his violent tendencies. Every time he thought they had things straightened out, something else happened to make her doubt their relationship.

"In the cave, I opened myself to you," he said in a thick voice. "At the spa I told your sisters about my parents. And that the Minot are doomed to be endlessly reincarnated unless they can stop the cycle. What else do you want?" He glanced across at the kitchen. "If I bring you a knife, I could lie still while you carved me up."

She shuddered. "I don't want to do that."

"What do you suggest?"

"I don't know," she answered, and he could see the warring emotions chasing themselves across her face. She'd been under the control of the Sisterhood all her life. Changing the rules had to be so hard for her.

In desperation, he asked, "Do you want to see one of my past lives?"

"You can show me?"

He swallowed. "I think so."

"All right."

Feeling trapped, he grabbed his shirt and put it back on before lying down on the bed. He'd made the suggestion. Now he wished he could take it back.

"How will I know you're not making it up?" she asked as she put on her bra and shirt.

"Maybe you won't. And you can go back to your sisters and tell them they were right," he bit out, unable to hid his desperation.

When he had wakened from dreams where his soul inhabited another body, he'd always struggled to throw off the memory. It reminded him of what he'd been. And he never liked the picture. Now he was going back to one of those times. Worse, he was going to take Sophia with him.

But how could he manage it with her as a distraction?

"What do we do?" she asked in a voice she couldn't quite hold steady.

"I think you have to let me get into another persona first, then touch me. Hopefully, you'll experience it with me."

"How will I know when you're there?"

"Probably because of the expressions on my face," he answered without elaborating.

This wasn't going to be a pleasant experience. It couldn't be. He had to be brutally honest, to let her see the worst of what he had been and what he could be again if she threw him to the wolves.

He tried to shut that last image out of his mind as he closed his eyes and struggled to pretend he was alone.

That wasn't so difficult. In his previous lives, he had always been alone, not really connected to the human race in any meaningful way.

As that eternal truth sank in, he shuddered. He wanted to open his eyes. To leap off the bed, flee the room if that's what it took to get away from his past.

But he knew he had to make Sophia understand how it had been for him—and all the men of his doomed race.

It had to be bad. The honest unvarnished truth, because Sophia would never believe less.

With grim determination he considered alternatives. He could have gone back a hundred years. Two hundred. Back to the Dark Ages where a short, violent life was the natural order of things.

Or he could have chosen the Crusades. The Hundred Years War. Czarist Russia.

Instead of going back through endless centuries, he chose something from less than a hundred years ago: America, the Roaring Twenties.

He'd wondered if he could drag himself into the scene. Not just as an observer, but back in the moments, reliving them. Even as he thought he couldn't do it, he was *there*. And he knew instantly who he was.

A mobster named Jamie Ferguson, high up in an organization making wads of money smuggling liquor into the states. Sometimes across the border from Canada, sometimes by swift boats that could outrun the Coast Guard if they were spotted.

Maybe there had been some good in him once, but he'd been seduced by the prospect of making all the dough he wanted and the adrenaline rush of living on the edge.

The gang he'd joined sold the booze in their own

speakeasies in cities along the East Coast, and they didn't hesitate to wipe out rival gangs who tried to cut in on their territory.

He went deep into that life, thinking that his strength and cunning had helped him get ahead as a thug. He was sitting pretty, in line to take over the business.

Somewhere along the way, he was aware of another presence beside him. Another mind linking into his. A woman, seeing, tasting, touching, hearing, smelling through his senses and at the same time experiencing all of his emotions. It was strange. He didn't understand it, but he accepted that he had invited the woman to come along with him.

He was caught up in the scene. Why had he ever tried to forget this? He was living big—like a movie star, or a captain of industry.

He had all the money he wanted. An expensive car, apartment in a swanky building, women, booze. Even Mary Jane and coke.

The excitement of living on the edge got him pumped. He loved the choices he had made. Except for one. There was a woman he wanted above all others, yet he sensed that she was out of his reach in the dog-eat-dog existence he was living.

A bunch of rivals tried to muscle in on his boss's territory. He and a couple of other guys ambushed them at a warehouse and machine-gunned them down with the casual savagery of men who will do anything it takes to maintain their positions.

Somewhere in his mind, he heard the woman with him gasp as the images assaulted her, but he was too busy to pay much attention.

She tried to intrude into his thoughts. *Jason.*

You want to stick around, you keep your trap shut, he growled.

He was too busy for dames at the moment. He'd gotten wind that the Feds were closing in on him, and he knew he had to lie low. A guy named Sid Lombardi offered to set him up in a hideout in Maine—for a stiff fee. It turned out that was just a down payment on what Lombardi thought he could score.

He and two of his friends slipped Jamie a Mickey Finn at the hideout. Turned out, they wanted to know where he'd hidden his stash of dough.

And when he wouldn't tell them, they thought they could make him spill. He woke up stripped naked, chained in a chair that was bolted to the floor, with his feet in a tub of water. Then they attached electrical leads to his penis and other tender parts of his body. It worked off a battery and a crank telephone. When they turned the crank, electricity shot through him.

Even with his strength, he couldn't free himself.

He was stuck. Although he tried to take the pain in silence, eventually he was screaming. And he could hear someone screaming along with him.

The woman. She was there, feeling some of the pain, but she couldn't do anything to get him out of there.

The torture went on and on. When he'd pass out, they'd wake him up with a bucket of cold water in the face. But he wasn't going to tell the bastards nothin'.

When they finally realized the electricity wasn't going to make him crack, they started using him for target practice. Starting with his right kneecap, then his left.

He knew he was going to die, and he also knew he was a tough SOB. He vowed not to tell them what they wanted, no matter what they did to him.

Finally, when they knew they had lost, they shot him in the heart, and he sagged against the bonds holding him in the chair. At the moment of his death, he knew he had lived many lives and died over and over again. And that it would all happen again. He was cursed, and there was no way to stop the endless cycle.

He would be in darkness for a while, then wake again,

to a new life. At first, it would seem that he had everything he wanted, until suddenly it would all go horribly wrong.

He didn't want to go back to that. All he wanted to do was drift for a time.

But two women were with him. He had thought it was only one. Now he realized they were sisters: one very close to him and the other far away.

Sophia and Tessa.

He didn't understand how he knew those names, but he understood that they were important.

He felt hands on his shoulders shaking him.

"Jason. Jason. Wake up."

He felt confused. He wasn't Jason. He was Jamie. Another man who had lived a dissolute life and died a horrible death at the hands of men even more ruthless than himself.

What kind of monster had he been? Not just then, but over and over down through the centuries. He wanted to deny that his past lives had anything to do with him, but he knew that would be a lie.

"Christ, no!" he groaned, the pain flashing back to him.

The woman groaned, too.

Was she the one named Sophia? Or Tessa? He was too confused to figure it out.

"Jason. Stop it. You've got to stop. I can't take any more. You're going to kill me if you don't pull yourself back to me."

Perhaps that was the one thing she could have said that would get through to him. Making a tremendous effort, he managed to open his eyes.

For a long moment, he lay there, trying to figure out where he was and why.

"What are you doing here?" he asked the woman who stared down at him.

Panic warred with determination on her face.

"Jason, we're in a cabin. You brought me here. We're hiding out from Cynthia and the other Ionians. Don't you remember?"

"I'm dead," he whispered. He remembered dying. That was the clearest thing in his mind.

"No. You're alive. You're Jason Tyron."

When he stared at her, struggling to focus on her words, she repeated the name.

"Jason Tyron. What do I have to do to bring you back to me?"

As she spoke, she threw herself on top of him, pressing her mouth to his for a frantic kiss while her arms gathered him close, her hands stroking over his back and shoulders.

The kiss broke, and he realized his face was wet—with her tears. While she'd been kissing him, she'd been crying.

"Jason. Please. I'm so sorry I put you through that."

"Sophia?" he murmured.

"Yes! Oh yes."

She sobbed again, and as she kissed him more frantically, he remembered what had happened.

"Tessa made you doubt me," he said against her lips. "You wanted proof."

"I'm so sorry."

"It's okay."

"No. That was horrible. But it made me understand that everything you've told me was true."

"It's hard to swallow."

"Worse than anything I could imagine," she gulped. "And I know something else, too. You never would have risked letting me into Jamie Ferguson's life if you didn't love me."

She had said what he'd been afraid to tell her.

"Yes, I love you," he said.

"And I love you."

The shock wave of those words left him gasping. "How could you? Now that you know what I've been. That guy Jamie Ferguson was . . . awful."

"Back then, you couldn't help yourself. It was your Minot traits and the curse."

"I'm still a Minot."

"I saw what you were and what you are. You've transformed yourself."

"I couldn't have done it without my mother. She made all the difference for me."

"Jason, she was important, but you had to want to change. And you've proved a Minot can do it."

When he started to speak, she went on. "And I've been fighting what I felt for you because I'm an Ionian. And I'm not supposed to feel anything but hate and fear for a Minot. But I don't. Not for you. I love you," she repeated.

He gathered her close, hanging on to her, rocking her in his arms, wanting to make love to her. So much.

But they couldn't. Not now.

"We have to go to Santa Barbara," he said.

"What?"

"Tessa is in Santa Barbara."

"How do you know?"

He shrugged. "She was here. Sort of."

"I didn't sense her."

"Because you were focused on the horror of Jamie Ferguson's final hours."

Her hands clamped on to his arms. "You're sure it's Santa Barbara?"

"Well, not right in town. He's got a big estate up in the hills."

"Okay."

"You didn't see her?"

"No."

"The two of you were hovering around me when I was in the . . ." He fumbled for a way to describe it and came up with, "The space between lives. She was just staring at me—probably in horror. You were telling me I had to come back here. And I understand why. We have to rescue her. And then we have to build a life together."

"Can we?"

"Yes," he answered, not even sure if it was true. She

might be like his mother—too bound to the Ionians to give up her relationship with them. But what if they could accept him?

He couldn't count on that. But he couldn't simply abandon the idea either.

"We'd better go," he said, pushing himself up, feeling his head spin. He'd dreamed of his past lives. Dark, disturbing dreams. But he'd never tried to get back into any of his previous personalities before. He hoped he didn't have to do it again. Because it had almost killed him, and next time it might.

"I need a drink of water," he said, feeling the dryness in his throat.

"I'll get you some from the pack."

Sophia started across the room, looked toward the window, and gasped.

CHAPTER TWENTY-NINE

JASON MOVED TO the side of the window and peered out.

He could see the high priestess staring in at him, a look of triumph on her beautiful face.

As their eyes met, he felt a terrible pressure constricting his head, making him feel like it was going to explode and send parts of his skull flying about the room.

"Damn you," he cursed.

"It's my fault. I made you prove yourself to me," Sophia whispered. "And while you were back there with Jamie Ferguson, she honed in on us."

"Not your fault," he managed to say.

The Ionians had silently gotten into position around the cabin. Maybe they'd gradually started exerting the pressure he was feeling now, and he hadn't even realized it because he was deep into the horror of his past life. Now it was almost too much to ask to stand up, let alone walk.

Yet he knew he had to. For himself. For Sophia and for Tessa.

"We're getting out of here."

"How?" she asked in a shaky voice, glancing from him to the window and back again. Her face was so pale that she looked like she'd been attacked by a vampire.

"You feel it, too?" he asked, struggling to get the words out.

"You mean the sensation that my head is going to explode? If something doesn't happen soon, I'm going to faint."

He was hanging on to consciousness by his fingernails. Anger surged through him. Anger that Cynthia was so determined to stop him and Sophia from doing the right thing.

Perhaps the anger gave him the will to keep fighting the bitch outside.

Putting his hands on the bed, he tried to move it. But he couldn't muster the strength. "Help me get this thing out of the way."

Sophia couldn't know what he had in mind, but she did as he asked immediately, and together they shoved the bed far enough to the right to reveal a trapdoor in the floor.

When he tried to lift the rectangle of plywood, it slammed back into position, but Sophia yanked on the handle with him, revealing a ladder leading down into a dark space below.

Weaving across the floor, he picked up the pack and thrust it toward her. "There's a flashlight inside. Go down."

"They'll find us."

"No, there's a tunnel. You go open the exit door. I'll be with you in a minute."

"You're coming?" she asked in a shaky voice.

"Yes. But I've got to make sure they can't follow us."

Reluctantly she began to climb down, and he wove across the room to the kitchen area.

Feeling like his head was going to explode like a pumpkin hit with a sledgehammer, he fumbled in a cabinet and pulled out a pack of old-fashioned kitchen matches along with the can of kerosene he used in the oil lamps.

With gritted teeth, he sloshed the fuel over the floor and onto the mattress, choking as the fumes rose toward him.

When he figured the cabin was sufficiently doused, he struck a match and tossed it into a pool of kerosene. It immediately flared up.

Knowing he had to get away, he staggered toward the trapdoor. But before he got there, a blast of psychic energy hit him and he doubled over, going down on his knees.

From below him, Sophia screamed.

What the hell was she still doing there? He'd told her to go down the tunnel and open the door. But she was right under the burning cabin, where the floor could fall on her head.

That thought sent panic shooting through him. He tried to push himself up and crawl toward the trapdoor, but he could barely move. Barely even see through the smoke that swirled around him.

"Get out of here," he tried to shout, but the words were little more than a whisper.

Sophia's head and shoulders appeared at floor level, and she gasped as she saw the flames and smoke.

"Get out of here," he tried again.

Instead, she scrambled up and grasped his shoulders, coughing as she dragged him toward the trapdoor. He tried to push himself along, but he knew he wasn't much help.

Flames rose all around them now, licking at the floor and the walls, coming closer. And smoke billowed from the surface of the mattress.

They were both choking as Sophia pulled him to the ladder; holding on to him, she began to climb down. Somewhere along the line, she lost her grip on his shirt, and he tumbled past her. He made a frantic grab for the rungs, but couldn't hold on and ended up hitting the dirt floor with a jarring thud.

Although he didn't lose consciousness, he felt time and space swirling around him.

Who was he?

Where was he?

Sophia scrambled down and knelt over him. "Jason, are you all right? Jason."

He lay breathing hard, trying to pull himself together. His head still felt like it was going to explode, and above him the fire roared. He couldn't stay here, but he needed to rest for a moment before he dragged himself up.

And go where?

He'd planned something, but he couldn't remember what it was.

OUTSIDE, the Ionians had kept their positions, until flames began to shoot up behind the windows and lick at the cabin walls.

Huddling in a group, they watched as fire enveloped the cabin. Window glass shattered, and they jumped back as smoke poured out.

Some of the women screamed. Cynthia struggled to hold herself together.

They'd picked up the mental vibrations Sophia and Jason were putting out, and they'd followed the fugitives here. Silently, while the two people inside the cabin were absorbed with each other, they'd gotten into position. Then they'd struck.

Cynthia had thought it was only a matter of time until the women could rush the cabin.

And now *this*.

The fire didn't look like an accident. Why had Jason started it? Because he wouldn't allow them to capture him? Or because he thought he could somehow get away?

She kept her eyes trained on the cabin, looking from the door to the window.

"Sophia," she whispered. "Sophia, get out of there."

Would Jason kill her? Was she already dead? She shuddered, angry with herself for not anticipating the desperation of a cornered Minot.

"They're going to die in there," Ophelia shouted. "We have to call the fire department."

"We have to get them out," Rhoda gasped.

"We can't!" In dismay, Cynthia watched the flames consuming the little building, knowing nobody could live through that conflagration.

Or could they?

"JASON!" Was that Sophia calling his name? He didn't even know.

He tried to open his eyes and look at her, but it was too much effort.

She leaned down. "Are you all right? Did you break anything when you fell?"

Again, it was too hard to answer. All he wanted to do was lie with his eyes closed while smoke drifted down from above. When Sophia shook his shoulder, he managed to mutter, "Leave me alone."

Were they back at the spa? He remembered the fire there.

Above the roaring sound from above, he whispered, "Did everyone get out okay?"

Sophia's hand tightened on his arm. "Jason, what are you talking about?"

He tried to focus on her words. "Is this the spa?" he asked, feeling his own confusion.

Sophia made a strangled sound. "No. This is your cabin. You set it on fire."

"Why would I do that?"

"To get away."

The answer didn't make sense. But he remembered that Jamie Ferguson had hid out in a cabin, and he'd died there.

She grasped him by the shoulder, shaking him. "Jason, you've got to start thinking straight. Jason."

Yeah, right.

He didn't even know who he was. Not for sure. But he was dimly aware that flames were licking through the wood above him.

Far away, he could hear women screaming.

"Jason. Please."

Then a burning brand fell, landing a couple of feet from his shoulder.

Sophia cried out, and his mind suddenly snapped back into gear.

The cabin. The kerosene. The fire. He couldn't stay where he was because he was putting Sophia in danger.

It took an enormous effort to get up, but he staggered to his feet, swaying on unsteady legs. He braced one hand against the tunnel wall to stay erect.

"Thank the universe," Sophia whispered.

She draped one arm around him and grasped the flashlight in the other. Together they staggered down the tunnel with her playing the flashlight beam ahead of them.

As he moved away from the fire, his mind cleared a little.

He remembered the pain in his head. It was gone.

"They must have stopped bombarding us."

"Yes."

They kept going until they came to the end of the tunnel. The way was barred by a wooden door. He lifted the lever and pushed against the barrier, but it wouldn't open.

"Crap," he muttered.

"What's wrong?"

"Something . . . I don't know."

Behind them, smoke billowed down the passageway, and he knew they didn't have much time. They were far enough from the fire to keep from getting burned, but the smoke was thickening, and it was going to overcome them soon.

CHAPTER THIRTY

THE OTHER MAN had arrived. Tessa had heard Rafe tell him to wait a few minutes until he could open the gate. After that he went into his bedroom. Did he have some kind of special equipment in there? Was that where he controlled his defense system?

She waited until he left the room, then peeked out of her own doorway, watching his back as he strode down the hall and out of sight. A few minutes later he was back with his visitor.

After they went into the library, she waited again until the door closed. Then, taking another chance, she hurried into the bathroom next door where she'd hidden before.

When she heard furniture creaking, she figured the men had sat down. Was it safe to get closer to the door? And what would happen if the housekeeper or butler came along and found her?

She knew she was taking a big risk. Probably they'd run to Rafe and tell him they'd caught her eavesdropping. But he had made her think that she had to do it, for herself and for her sisters.

Still, her heart was pounding as she opened the bathroom door and looked into the hall. Just as she was about to step out, plump Mrs. Vincent bustled down the corridor. Tessa waited with her pulse pounding until the woman was out of sight. After another half minute, she tiptoed down the hall to the library.

"Can I get you a drink?" Rafe said, and she tensed, hoping he wasn't going to call for someone to serve them.

"Bourbon on the rocks," the visitor said.

Rafe's footsteps came toward her, and she went rigid, but he was only crossing the room to close the door. Still, her hearing was excellent, and she followed his steps to the bar that she'd seen in the corner. Ice cubes clinked, followed by the sound of liquid being poured.

"Now that you're here, I can tell you what I'm planning. The death of the Ionians," Rafe said, and Tessa had to take her bottom lip between her teeth to keep from gasping.

Her head was spinning, and she steadied herself against the wall, stiffening her legs to keep from falling over.

Had she heard him right? No, that couldn't be what he was planning.

More words came to her from the office.

"Is it necessary to destroy them?" the visitor asked. "I mean, you've got what you want, haven't you?"

"I thought you wanted revenge."

Sidestepping the question, the other man said, "For years, I was a man of peace."

Rafe laughed. "No Minot is a man of peace."

"Perhaps, but you can train yourself to behave in a more civilized manner."

"I am what I am," Rafe said with a finality that sent cold flowing through Tessa's body all the way to her bones. He'd been tender with her. Now it sounded like he'd only been putting on an act to lull her into submission.

"I want her pregnant before I move on the others."

She struggled not to react aloud. Pregnant with his child! Never in a million years. She had started to doubt him. He'd just given her proof of his true nature.

She needed to find out more, but she thought she had heard the important part. This man was planning to kill her sisters, and she had to warn them.

WITH her heart in her throat, Sophia watched Jason trying to push the door open.

"Get down," he rasped. "Where the smoke is thinner."

She crouched beside him, coughed, then asked. "Can I help you?"

"I doubt it."

With dogged determination, he rammed his shoulder against the door, but still it didn't give. Then he tried pulling inward.

"There's a little movement," he muttered.

He kept pulling and pushing, trying to make the damn thing open one way or the other. Finally with a heaving sound, the boards splintered and he crashed partway through.

Fresh air rushed in, and Sophia took a grateful gasp.

Jason peered out. Over his shoulder, Sophia stared at the outside world. The tunnel exit was in a wooded area, and she could see that a tree had fallen across the doorway.

He began tearing at the boards, throwing them into the tunnel behind them. Although Sophia wanted to help, there wasn't room for two people to work there.

But she could see the demolition was having an effect. Soon there was an opening in the middle of the door that was probably big enough for her to crawl out.

"You first," he told her. "But make sure the coast is clear."

Sophia stuck her head out and looked around.

"Are we alone?"

"Yes."

"Okay. I don't think they'll find us. We're pretty far from the cabin, and there are trees and big rocks in the way."

She eased her shoulder through the gap, then pushed upward, wiggling through the opening and half falling out onto the ground. For long moments she lay dragging in lungfuls of the untainted air.

Looking up, she expected to see Jason coming after her. He stuck his arm through, but his shoulders were too big to fit. Withdrawing, he began pulling at the boards again.

She could hear him coughing as he worked, and her heart leaped into her throat.

"Take a breath through the hole," she called out.

He did as she suggested, then went back to trying to dismantle the door. Scrounging around for some way to help him, she found a large rock. But when she raised it to pound in the door, she stopped herself. If she started making noise, Cynthia and the others might find them. All she could do was wait with tension singing through her while Jason worked.

Finally he enlarged the opening enough for his shoulders to fit through.

When he disappeared again, she wanted to scream, but he reappeared quickly. "Stand back."

After she did, he threw out the pack he'd dragged with him, even when he was half choked and blinded by smoke. Then he wiggled out, and she kept him from hitting the ground hard by easing him down.

She crouched beside him, and he wrapped his arms around her, holding on tight. They rocked in each other's arms, both thankful that they had made it out of the cabin and out of the tunnel.

After a quick kiss, she murmured, "I was so scared."

"We're safe now."

"Do you have another car stashed somewhere?" she asked.

"Sorry."

"I guess that was too much to hope for. What are we going to do?"

"For starters, we've got to get out of Sedona before they find us again. It was a mistake to stay here."

"My fault. I should have realized they'd zero in on us."

"Let's not waste time on blame. We've got to focus on getting away."

"Won't they think we're dead?"

"Not when there are no bodies inside the cabin. And not if we try to contact Tessa."

He sat up, bringing her with him, and brushed dirt from her shoulder. "Burning the cabin didn't work out quite the way I expected."

"Did we have a better option?"

"No."

"Okay, but . . ." She flapped her hand in frustration. "We still have no idea who took Tessa."

"But we know where the guy lives. And we can find him. And find her."

"Before it's too late?"

"Too late for what?"

She swallowed. "I don't know. But the Ionians do have some sense of the future, and I can't help worrying that something horrible is going to happen."

"We'll stop it!"

The determined look on his face made her heart melt. He was doing this for her. For the Ionians. And they kept trying to stop him.

He started walking through the woods, and she followed him, glad that he knew where he was going.

"Did he drive her to Santa Barbara, do you think? Or did he fly?" Sophia asked.

"I don't know. But we're going to drive. Less chance of someone figuring out where we're going."

"What happens when we get there?" she asked as they skirted around a large boulder.

"I guess that will depend on what we can work out."

She nodded, wishing they had some kind of concrete plan. But that would have to wait until they had a better idea of the situation.

Jason turned toward her. "When we get to the road, I'll leave you somewhere safe and get a car."

"How?"

He patted the backpack. "I brought more than a flashlight and water. I've got money—and credit cards in another name. Also a matching driver's license."

"You were prepared."

"I guess it's a Minot trait!"

"You've got more than Minot traits. You're an extraordinary man who overcame his background."

He shrugged. "You've heard of nature versus nurture?"

"Of course."

"My mother made the difference. Without her, I would have been like the rest of them."

She had trouble believing that was the only factor, but she wasn't going to argue. Not when their lives were in danger.

As they approached the road, he slowed. "Will you be all right alone?"

She wanted to say, "Yes." But she heard herself say, "I wish I could come with you."

"So do I. But I've got to make it fast. And I don't have the strength to carry you this time."

She pressed her hand to her mouth. "Sorry. I wasn't thinking straight. I don't want to make this harder for you. How long will you be?"

"I'll be back as fast as I can." He got out a bottle of water and gave it to her.

She reached for him, and they clung together. She had the awful feeling that if he left her here, she was never going to see him again, but she didn't voice the thought. Had he heard it anyway?

Finally, he eased away. "Let's get you comfortable."

He found her a place to sit that was sheltered from the road where she'd have her back to a tree trunk. Together they gathered a bed of leaves for her to sit on. When they were finished, he hugged her again before fading back into the woods.

Settling down, she leaned her head against the trunk and closed her eyes. She might be here for hours. There was no way of knowing.

At first she tried not to check her watch, but as time crawled by and the sun dipped low in the west, she started sneaking peeks at the dial. It would be dark soon, and she hadn't been out alone at night since the incident on the road.

But that guy who'd assaulted her wasn't even here. He'd taken Tessa to Santa Barbara—if Jason was right, which she didn't even know. Still, going there seemed like their only option. Too bad they didn't dare to join their minds until they were away from Sedona.

She pressed her back against the tree trunk, wishing she could get a little sleep, but she couldn't doze off. And she couldn't shake the notion that someone was stalking her as she listened to the wind in the trees and the sounds of branches crackling nearby. She tried to tell herself it was just little animals in the underbrush, until she realized she must be listening to footsteps moving closer.

The hairs on the back of her neck prickled as she peered into the darkness.

If it was Jason coming back, why didn't he call out to warn her?

She sat as still as possible, her heart pounding, wondering if it would do any good to run.

When a black-clad figure glided into view, she gasped. It was Ophelia.

Scrambling to her feet, Sophia prepared to flee.

"Don't. We're not here to harm you."

"We?"

Eugenia stepped forward, and Sophia had to press her back against the tree trunk to keep from swaying.

"Are you here to drag me back to the spa? Where I won't be under the influence of the evil Jason?" she asked, her voice dripping with sarcasm.

"No," Eugenia answered.

"Then what? Kill me out here so I don't cause you any more trouble?"

"We've had a close relationship since you were a little girl. You think I would do that?"

She turned her hand palm up. "I don't know anymore. Not after the way Cynthia attacked us."

Eugenia sighed. "A group of us is hoping you can find Tessa, and bring her back."

As she tried to take that in, she asked, "How did you find *me?*"

Eugenia gave her a sympathetic look. "You're nervous and upset, and you're giving off enough vibrations to take down a major rock formation."

"I didn't know."

"Most people wouldn't pick them up."

"But you're not most people." She looked at Ophelia. "A while ago, you were working with Cynthia, making my head feel like it was going to split open. Is she waiting around the corner?"

"No. She doesn't know I'm not back at the spa. And she'll be angry when she finds out I'm missing."

"Why didn't *she* find me?"

"She called in the incident at the cabin," Eugenia answered.

"The incident!"

"And she's busy with the fire marshal and the police."

Sophia kept her gaze steady. "Why are you defying her?"

"Because we don't want to leave one of our sisters in the hands of a Minot, and we think you have a chance of bringing Tessa back," Eugenia responded. "You said three Ionians had disappeared. One was Jason's mother, Julia. We don't know anything about the others."

"I thought you might."

Eugenia shook her head.

"What about them?" Sophia asked.

"We need to know if they were . . . captives. Or if they lived happy lives."

"With a Minot?"

Eugenia shrugged.

Sophia raised her chin. "I'm with a Minot."

"Do you trust him?"

"Yes," she answered immediately. "He could have left me. He could have hurt me. He could have tried to mess with my head. He hasn't done any of that. Instead he's been trying to help us. And look what he's gotten for his trouble."

From the darkness, a deep, male voice said, "I'm glad to hear the vote of confidence."

It was Jason. She ran to him and clasped him tightly, not caring what the other two women thought. "Thank the powers you're back."

"And I see two of your sisters have joined the party." He pressed her against his side as he faced the other Ionians.

"Do you know where to find Tessa?" Eugenia asked.

"We think we know the city. That's as far as we got."

"We'd like to help you rescue her."

Jason kept his voice even. "I think we have to find her first. And I think our best chance of that is if we're alone. Because the more people involved, the more likely Cynthia will find us."

Eugenia pressed her palms against her thighs. "I was hoping to go with you, but you may be right. If the four of us were together, Cynthia might be able to track us."

"Thank you for not arguing," Sophia said.

"But if you need our help, I hope you'll ask for it."

"Maybe," Jason answered.

"I understand why you might not trust us."

"At least you're insightful." Jason's voice held the same sarcasm that Sophia hadn't been able to repress earlier. He took her hand. "We'd better split."

Without a backward glance, she walked with him out of the forest. When they reached the road, she saw the car he'd parked in a turnoff. It was a midsized Ford only a few years old.

They climbed in, and he headed away from town.

"Where did you get the car?" she asked.

He laughed. "Craigslist. For a nice fee, the guy agreed to keep it in his name for the time being."

"Is that legal?"

"Well, I'm just borrowing it. He's getting a good deal."

They headed for Route Forty, then west.

"I think we can make Lake Havasu City," Jason said.

Sophia had never been to the resort area, but many of the spa guests had spoken about it. Some had combined trips to the Seven Sisters with visits there. "Isn't that almost two hundred and fifty miles away?"

"Yeah."

"You can run fast, but if you try to do a hundred miles an hour on the road, you'll get a speeding ticket. In a car that's registered to someone else."

"Point taken, but I want to get far enough from Sedona so they can't tune in to us."

"If that's possible," she answered.

He looked toward her, then back to the road. "Do you trust Eugenia?"

She thought about everything that had happened. Wishing she could be more positive, she admitted "I don't know."

CHAPTER THIRTY-ONE

"YOU THINK THEY'RE telling the truth about wanting to get Tessa back?" Jason asked in a gritty voice.

Sophia clasped her hands together in her lap. "If you had asked me last week, I would have said 'yes' with no hesitation. Now I'm not so sure."

Jason had been expecting the answer. "So we've got to do this by ourselves."

"That's probably right."

He dragged in a breath and let it out before saying, "And our first job—if we can get back into contact with Tessa—is to convince her that I'm on her side."

She reached to clasp his arm, holding on tight. "We'll do it."

"Maybe."

They rode in silence for several miles.

When he slowed, she gave him a questioning look. "Now what?"

He gestured toward a fast-food restaurant. “We haven’t had much to eat today. We’d better grab some burgers.”

“And milk shakes,” she said. “We could use the calories.”

“I’m learning your secret vices.”

She gave him a mischievous grin. “Which is worse? Milk shakes or S and M?”

He laughed. “Depends. If you tied me down, dripped cold milk shake on me, and licked it off, I’d be able to give a better evaluation.”

“Stop!” she begged.

“Okay.” But he was secretly pleased that they could joke around, even under the present circumstances.

After paying for the simple meal at the drive-through, they kept driving while they ate the burgers and drank the shakes.

As she bundled up the trash, he said, “It’s been a hell of a day. You should get some sleep.”

“You had the same day. Worse, actually. If you’re going to stay awake, so will I.”

Despite what Sophia had said, he watched her lean back, watched her eyes drift closed. When her breathing became even, he focused on the road, glad that she could get some rest.

He was tired, too, but he wanted to get as far from the Ionians as he could. He’d known they were cautious and clannish. He understood that they could be vindictive. He hadn’t realized the lengths they’d go to get their way. Or maybe it was the old Ionian–Minot thing? They couldn’t let their sworn enemies win? At least that was true of Cynthia. The one named Eugenia seemed more reasonable.

And he knew they weren’t all the same. His mother had been different, or she never would have gone off with his father. He prayed that Sophia had the same courage of her convictions. Still, in the end, his mother had lost the battle for independence. He thought about his father again. What had made him different from the average Minot? Did he have Ionian blood, too? It was an interesting question. One he might never find the answer to. He shuddered.

When he reached the outskirts of the city, he drove past the first few motels and turned in at a well-known chain where the rooms were all on the outside. As he pulled to a stop under the portico, Sophia's eyes blinked open, and she looked around.

"We're here?"

"Yeah."

"I told you I wanted to stay awake."

"It worked out."

She pushed herself up. "We don't have any luggage."

"Actually, we do. Before I picked you up, I made a quick run to a discount department store. I've got basic toilet articles and clothing."

When she started to get out, he put a hand on her arm. "Stay here. If someone's looking for us, it's better if the desk clerk doesn't remember a man and woman checking in together."

"I didn't think of that."

"You're not used to being devious."

Ten minutes after he'd pulled into the parking lot, they were in their room.

He sat down on the edge of the bed and wearily pulled off his shoes. "I've got to get some sleep, but I feel like I've spent the day in a chimney."

"Go get cleaned up. I'll wait."

He took a quick shower, feeling refreshed for the first time since they'd escaped from the tunnel.

The fates allowed him a few hours of rest. Then a nightmare seized him.

He was Jamie Ferguson, the Prohibition Era gangster again, stripped naked, chained in a chair that was bolted to the floor, with his feet in a tub of water and electrodes attached to the sensitive areas of his body.

His torturer turned the crank on an old-fashioned telephone, and pain ripped through him.

He wouldn't scream. He wouldn't tell them where he'd hidden his stash. But his body jerked as the pain stabbed into him.

Then the bastards started shaking him and calling his name.

Only they weren't calling him Jamie. It was Jason.

His confused mind struggled to grapple with that. When he tried to strike out with his hand, he found that the chains holding him down weren't all that secure.

He slammed a mighty blow into his torturer, hearing a satisfying gasp of pain and surprise.

"Jason. Don't. Jason, you're having a nightmare."

He was still confused. He'd thought he was in a chair. Instead he was lying down.

When a warm body pressed on top of him, he bucked.

"Jason. Wake up. Jason."

Jason! Stop it. You're hurting me.

The voice in his mind got his attention. Maybe he wasn't back in the 1920s. Unless the gangsters had powers he didn't know about.

His eyes blinked open. In the dim light, he saw Sophia above him, staring down. She was trying to hold his arms, but of course she was no match for his strength.

"Sophia?"

Her hands tightened on his arms. "Thank the universe."

A wave of guilt swept over him as he stared at the red splotch on her right cheek. "I hurt you."

"You were having a nightmare."

He made a rough sound. "I was back in the world of that gangster—Jamie Ferguson."

"I'm sorry. It's my fault. You went back there to prove something to me, and now it won't let go of you."

He gently rolled her off of him, then sat up. "I thought it was safe for you to be with me. It seems I was wrong."

She caught her breath. "You're not wrong."

"Like I said, I hurt you."

"You thought I was someone else in the dream."

"That's no excuse."

When he started to climb off the bed, she grabbed him. "Don't run away from me. Not when . . ."

Her voice trailed off.

"What were you going to say?"

"It wasn't the right thing."

"You were going to say you'd given up everything to be with me."

"I have no right to make you responsible for my decisions."

"We both know what you've given up. We both know what happened to my mother."

"Let's focus on what I've gained, not what I've lost. Come back to bed. Help me get through to Tessa."

"It didn't work so well last time."

"It will now."

"Why?"

The determination in her eyes made his throat tighten.

"What if you stay in the background? You help me reach Tessa, and I'll do the talking."

"You really think she won't know?"

"Jason, we've got to try!"

He understood that desperation was driving her, but he had to ask, "And you think we're far enough from Sedona to keep them from finding us again?"

"That's another chance we have to take. They might have wanted to follow us, but they have no idea which direction we took. They could be farther from us than just the distance to Sedona."

He wasn't sure that was true. Or if her plan would work, but the pleading look on her face tore at his heart.

When he held out his arms, she came into them, nestling against him.

"We're going to try what we did before?" he asked.

"Yes."

He nodded against the top of her head.

When she lifted her face, their lips met in a kiss that was as frantic as it was passionate. And in that moment, he knew what she was going to say to Tessa.

"Okay," he murmured as he stroked her hair, her back, her arms, letting the feeling of closeness between them build along with his arousal.

Nothing had changed in that department. He wanted her with the desperation of a man who understood that the thing he craved most in the world could be cruelly snatched away from him. She might think she wanted a life with him. That might turn out to be impossible.

Never. You spent a lot of time planning how to get close to me. Don't throw it away.

He knew she was right. He wouldn't give her up without a fight. So he let the passion build, and tried to drift above the physical need gnawing at him.

Then from far away, he heard another voice. Gritting his teeth, he struggled to stay quiet and hidden.

Sophia?

Yes.

Thank all the ancient powers. I've been calling to you, but I couldn't get through.

I'm closer.

You know where I am?

Santa Barbara. I don't know any more than that.

I'm with . . .

He heard a gasp. Felt her start to pull away. *You're still with him! And he's . . . a . . . a gangster. Jamie Ferguson. Or did I dream that?*

You didn't dream it. But that was a past life. He showed it to me. You must have joined us in a dream. Stay with me now. He saved my life. We were in his cabin, hiding out from Cynthia, and she found us. She brought some of the others, and they were using their powers to crush our minds.

Cynthia did that?

He felt Sophia opening herself, letting Tessa see everything that had happened.

The other Ionian gasped.

All that's true?

How could I lie in my thoughts?

He heard Tessa's silent acknowledgment.

Tell us the name of the Minot who has you, Sophia begged.

Jason clenched his hands on Sophia's arms, and pressed his lips together, fighting to stay out of the conversation. He wanted to demand the man's name, but he understood that she wasn't going to tell *him*.

After long moments, Tessa answered, *Rafe Garrison.*

Jason had expected to feel some kind of shock wave roll over him, but there was no sensation of hearing a revelation. The guy hadn't been on any of the property or rental records he'd searched in Sedona.

And there's another one with him. I don't know his name. He introduced him as John, but that might be . . . an alias. They're plotting something together. This other guy hates the Ionians. He . . . he's going to help Rafe kill the rest of our sisters.

Sophia gasped. *No!*

You have to stop them. But I don't know how you're going to get in here. He's got . . .

Before she could say anything else, the transmission suddenly cut off, and he was left holding Sophia in his arms.

"What happened?"

"I don't know."

"Could he have heard her talking to you?"

"I don't know!" Sophia's voice went high and thin in her frustration.

"We'll get there."

"We still don't know exactly where."

"While you were focused on talking to her. I got a picture from her mind. She traveled a long way through hills covered with dry grass and scrubby vegetation. She's out in the country. If it's around Santa Barbara, it's probably north."

"How do you know?"

"The population density is pretty high to the south. There'd be nowhere like what she saw."

"You're sure?"

"I visited there with my parents when I was younger."

She sighed. "Okay."

He cradled her in his arms, still wanting her as much as he had a few minutes ago. But he could tell that she was no longer aroused.

"You're upset."

"I just heard about a plot to kill my sisters. I have to warn them."

"You can't."

"But we have to assume she overheard the two men talking about their murder plans. They could be going right to Sedona."

"No."

"Why?"

"Don't you think the Garrison guy would be taking a chance if he didn't establish his relationship with Tessa better before he went off to kill her sisters?"

Sophia nodded against his shoulder, clinging to him. "That could be right. But if it's wrong . . . my sisters could die."

"They have defenses."

"He must think he can get past them."

Jason dragged in a breath and let it out. "If you contact your sisters, they'll stop you from rescuing Tessa."

She moaned. "I don't know what to do!"

"We're not far. We'll get to his place and stop him."

Her mouth firmed. Pushing herself up, she looked at the clock on the bedside table. It said seven a.m.

"Let's get back on the road again."

"I need to do a little research first." He got up and picked up the carry bag he'd brought. From it he produced a minicomputer.

"Did you think of everything?" Sophia asked.

"I tried to."

CHAPTER THIRTY-TWO

TESSA LOOKED UP as Rafe walked into her room without knocking. She'd been talking to Sophia, but she'd broken off when she heard the knob turn.

"I wasn't expecting you," she managed to say.

"Are you feeling all right? You look . . . upset."

"I guess I'm still recovering from the trip," she said, wondering if that sounded too lame.

"I'm going to show my friend around the compound."

"Okay."

"We can all have breakfast together later. Perhaps you should rest now."

"That's a good idea."

He stood looking at her for a long moment, then he turned and left her alone.

As soon as he was gone, she got out of bed, crossed the room, and listened at the door, hearing voices in the hall. When they faded away, she pulled on sweat clothes and hurried down the hall to the library where the two men had been talking the night before.

One thing she'd discovered: the servants stayed out of the way as much as possible, which was lucky for her.

After glancing over her shoulder, she entered the room and looked around. Could she find some proof of his plans? Proof that she could show her sisters—if she could get off this estate.

A door at the far side led to a small private bathroom. She gave it a quick once over, then began opening drawers and cabinets.

But it seemed Rafe wasn't going to leave evidence lying around. She was about to leave the room when she heard footsteps in the hall. With her heart pounding, she looked for a place to hide. Her only choice was behind the draperies.

SOPHIA dressed while Jason connected to the motel's wireless network and Googled Rafe Garrison.

"What can you find?" she called from the bathroom.

"He didn't make any attempt to hide his identity. He's very well off, with an interest in a score of companies. And . . . wait for it, he lives on an estate above Santa Barbara, California."

"You found all that online?"

"Yes. Which means the place must be well defended."

He skimmed more of the sites with references to Rafe Garrison. He was a darkly handsome man who looked to be about Jason's age. But there was no more information that would help them deal with the guy.

TESSA stood behind the draperies, praying that Rafe wouldn't hear the pounding of her heart.

As he crossed to the far side of the room, she cautiously

moved the fabric aside so she could see out through a narrow slit.

He opened a cabinet. Behind it was another door with a combination lock.

When he turned the dial on the combination, she was at the right angle to see which numbers he stopped on. Starting with fifteen, then spinning to the right to nineteen. Then left, twice around to seventeen.

While she silently repeated the numbers, he opened the double doors, and checked some equipment. Something electronic.

He closed the door, and she eased the curtain back into place, praying he wouldn't discover her. Instead he went into his private bathroom and closed the door.

Taking the opportunity he'd given her, she leaped from her hiding place and dashed across the room, making for the door to the hall.

JASON and Sophia came down to the lobby, where the staff had set out coffee and baked goods. They both poured coffee and ate some muffins.

As they drove out of town, Jason said, "We should make some plans."

"We've got to find his place first."

"Then what? We've got two bad guys to neutralize."

"Minot rely on their strength and cunning. They're not going to expect a mental assault," she said.

"You mean like what Cynthia did to us at the cabin?"

She nodded.

"You think we can fight them that way?"

"I don't see any alternative. If Tessa joins us—that will be extra power."

He wanted to say it wasn't enough. Particularly since he'd never tried to stop anyone with a blast of mental energy. But he didn't have any other brilliant suggestions. He'd beaten

Rafe Garrison in a fight before, but who knew what the guy might have available on his own territory. And that didn't take the other one into consideration. Another Minot had joined Garrison. Obviously for his own reasons. Could they use him? Turn him against Garrison? But how would they get to him?

And what had the Ionians done to him to make him angry enough to kill them?

They made good time, with only a couple of quick stops, arriving in Santa Barbara around eleven.

"We could get another room, lie down, and try to contact Tessa," Sophia said.

"Or just drive north into the hills. Toward his house."

"Okay."

They headed for San Marcos Pass. Soon after that, development grew sparse, probably because the steeply sloped mountains would make building difficult.

According to the GPS, they were making for a place called Los Olivos that must be out in the middle of nowhere.

The farther they got into the brown landscape, the edgier he felt.

"The scenery's got some desert qualities," Sophia observed.

He tried to think about the vegetation, but his senses were tuned to danger he couldn't yet see.

To distract himself, he answered, "Some of the same plants that don't need much water. Even sycamore trees."

They were high on a mountain road when Jason rounded a curve. Suddenly he couldn't breathe, couldn't see. Couldn't control the car.

CHAPTER THIRTY-THREE

SOPHIA SCREAMED AS the Ford veered across the blacktop, headed for the shoulder, then toward a steep drop-off.

"Jason! Jason!"

He was inert in the driver's seat, and her only option was to lunge across him and grab the wheel.

Although it was almost impossible to steer from that position, she pulled them back onto the blacktop seconds before the wheels reached the side of the cliff.

But they were still going much too fast. As she struggled to control the car, she tried to move Jason's leg away from the accelerator. The limb felt like lead, pressing down far too hard on the gas.

Because she knew their lives depended on slowing the car, she kicked desperately at his foot and finally succeeded in dislodging it.

If she could only move the seat back, she could get into

a better position, but the controls were on the wrong side, and she had to keep her eyes on the road.

She tried to hug the side away from the cliff as they careened downhill, but the car was picking up speed on its own.

"Jason," she called again. "Jason!"

He was slumped against the seat back, and when he didn't respond, fear leaped inside her. Had all their mental bonding given him a stroke or something? She'd never heard of anything like that with her sisters, but maybe it was different with a man.

Fighting her panic, she kept trying to control the vehicle. When she saw a road leading off to the side, she yanked at the wheel, changing their direction.

As they turned a corner, she saw that they were heading straight toward a huge rock, but she managed to maneuver around it.

The road wound back the way they'd come. When they'd traveled about five hundred yards, she felt Jason's body jerk.

"What the hell?"

"Thank the universe," she gasped. "Slow us down. I'll keep steering."

He did as she asked, moving his foot onto the brake, decreasing the forward momentum of the car with a series of jerky motions.

Finally they came to a stop in a little valley shaded by gnarled trees with leaves that looked something like oaks but smaller.

He pulled off the road and sprawled in the seat with his eyes closed. They were both panting.

When she'd caught her breath, she turned to him, studying his face. His skin was pale and covered with a sheen of perspiration. "Are you all right?"

"I think so." He swiped a sleeve across his face, breathing in and out slowly.

"Rest for a minute."

As he sat with his eyes closed, she found his hand and squeezed. "That was scary."

It was reassuring when he squeezed back.

She tightened her grip on his hand. "What happened?"

"I don't know. Something . . . hit me. One minute I was okay and the next I was . . . out of it."

"Was it something like when Cynthia and the others attacked us?"

"Similar, I guess. But not exactly." He laughed. "Stronger. If that's possible."

"You said Minot didn't use . . . psychic powers."

"Yeah. I never heard of it. Except what my parents were doing together." He stared off into space, and she thought he was trying to give her a better description of what had happened to him. Finally, he said, "Tessa told us something."

"That could explain what happened to you?"

"Maybe. When she talked about the other Minot who was coming to join him, she said the other guy couldn't come in unless Garrison lowered some sort of barrier. Maybe something he was generating with electrical equipment?"

"You think *that* was it?" She sucked in a sharp breath as the implications sank in. "You think he knows we're here?"

Jason considered the question. "Not necessarily. I think he's got defenses against Minot around his property, and we came up against them. I think I only glanced against it, so hopefully it didn't trip any alarms."

Sophia finished for him. "But we can't get onto the property."

"Maybe Tessa can help us."

"How?"

"By turning it off."

"Assuming that she could figure out where it is—and somehow distract him. Then get away and shut it down."

Sophia stared at him. "I guess that's a lot for her to manage," she said slowly.

"All we can do is lay it out for her."

"After we figure out where his property starts." He looked back the way they'd come. "There must be some kind of line. I'm going to try moving in closer again and see if I can figure it out."

She gripped his arm. "You can't do *that* again."

"I have to know the parameters."

She kept her hold on him. "If you didn't trip an alarm this time, you could do it the next. You think it's a good idea for him to figure out we've come to rescue Tessa?"

He gave her an apologetic look. "No. I guess I'm not thinking too clearly."

TESSA hurried back down the hall to the bedroom wing. As she rounded the corner, she almost collided with the other Minot, the one who was working with Rafe. He had stepped out of Rafe's room and stopped short when he saw her.

For a long moment, they stood staring at each other.

She didn't dare ask what he was doing.

He was the one who spoke in a low voice. "There's a canister of gas in his dressing room closet. With a tube going to your room."

She dragged in a breath, wondering if she had heard him correctly.

"What is it?" she managed to say.

"We can only speculate."

"Why are you telling me?" she whispered.

"So you'll have all the facts."

Before she could ask another question, he walked quickly down the hall and around the corner.

Forcing herself to move, she stepped into her own room and closed the door.

A canister of gas. For what?

With a sick feeling, she crossed to the wall between the two rooms and began to run her hand over the vertical surface. Just under a wall sconce, she found a small hole that was camouflaged by the wallpaper pattern.

She thought back, trying to remember her reactions when Rafe had come in and awakened her after they'd arrived here.

She'd wanted him, but she hadn't felt like herself. Now she had a good idea why.

Sitting down on the side of the bed, she lowered her face into her hands, knowing she was in worse trouble than she'd imagined. She'd thought she was making her own decisions. Apparently, he'd been worried that she wouldn't make the correct ones—at least as he saw them.

Her chest tightened as she thought about how it had been when they'd made love. She'd touched his mind, and she'd been thrilled to do it.

Now she acknowledged the hesitation on his part. Maybe if he'd embraced the connection, things would be different. Instead, he'd pulled back because that wasn't what he really wanted. He'd known all along that he'd have to hide his true intentions from her.

He'd been kind to her. Considerate even. But the longer she stayed with him, the more she understood that he was just putting on a show of civilized behavior.

She clenched and unclenched her fists. She had to get out of here, and she couldn't do it by herself. But could she act like she didn't suspect a thing until Sophia arrived? If she arrived.

"WE need to find a place where we can contact Tessa," Jason said.

"You're right."

"This time, I'll drive," Sophia said.

As they headed back toward town, neither one of them spoke, and Sophia assumed they were both worrying about what was going to happen next. They'd come here to rescue her sister, and they'd hit an immediate obstacle. What other defenses did Rafe Garrison have?

As they approached a motel chain north of town, Jason gestured. "Stop here."

He got out and paid for a night.

When they'd stepped into what looked like a three-star motel room with a bed, a chair, and a television set, he turned to Sophia.

"Let's see if we can change the rules a little bit."

"How?" She was the one who'd been practicing mental communication all her life, but he seemed to have more creative ideas.

When he held out his arms, she came into them, clasping him tightly and laying her head against his shoulder.

They swayed together in the center of the room, both overcome with emotions—and longing. But she knew they had to stick to business.

"Do we have to stand up?" she asked.

He laughed again. "Comfortable is good."

Turning, he pulled down the spread and blanket. They both kicked off their shoes and lay down, reaching for each other again.

She closed her eyes, absorbing the feel of him and at the same time trying to connect with his mind.

The process was becoming familiar, and she was able to link with him quickly.

Try it with less physical connection, he suggested.

Sophia eased away from him, keeping their hands as the only physical link.

When the mental connection held, she felt his satisfaction.

Slowly he drew his hands away, his fingers inches from hers. She felt the connection waver, but it still held.

Can we still do this while we're running around out there in the hills?

I hope so.

Too bad we don't have a lot of time to practice.

He took her hand again. This time, by mutual agreement, they reached toward Tessa—and found her waiting for them.

Thank the fates.

Are you all right? Sophia asked urgently.

I have to get out of here.

We're very close. But we can't get into the estate. Garrison has some kind of barrier that keeps out Minot.

Some kind of electrical thing?

Do you know where it is? Jason asked.

She gasped when she heard his voice.

You!

You don't think Sophia can do this by herself, do you?

Tessa made a moaning sound. *I don't know what to think. What to do.*

Help us, he said. *Can you turn off his device?*

I don't know.

Sophia spoke. *Please. We need your help to get in.*

I'll try. I have to go. He's expecting me at lunch.

Jason entered the conversation again. *I just got caught in the edge of his shield. Did he act like he knows I'm out here?*

I don't think so.

Okay. Try to turn it off as soon as it's dark outside. Then keep him busy.

How?

Be creative.

I . . .

The communication snapped off, and Sophia rolled away from Jason, staring at him.

"You know what you're asking her to do?"

"Yes."

"Suppose she . . . can't."

"Then we're in trouble."

"You are, already."

Both of them looked toward the door, where the speaker stood, trapping them in the room.

CHAPTER THIRTY-FOUR

IT WAS EUGENIA. In back of her were Ophelia, Adona, and Vanessa.

Jason and Sophia sprang off the bed. He drew her in back of him, for all the good that would do if the Ionians attacked.

"You said you wouldn't follow us," Sophia said in a shaky voice.

Eugenia shrugged. "I needed you to find Tessa, and I needed to see how you would proceed. I think it's clear you can't get her back by yourself."

Jason kept his gaze fixed on her. "We're going to give it a try."

Eugenia's voice turned scornful. "You can't even get in there. He's got some kind of device that stops Minot."

"Tessa's going to turn it off. We asked her to do it as soon as it got dark."

"If she can; if she has the will. Maybe she's switched sides."

Sophia raised her chin. "She told us he's planning to kill all the other Ionians. She wouldn't have said that if she wasn't on our side."

Eugenia gasped. "Is that true?"

"She thinks so."

"It could be a lie. I don't know what tricks a Minot is going to play," Eugenia snapped.

"Because it's been drummed into you for years that we're evil."

They glared at each other.

Jason forced himself to calm. Getting into a fight wasn't going to help Tessa—or him and Sophia. "Be logical. Making Tessa terrified for her sisters isn't a smart move on Garrison's part."

Eugenia nodded. "All right. That makes sense. But she may not know she's under his control."

Sophia grimaced, hating to think that was true. She knew that making assumptions about Tessa's loyalties or her abilities was dangerous, yet at the same time, she knew that they needed her help to get inside the estate.

"We'll all go there tonight," Eugenia said. She looked at Jason. "If you can get in, you can keep him occupied. Let him think you're the main threat. We'll find Tessa, then surprise him with the same technique that we used on you. Only we'll turn up the volume."

"Phasers set to kill?" Jason asked.

"Something like that. If Tessa's right, he's too dangerous to walk the earth."

Would that turn out to be true of him, too, when the emergency was over? He'd like to discuss that point, but he didn't have the luxury at the moment.

"We've been digging into his background," Eugenia said. "We found the Web site of the architect who designed the house. We have the plans. And the location of the house on the property."

She held up the minicomputer she'd been carrying in her right hand.

"All right. That will help," he said in acknowledgment, hating that they were running the show. Too bad he and Sophia had come here without any firm plans. Maybe he'd been assuming that he and Garrison would fight—hand to hand the way they'd done in the desert.

"There are two Minot there," Sophia said.

Eugenia blinked. "How do you know?"

"Tessa told us."

"You're sure?"

"She mentioned him several times," Sophia answered.

"Why has he joined with Garrison?" Eugenia asked.

"He hates the Ionians," Jason answered.

"Why?"

Jason couldn't stop himself from saying, "I can imagine the order did something nasty to him. Hell, for all I know, his father could have raped his mother. He could have been a boy baby born at the spa, and they left him out in the desert to die."

"No! You're angry and making assumptions. We would never do anything like that.

"Maybe he wanted to hook up with one of those other women who left the order, and the Ionians killed her."

"Impossible."

"Would you have thought Cynthia would veto getting Tessa back?"

"No," Eugenia said again.

"The guy calls himself John. Does that mean anything to you?" Jason asked.

"Nothing." She snorted. "Maybe John Doe?"

"It appears we can't figure out who he is," Sophia broke in. "Let's hope we can get Tessa out of there."

"And make sure Garrison can't kill any Ionians," Eugenia reminded them.

"What about the other guy?" Jason asked.

"We have to assume he's just as dangerous." She switched back to the invasion plan. "We can get close because a hill hides the road from direct line of sight."

"Garrison's got to have security cameras," Jason said.

"We can park about two hundred yards away and walk to the property line. And wait for the signal that the"—Eugenia flapped her hand—"let's call it a force field—is down."

Jason didn't ask what would happen if Tessa couldn't drop Garrison's shield—or distract him.

"We'd better get some rest," Eugenia said. "We have rooms at this motel." She looked at her watch. "We'll come back here a couple of hours before dark, have something to eat, then drive out to the compound."

"You've got it all figured out," he said dryly.

"You and I both know something will go wrong," she answered.

"Yeah. One thing we won't know in advance is if the barrier is down. I'm going to have to try going through. And if I pass out, you and Sophia will have to drag me back."

AFTER Eugenia and the other Ionians left Sophia and Jason alone, he was too restless to sleep. He'd transferred the house plans to his own computer and spent some time memorizing them. It was a sprawling property, and he hoped they could locate Tessa.

Finally, he joined Sophia, who'd been lying on the bed with her eyes closed. As soon as he eased down beside her, he knew she wasn't really sleeping.

He reached for her and pulled her close.

"We're supposed to be resting," she murmured.

"If something goes wrong tonight . . ." He stopped and started again.

She might have been thinking the same thing, because her mouth came down on his for a kiss that turned frantic the moment their lips touched.

"Slow down," he murmured, his lips against hers. "We both want to enjoy this."

Turning his head, he nibbled at her ear, then slid his lips to her jaw, her neck.

In the darkened room, he gathered her closer, marveling at how perfectly her body fit against his. Swaying her in his arms, he slid her breasts against his chest as he sucked her lower lip into his mouth.

Do anything you want with me, she whispered in his mind. *Everything you want.*

Oh yes.

He kissed her deeply, drinking from her essence, trying to hang on to his will to go slowly and savor every moment of this time they had together. Perhaps the last time.

His hands went to her bottom, cupping her sweet curves so that he could press her center to the erection straining at the front of his slacks.

If Eugenia barged in again, she was going to be embarrassed, he thought as he unhooked Sophia's bra, then eased away from her to pull up her T-shirt and suck one of her hot, distended nipples into his mouth while he tugged and twisted the other one with his thumb and finger.

His hand went to the button at the top of her jeans, pulling it open and lowering her zipper.

Impatiently, he reached inside, dipping into the folds of her sex, loving the way she had turned wet and molten for him.

When he slipped two fingers into her, stroking in and out, she answered with a muffled sob as her hands went to the front of his jeans and began struggling to get them off of him.

As she lowered his zipper, he couldn't hold back a cry of gratitude. And when she freed his cock and wrapped her hand around him, he fought not to lose control.

It felt good. Too good.

He wanted to take her now, but they were still both half dressed, and he knew it would be better naked.

Naked, she echoed in his mind.

He rolled away to tug at his shirt and jeans, and she also finished undressing. When they were unencumbered, she came back into his arms, both of them crying out as they clung together.

She looked at him, her eyes dazed, as he reared up, then kissed his way down her body, finding the delicious core of her, lapping and sucking on her, feeling the fluttering vibrations of her approaching climax.

"Not that way," she gasped.

"Let me."

She tensed, then lay back, and he kept up the caress, bringing her to a rocking climax. Then he came back beside her and started arousing her all over again. When he knew she was ready, he thrust deep inside her. As she began to move in a jerky rhythm, he cupped his hands around her bottom, pushing deeper into her, watching her face as her inner muscles clenched around him.

"Jason. My love. Jason."

He heard the words echo in his mind, and returned them to her.

I love you. I will always love you. No matter what happens.

As he felt her coming, he let himself go, joining her in an explosion of ecstasy that left them both limp and panting.

He gathered her in his arms, kissing her face, her hair, her jawline, wanting to memorize every tiny detail of her.

"I've never let a lover take charge like that," she murmured.

"Was it okay for you?"

"You know it was."

She nestled beside him, and as he held her, he knew their thoughts were running along parallel lines.

We could leave.

Disappear.

No one would know where we had gone.

Tessa got herself into trouble. We don't have to rescue her.

Or the rest of the Ionians? He's coming after them, too. We can't let him wipe them out.

Sophia held him more tightly, wondering what it would have been like to be a normal woman, free to choose a life with the man she loved.

Jason moved his cheek against hers, still speaking in her mind. *We don't want to end up like my parents.*

I know.

We'll rescue Tessa and make peace with the rest of the Ionians.

If the spirit of the universe is willing.

TESSA had excused herself for the afternoon, saying that she needed to rest. But as she lay on her bed, she kept listening for the telltale hiss of gas. What if he used it again? Then came in and started making love to her. He'd leave her drugged and sleeping.

Then she wouldn't be able to help Sophia and . . .

She couldn't bring herself to think too much about the Minot with her. Sophia trusted him, but what if he'd drugged her the way Garrison had drugged her?

She climbed off the bed and went into the bathroom, closing the door behind her. Would it block the gas if he decided to use it?

Another sickening thought grabbed her. Probably he had a camera in the bedroom. What if he had one in here, too?

Would he do something so disgusting?

She didn't know, but perhaps she should draw a bath and pretend that she wanted to relax in a tub of hot water.

SOPHIA wasn't hungry, but she forced herself to eat some of the Mexican food Eugenia ordered for everyone.

An hour before dark, they set out in two cars. Sophia was hoping that Eugenia was right—that their approach couldn't be seen from the estate. If the senior Ionian had calculated wrong, Garrison and his friend could be waiting for them.

With guns? Or something worse?

The sun had set when they pulled off the road, but there was still enough light for them to make their way across the dry grass and through the scrubby vegetation toward the estate.

Jason walked cautiously, ready for the sensations he had experienced before.

He wasn't disappointed. One minute his head was clear. In the next, he felt as though he was falling through time and space.

He didn't know he'd actually started to fall until he felt hands on his arms holding him up and pulling him back a few yards.

"Are you all right?" Sophia asked urgently.

He dragged in a breath and let it out. "Yeah. Thanks."

"I guess Tessa couldn't lower the barrier," Eugenia said.

"It's barely dark. We should give her a few minutes," Sophia answered.

"THAT was an excellent dinner," the other Minot said. The one who claimed his name was John.

At dinner, the two men had talked about the financial markets, as though they weren't actually plotting murder.

She'd tried not to stare at the visitor. He looked even more familiar than he had earlier. She'd caught him looking at her, too, but each time he'd glanced away.

Who was he really? And what was his role in all this?

He seemed to be Rafe's friend, but he'd told her about the gas. Did he want her for himself? Was that what was going on?

Rafe broke into her thoughts.

"Would you excuse us?"

"Of course," she answered as one of the servants came in to clear the table. They'd dined on Beef Burgundy, which she'd hardly been able to taste. The same for the Crème Brûlée and coffee at the end of the meal.

As the two men exited the room, she focused on Rafe's broad back, wondering if Jason could beat him in a fair fight. No, beat two of them.

And could he even get in here? She'd resolved to distract Rafe. Maybe she wasn't going to have to do it, because Rafe was busy with his guest.

She sat at the table until they'd left. Then she walked down the hall and into the library.

Wondering how she was going to sabotage the equipment in his closet, she reached for the dial of the combination lock, just as the door behind her opened and the other man, John, walked into the room.

"What are you doing here?" he said in a hard voice.

SOPHIA, the other Ionians, and Jason waited in the gathering darkness.

"I think she's not coming through for us," Eugenia whispered. "We have to go in."

Jason turned to her, his voice urgent. "You can't do it alone. You have no idea who or what you'll find in there."

"Then perhaps we should focus on getting you through the barrier," Eugenia answered.

"How?"

"Put up a wall around you, the way we did when we discovered you at the spa."

"Will it work?"

"I don't know. But we have to try," Sophia answered, struggling to control her own fear. If they got Jason in, how would he get out again? They'd have to find the machine and turn it off. Or could they all regroup and reverse this process?

"Let's get on with it," Jason growled. "What do you want me to do?"

"Don't fight us," Eugenia murmured.

He'd like to oblige, but this was the woman who had tried to kill him. At least, that's what it had felt like at the time.

This is different.

The words echoed in his head, and he knew they came from Eugenia. *Don't fight us*, she silently repeated, and he realized he could speak to her in his mind, the same way he spoke to Sophia.

That brought a shiver skittering over his skin. He hated being open to this woman, but it seemed he had no choice if he wanted to get into the estate.

With a silent sigh, he struggled to open himself to their attack.

Not an attack.

Whatever.

They still grasped him by the arms, and he held himself rigid, waiting for the pain of their invasion to hit him.

The pain didn't overwhelm him, but he couldn't call the sensations that enveloped him pleasant. He felt swaddled by layers of gauze. Along with the sense of confinement, his head seemed to be filling up with something soft and mushy, like cream cheese, maybe.

He tried to focus on that. Tried to describe the sensation to himself, but it was beyond him now.

The Ionians were doing this to him, and he wanted to shout at them to let him go.

Relax. Don't block us. We're trying to help. You want to get into the estate, don't you?

It was Sophia speaking to him, and he struggled to focus on her words.

But his mind simply wasn't working in any kind of normal fashion.

Panic seized him. It was like someone had suddenly damped down all his senses along with his ability to think coherently.

He wanted to scream, but no words came out of his mouth.

Stop! he silently shouted.

He felt Eugenia wince, reacting to his plea.

Maybe he was hurting her. He hoped so. As soon as he thought about it, he realized she could probably hear him, and in his dimmed mind, he realized something else. If he was hurting Eugenia, he must be hurting Sophia.

He struggled not to do that again.

As they moved him forward, he seemed to come up against an invisible wall that made every cell in his brain sizzle. And he knew that whatever the women were trying wasn't working.

Then all at once, the pain stopped.

What happened?

He thought the question came from Eugenia.

Something changed.

Maybe Tessa turned off the barrier.

Panting, he crashed to the ground, bringing down Sophia and the woman on the other side of him.

They lay in a tangled mess while he struggled to catch his breath and take stock of his faculties.

"Are we . . . on the other side?" he panted.

"Yes," Sophia answered.

He hated lying on the ground surrounded by women who all wanted to know how he was feeling.

Gritting his teeth, he pushed himself up.

"I don't like it," Sophia murmured. "What if it's a trick?"

"We have to assume we're in the clear."

He peered into the darkness. Garrison's house was still hidden from view. And he couldn't help wondering if there was some factor they hadn't counted on.

What about servants? Bodyguards? Would they leap to Garrison's defense or head for the hills?

When they reached the top of the rise, they saw the house.

A few dim lights burned in what must be the bedroom wing. The general living areas were more brightly lighted.

They moved silently forward. When they were still fifty yards away, Jason motioned for them to stop. Reaching for Sophia's arm, he sent a silent message: *Wait here. Let me find out what's happening inside.*

He could see she didn't like the plan, but Eugenia must have heard, too, because she put a restraining hand on Sophia's other arm.

I can call to Tessa, Sophia said.

Better not, he answered. *Not if she's with Garrison.*

Sophia scowled at him, but she let him leave her and the other women behind a towering clump of pampas grass.

He crouched low, heading for the house.

When Jason was still about twenty yards away, a man stepped out, and Jason froze, ready to fight the guy.

But it was only one of the staff, taking a plastic bag down a flagstone path to a fenced-in area.

Jason waited until he'd left the bag of what was presumably trash, then grabbed the guy and clamped a hand over his mouth.

"I'm going to take my hand off your mouth so you can answer a question. If you call out a warning to Garrison, I'll kill you. Nod if you understand."

The man nodded.

"Where is Tessa Thalia?"

The man hesitated, looking frightened.

Jason yanked his arm painfully behind his back. "Where?"

"In her bedroom. With Mr. Rafe."

A flurry of movement informed Jason that Sophia had joined him.

"I told you to wait."

"I'm coming with you."

Cutting his losses, Jason turned back toward the man. "Where is the bedroom?"

Before the guy could answer, they heard a scream.

"Tessa," Sophia gasped, jumping up.

He tried to grab her, but she dodged out of his way and pelted toward the house, bent on reaching her sister.

The other women came streaming after her, and Jason knew that whatever advantage they'd hoped to gain from surprise had just been lost.

Floodlights switched on around the property as Tessa burst from a doorway and ran toward them. She was wearing a sheer nightgown, and her eyes were wild as she looked around.

Garrison was right behind her, dressed in only a pair of boxer shorts. Behind him must be the man Tessa had told them about. The Minot named John.

When Jason saw him, he gasped.

CHAPTER THIRTY-FIVE

THE SECOND MINOT spotted Jason and stopped short.

All around them, people were moving, including the servant, who had taken off into the night.

But Jason's focus was only on the man behind Garrison.

Not some guy named John.

His father. Paul Castle. Who was supposed to be dead.

But Jason had never recovered his body, and now, here he was. He must be the man Tessa had been talking about. The one who hated the Ionians, and Jason certainly understood why.

All that flashed through his mind in a blinding instant.

He knew his father saw him and knew who he was because an expression of satisfaction gathered on his face.

It changed to fear as Garrison raised his gun and pointed it at Jason.

No hand-to-hand combat, like the last time in the desert.

Apparently Tessa's kidnapper wasn't taking any chances on losing this fight.

Before Garrison could fire, Paul Castle shouted, "No," and leaped forward with Minot speed, reaching for the gun as he bore down on Garrison.

Jason sprang forward at the same time, trying to get the gun. But Garrison had already spun around, pointing the weapon at Jason's father.

Jason leaped onto Garrison's back, struggling to wrench the gun away from his father's direction. The weapon discharged, but Paul had already dodged to the side.

It was all happening fast, faster than a normal human being could move.

Jason could hear women screaming. Tessa and Sophia.

Get back, he silently shouted at them. *This is between us and him.*

Maybe they got the message. Maybe they did as he asked. At the moment, he was busy trying to keep Garrison from hurting anyone.

Jason and his father had worked as a team before. They fell back into old, familiar rhythms.

Together they tackled Garrison, both of them coming down on him, Jason on top of Paul.

But Garrison still had his finger on the trigger. The gun discharged again, and Jason felt the impact, even as he knew the bullet had hit his father, not him.

"Dad."

Jason rolled his father to the side, ignoring the gun that was now pointed at him.

Before Garrison could fire, he screamed, his face contorting in agony, and Jason knew that the Ionians had sent him a blast of powerful energy.

Jason wrenched the gun from his hand and flung it away, then lifted Garrison into the air and smashed him onto the ground with bone-jarring impact.

Figuring the women would finish the job, Jason turned away and knelt beside his father on the ground. He was lying very still with his eyes closed. A red stain spread across the front of his shirt.

In the background Jason heard Garrison begin to choke and writhe on the ground.

"Get the . . . hell . . . off me," he gasped.

Jason bent to his father. "Dad. Dad. What are you doing here?"

"I knew you were in Sedona. Thought you . . . were coming here."

Behind Jason, Tessa screamed. "Don't kill him."

"He's turned you," Ophelia muttered, a note of derision in her voice.

"No. You don't understand," Tessa protested, grabbing for Eugenia and trying to push her away from Garrison. "You've got to listen to me."

Paul Castle was barely breathing, but his eyes focused on his son.

Anguish tightened Jason's throat, but he managed to say, "Why did you pretend to die? Why did you join Garrison?"

"My . . . hate would have contaminated you. I would have. . . undone everything your mother taught you."

"No."

His father was silent for a moment, then began to speak again. "I . . . was eaten up with . . . anger . . . I wanted . . . revenge for your mother's death. Then I found out you were coming to rescue . . . Tessa. I . . . couldn't let him hurt . . . you." Blood trickled from his mouth as he spoke. "I . . . turned . . . off the shield . . ."

Jason was aware that Sophia had knelt beside him.

"Your father?" she wheezed as she tore open his blood-soaked shirt, catching her breath as she saw the extent of the wound beneath.

"Yes."

Paul's eyes fixed on Jason. "I'm . . . finished. I'll finally be with your mother. Run."

Eugenia joined them. "Garrison's done for. We've won." She looked at the man sprawled in front of Jason. He had stopped breathing, and his eyes were staring into nothingness.

"Is that your father?"

"Yes."

"You said he was dead."

"I thought he was," he choked out, trying to grapple with what had happened. He'd lost his father years ago. And now he'd lost him again.

Tessa ran over to them. "Rafe's got a bomb. It's linked to his physiology. It's going to go off if he dies."

Jason didn't ask how she knew. He simply picked up Sophia and started running.

The Ionians who had been pounding Garrison with psychic energy leaped up and followed.

How long did they have?

Jason didn't know. All he could do was run, hoping the bastard would live for a few more minutes.

He heard the Ionians pelting after him. They hadn't listened to Tessa's warning, and they hadn't understood the danger of killing Garrison.

Jason headed for the hill, bent on putting it between himself and the house.

Before he reached it, a massive explosion shook the structure behind him, sending a shock wave toward them and deafening him as he threw Sophia to the ground, sheltering her under his body.

Debris rained down around them, and a large chunk of wood landed nearby. But only small pieces hit him on the head and back.

Finally, it was over, and Jason raised his head. When he looked back, the house had disappeared in a pile of smoking rubble. Had all the servants gotten out? He didn't know.

He rolled off of Sophia. "Are you all right?"

"Yes." She lay still for several seconds, then raised her head and looked at her sister. "How did you know about the bomb?"

Tessa spoke in a shaky voice. "John . . . I guess he was really Paul, your father, said Garrison was bragging about it. Paul was sure you'd come to rescue me. He said to be ready to get out of there."

"He was expecting us?"

"Yes. But I didn't get a chance to ask . . . him any questions. And I didn't tell him I'd been in communication with you and Sophia—in case." She gave Jason an apologetic look. "In case he was going to . . . double-cross me."

"I understand," he answered, still shell-shocked by what had happened. "After what Garrison did, you couldn't trust me, and you couldn't trust my father. Not completely," he added in a gritty voice.

"But I trusted him enough to work with him. I opened the locked cabinet where Rafe kept the electronics. John told me to keep Rafe busy while he turned off the shield." She gulped. "I had to pretend I wanted to make love again."

"Don't think about that now," Sophia said. "It's over."

Tessa nodded then focused on Jason. "I kept thinking John looked familiar. It was because he looked like you." She gulped. "It's my fault he's dead."

"No," Sophia said automatically.

"He made his choices," Jason added.

"So did I," Tessa said. "And I never should have left the spa." Her gaze swung back to Eugenia. "I want to go home. So much. Can I?"

Eugenia nodded. "Of course."

But Jason heard an edge of doubt in her voice. Would Cynthia really permit Tessa back into the order? Would she punish everyone who had participated in the rescue?

He watched Sophia and Tessa embrace, saw them whispering together, then watched the women gather round the sister whom they'd saved.

He could see how close they were, how the order drew them back together.

Sophia glanced at him, an uncertain look on her face. Detaching herself from the group, she came over.

"I've got to ride back with Tessa. She needs a lot of support now."

"I understand," he answered before clearing his throat. "I want to bury my father."

"Yes. I'm so sorry about him."

"I lost him a long time ago. Seeing him again was a shock."

Sophia reached a hand toward him and let it fall back. "I have to go. Can you meet us at the spa?"

"Okay." He wanted to ask what would happen then. He wanted everything settled, but what if it all went the wrong way?

He couldn't deal with that now.

"We should get out of here before someone comes to investigate the explosion," Eugenia said.

"What will the police think happened here?" Sophia asked as she craned her neck toward the wreckage of the house.

"Hopefully they'll think it was some sort of accident," Jason answered. He looked at Garrison. "Maybe they'll think he had a stroke." He walked to his father's body, picked him up in a tender embrace, and started for the cars without looking back toward the women.

Jason drove directly to his ranch, speeding ahead of the Ionians. He wanted to be alone with his grief. No, that was a lie. He ached to have Sophia with him, but she'd gone with her sisters instead.

Darkness seemed to hang around him as he began to dig a grave in a spot not far from the labyrinth. After wrapping his father in one of the native rugs he'd bought for his house, he laid him carefully in the grave and covered it with dirt.

When he was finished, he bowed his head and asked the spirit of the universe to grant Paul Castle peace at last.

As he walked away, he wondered if there was any point in going to the spa. Sophia had risked everything to rescue Tessa. Then he'd watched her rush back to her sisters when the crisis was over. He'd seen how important they were to her, and the longer she was with them now, the more likely they'd turn her around to their point of view again.

She'd only known him for a few weeks. Weeks that had been a pressure cooker of intensity. Now that the crisis was over, how could their short relationship compete against the life she'd always known? The life she'd been born for. Raised for.

His chest tightened painfully as he thought of all the reasons why he had lost her. His father was one of them. He'd initially talked to Garrison about a revenge plot. Finding out his son was involved with an Ionian had changed his mind, but that didn't speak very well of his initial motivation.

Jason turned back toward the grave and grimaced. His father had lost the woman he loved. Jason was sure he had, too.

But he'd be a coward if he didn't drive to the spa and hear about it in person.

CHAPTER THIRTY-SIX

JASON'S STOMACH MUSCLES clenched as he pulled up in front of the main spa building. He was dreading the coming confrontation, but he didn't want to postpone it either.

When he got out and saw Cynthia waiting for him, he steeled himself for the worst.

From her expression, it looked as if she was planning to boil him in oil. Instead she said, "Come in," before turning abruptly and going inside.

He followed, willing his face not to give anything away.

When he got to the lounge, he found all the sisters assembled. The ones who had gone to Garrison's house were in a separate group, with Sophia among them.

"Sit down," Cynthia ordered.

He looked toward Sophia, meeting her gaze but unable to read her expression. He ached to go to her. He wanted to lift her into his arms and carry her away—very far away.

But he knew there was no point in proving he was an overbearing lout.

Instead he took the only seat available—which was off to the side of the group.

So what was this going to be? A trial?

He thought Cynthia was going to start in on him immediately. Instead she swept her gaze over the disobedient Ionians.

"You defied me," she said.

Sophia raised her chin. "I couldn't leave my sister in terrible danger."

"And I couldn't allow it either," Eugenia added.

"You *couldn't allow*," Cynthia said, her voice deadly calm.

The two women stared at each other. It was Eugenia who looked down. "I am sorry I overstepped," she said, her words stiff. "But I felt we needed to get Tessa back if we could."

"You could have all gotten killed," Cynthia said. "You and everyone who went with you. That was an unacceptable risk."

Tessa spoke for the first time.

"If they hadn't come to get me, you wouldn't know that Rafe Garrison was planning to impregnate me and kill the rest of the Ionians. You'd all be dead."

Cynthia blanched. "Is that true?"

"Yes. I needed time to think, but I made a mistake by leaving the spa. Garrison found me almost at once."

"And Jason's father—a Minot—played a key part in saving her," Sophia added. "He gave up his life for us—and Jason."

Cynthia looked at Jason. "The last I heard, you said your father was already dead."

"I thought he was. That's what he wanted me and everyone to think. He faked his death. He said because he was afraid his anger would contaminate me. He was at Garrison's house." He swallowed, before continuing with brutal honesty, "I think at first he was planning to get revenge on the Ionians. Then he found out I was involved, and he changed his mind."

Sophia spoke up. "For centuries, we've been protecting ourselves from the Minot. Maybe it's time for us to figure out how to work with them."

"Impossible," Cynthia answered. "They can't be trusted."

"Jason can," Sophia shot back, and his heart leaped to hear her defending him.

"We don't know that."

"And you won't unless you give him a chance to prove it," Sophia said.

"He could live with us for years and turn out to be a traitor. Like those Russian spies who were in the U.S. for years until the FBI arrested them," Cynthia answered.

Eugenia entered the conversation. "It may be time for us to think about how we need to change—to exist in the modern world. These are complicated times."

Cynthia gave her a dark look, and Jason knew she didn't like being challenged, but she was a practical woman. And perhaps she saw that the order was under new pressures that demanded new solutions.

But Cynthia wasn't ready to give up. She glared at Sophia, then swept her arm toward Jason.

"You think this Minot wants a warm, close relationship with you. What if he only wants to lift the ancient curse he says the Scythians placed on him and the others of his kind?"

Jason jumped up, determined to defend himself. When he started to speak, Sophia shook her head.

Let me, she said. *I hope she'll listen to me.* When he realized she was speaking silently to him, his heart squeezed. They could still do it! She still *wanted* to do it.

As he gave an almost imperceptible nod, she addressed Cynthia again.

"I think he already lifted it."

Had he heard that right?

How?

"By changing everything about himself," she continued aloud. "He says his father and mother discovered the curse. I think they didn't figure out what it really meant."

Jason waited with his heart pounding. What was she talking about?

"At the cabin, when I was starting to doubt him, he took me back to one of his past lives and let me see what it was like. It was awful. More horrible than you can imagine. His enemies did unspeakable things to him." She gulped. "But it was as much his fault as theirs. He was leading a violent, immoral life, and that violence came back to destroy him."

His heart sank. Was she getting ready to walk away from him after all?

She turned to him, her face grave. "But I know that he's a different man now. He's proved through his actions that he's conquered his Minot heritage. And he did it by himself."

She got up, crossed to him, and clasped his hand, holding tightly to him in front of all her sisters.

"I've had a lot of time to think about the Minot. Jason believes the curse was only about repeating his mistakes over and over. I think it was also about taking away the ability to change. He's done that! By himself—because he wanted a different life."

"You have no proof of that," Cynthia said.

"Yes I do. Everything he's done in the past few days proves it. He had the courage to tell me he wanted a relationship with me. He had the courage to show me what he had been in the past. And the courage to ask for my love—not demand anything from me. Then he risked everything to help us rescue Tessa. What Minot could do that unless he'd overcome the curse?"

She stretched out her hand toward Cynthia. "Don't deny us the chance to show you that an Ionian and a Minot can make peace with each other. Real peace," she pleaded.

Every muscle in his body was rigid as he waited for an answer.

"We cannot allow him to live here at the spa," Cynthia said.

Jason's hopes sank, but Cynthia went on. "I would make a concession, though. He can live near us at his ranch. And you can live with him and come to the spa to work here—and perform your other duties."

He felt light-headed. Had he heard that right?

He must have, because Sophia pulled him into her arms, holding tight. "Thank you," she said, and he echoed the heartfelt words.

SOPHIA clung to the man she loved, rocking in his arms, her joy overflowing. Raising her head, she looked at Cynthia. "I know that was a hard decision. A decision only a wise and good high priestess could make. Thank you so much," she murmured.

Even as she spoke, she understood that some of her sisters would never accept the new order.

Yet she knew she had changed. And the Ionians had changed, too, although they might not admit it yet. The blending of those two truths might be their salvation.

The meeting was over quickly. As many of the sisters gathered around Tessa, Sophia and Jason slipped away. At the spa exit, when the guard raised the gate, she breathed out a deep sigh.

Jason looked at her. "I thought I had lost you."

"I was frightened, too."

"I'm glad she didn't force you to choose between me or your sisters."

She gulped. "I would have gone with you. Not far away, but to your ranch, close to the spa. I would have kept hoping that Eugenia and Tessa could change Cynthia's mind."

The words astonished him. “You would have chosen me?”

“Yes. But we don’t have to worry about that now. And we’ll show them that our life can be a model for the order.”

“It’s going to be a little strange when the Ionians are almost like nuns.”

She laughed. “Nuns with sex.”

“Uh-huh.”

“If you’re thinking about pulling off the road and making love with me, it’s only a ten-minute drive to your house—where we can be comfortable.”

He grinned, clamping his hands on the wheel as he headed for his ranch. “What about Tessa? Will she be all right?” he asked.

“I hope so. She has a lot of healing to do, but our sisters will help. If she comes through this, it will make her stronger.”

“And do you think Eugenia is going to shove Cynthia out?”

“Maybe. It’s hard to say. All I know is that the order isn’t going to be the same.”

“Maybe Cynthia will take a leaf from our book and move in with her boyfriend.”

“Impossible! Not the high priestess.”

He shrugged. “You know a lot more about the order than I do.”

After pulling to a stop in the parking area and cutting the engine, he reached for her, and she came into his arms, clasping him tightly.

“This is what I longed for,” he whispered. “Since I was young.”

“It’s what I never dared hope for. You had to show me what I could have—if I had the courage.”

After a long kiss, he asked, “Do you think she’ll let us marry?

“I hope so, but we’d better take this one step at a time.”

“Starting with a lifetime commitment. Maybe we can have a private ceremony—in that cave of yours.”

"Something creative."

She hugged him more tightly, overwhelmed with happiness. Until a few weeks ago, she'd been sure of the future laid out for her. Now it was taking a completely different direction. One that she could never have imagined, but one that she would embrace with all her heart.

Turn the page for a preview of a new novel in Virna DePaul's Para-Ops series

CHOSEN BY FATE

Available October 2011 from Berkley Sensation!

SEVERAL WEEKS LATER
AN ABANDONED WAREHOUSE
WASHINGTON, D.C.

CALEB'S HANDS MOVED swiftly and efficiently as he set up the mobile radar equipment he'd spread out on the roof. The building below his feet had been swept and a perimeter established. Now all Caleb had to do was determine who was in the room with Mahone and whether Mahone was still alive.

Briefly, he glanced at Ethan Riley, leader of Hope Restored Team Blue, and the four men, skilled in entry and perimeter surveillance, who'd accompanied them here. Only hours had passed since Caleb had left his teammates in the Vamp Council's chambers in Oregon and, despite the grueling activity of the last few days—which had included parachuting into North Korea, hiking miles in the snow, rescuing several Otherborn, and tracking down what just might be an antidote to the vamp vaccine—Caleb felt the same focused energy he always did when on a mission. "Did you get in touch with the Para-Ops team?"

Riley looked up from checking his rifle. "They've detained

the vampire Dante Prime. Devereaux tried to teleport here, but he'd depleted his powers in Korea . . ."

Caleb snorted. "No shit." Although vamps could teleport to and from anywhere in the world, provided they'd been there before, that kind of travel drained them. Before Knox Devereaux and the rest of the team had interrupted the Vamp Council to question Dante Prime for treason and conspiracy to commit murder, the dharmire had spent several hours teleporting between North Korea and the United States. Each time, he'd carried a wounded Otherborn or one of his team members back with him. Beat him how the vamp was even capable of talking at this point. Add everything else that had happened to him—

"Is it true you found his father? And that he'd been turned into a vampire?"

Caleb didn't even look up. The Para-Ops team had trained with Team Blue's aerial experts before dropping into North Korea. At the time, Knox's father hadn't even been on their radar—and for good reason—since everyone believed he was dead. How the hell news of Jacques Devereaux's return had spread so fast, Caleb didn't know. Still, Riley had to know how fruitless his question was. "No comment."

He sensed Riley wince. "Sorry."

Caleb shrugged. Just because a person expected a particular result didn't mean he shouldn't try to get around it. Caleb was always trying to get a different reaction from his teammate Wraith, regardless of how unlikely that was. For one horrific moment, Caleb felt the same fear that had constricted his chest when he'd realized Wraith planned to blow herself up to get them inside the North Korean compound. It wasn't easy, but he pushed the feeling away.

Wraith was okay. He'd seen that for himself. He'd felt it when he'd pushed her down and covered her body with his. He'd savored it when she'd kissed him back, right before she'd kneed him in the balls.

Clearing his throat, he returned his attention to Riley and

the other man's apology. "No worries. I'm as human as you, remember?"

Now it was Riley who snorted, prompting Caleb to smile tightly.

Okay, so maybe he wasn't quite as human as Riley. They shared the same DNA, but being able to communicate with his ancestors, hear the Great Song, and occasionally walk the Otherworld made him a little different.

Different didn't always mean better.

His fingers moved faster. Almost there. Glancing at his watch, Caleb clenched his teeth. A bead of sweat trickled down his temple. He knew they couldn't go in blind, but—

"What about your wraith? Was she what you expected her to be?"

Caleb paused for only a fraction of a second before continuing his task. "She's not my wraith. She's a wraith who decided to keep the name 'Wraith' just to be ornery. And she's exactly what I expected her to be." What he didn't say was that she was also far more than he'd expected. A heinous bitch, yes, but one whose attitude and mouth were designed to hide something textured and complex and—

Disgusted with himself, Caleb pressed his lips together and once again pushed thoughts of Wraith out of his head.

Get Mahone out. That's all he could think about right now.

"Finally!" Snapping the last wire in place, Caleb flipped on the power and adjusted the radar settings, then scanned the building's interior until the radar picked up body heat. "Bingo."

Caleb immediately zoomed the camera in and got a good look at Mahone.

Dear Essenia, he thought, automatically invoking the name of the Earth Goddess to give him strength. Although humans believed Essenia was an Otherborn deity, few knew Earth People—like Caleb's own Native American tribe—had prayed to the same deity for centuries. Besides, from what Caleb saw, Mahone needed all the prayers he could get.

With his wrists shackled to chains hanging from the ceiling, Mahone looked like he'd gotten into a fight with a chipper machine and lost. His face and body were covered in blood, and what was left of his clothes hung in shreds from his battered body. From his position on the rooftop above, Caleb once again adjusted the settings on the mobile radar equipment. His adjustments made the image on the screen zoom out, losing detail and focus until it captured the entire room, providing grainy outlines of Mahone, a desk, a table, and one other individual whose silver hair, height, and slim build proclaimed him to be a vampire.

When Caleb and the five members of Hope Restored Team Blue had arrived at the isolated warehouse twenty minutes earlier, Caleb had figured Knox, leader of the Para-Ops team, had made a mistake by not sending any Others with him. That, or Knox simply had faith in Caleb's ability to take down anything that got in their way, human or not. Either way, Caleb was getting Mahone out, and he planned for both of them to be breathing when he did it.

Caleb thought of the first time he'd met Mahone and the vision he'd had. He'd had the same vision several times since, and the moment he'd met Wraith, he'd become convinced that the black and white aura that hovered near his own had to be hers. Upon their meeting, he'd felt a sizzling arc of connection that had only intensified with time. Apparently she hadn't. In fact, she seemed to have no use for him and spent most of her time pushing him away. Maybe the aura belonged to Mahone, instead, and the vision had been a premonition of this very moment—Mahone straddling the line between life and death, waiting to see whether Caleb could save him.

Luckily for both of them, Caleb had come prepared.

He looked at Riley. The man might be a little chattier than Caleb liked, but he'd had no problem taking Caleb's lead on the current mission. He was smart and he was a clean shot. That's all that mattered right now. "Mahone's in bad shape. We need to get in there fast. I'm hoping the vamp will teleport as soon as he knows he has company, but I need you and your team to cover me in case he decides to stick around. Are your shooters set up around the perimeter of the room?"

"They've all checked in and are in the crawl space with their weapons ready."

"Obviously your bullets won't kill him, but along with the Hyperion gas, they may buy me enough time to get to Mahone and extract him."

"How long does it take for the Hyperion to immobilize a vampire?"

The Hyperion was something Caleb had developed toward the end of the War. The government hadn't known about it, and he'd only used it a few times before peace had been declared. The testing he'd conducted had been limited, but he felt fairly confident it would work.

At this point, he figured his odds of getting out with Mahone were only slightly below average. "Usually about sixty seconds, but that's with a vamp who's been weakened by the effects of the vampire vaccine. From the looks of this one, he's had pure blood recently. Still, he might not be at full strength."

"If the vamp's immobilized by the Hyperion, how do we keep him contained while we take him in?"

"We don't. That's not what we're here for. Our sole objective is to rescue Mahone."

Riley nodded, but looked troubled. "You said he's doing bad . . ."

Caleb tried to keep his expression blank. "Doing bad" was an understatement. Mahone probably had less than five minutes of life left in his broken body. "Just get me to him. I'll take care of it from there. You ready?"

Riley communicated with his men, then nodded. "It's a go."

Slipping the small gas pellet from his pocket, Caleb held it up. "Remember, you have to stay back. Help me hold back the vamp, then get your men out. You're maintaining the perimeter, not going in. This gas immobilizes vamps and weres, but it does far worse to humans once enough of it is absorbed in the bloodstream."

"What about you?"

"I've built up a resistance. It's not extensive, but it'll give me the five minutes I need. If we don't make it out, it'll take two hours for the gas to dissipate. Don't come into the room until that much time has passed. Understood?"

Riley nodded and held out his hand. O'Flare shook it, then strode to the door that would lead him from the roof to the room below. He moved quietly, his breathing low and shallow, his gun held at the ready with the gas pellet in his other hand. He'd activate it as soon as he got close enough that it could work its magic on the vampire.

When he entered the room, he immediately saw Mahone. Even the radar's enhanced imaging hadn't prepared him. The vampire wasn't touching him, but Mahone's facial features were contorted in agony, his body writhing and jerking even as he remained silent. Fuck, Caleb thought when he saw the blood seeping out of Mahone's eyes and ears.

"Hey, vamp." He shouted at the same time he threw the pellet, which would emit a toxic but invisible gas. The vampire whirled around, his eyes flashing red the instant he saw Caleb. The vampire bared his fangs and came at him, his feet gliding above the ground. Caleb fired a round directly at his chest, causing him to fall back. At the same time, Riley and his men fired, as well. As the vamp jerked with the impact of the bullets, O'Flare ran for Mahone. He reached up and felt his pulse.

It was barely there. Caleb felt the man's life literally bleeding out of him.

Laying his hands on Mahone's bloody chest, Caleb closed his eyes. Bullets still fired around him, some coming too damn close. Damn it, Riley's men had to get out before the gas reached them in the crawl space. "Get out!" he yelled.

"The vampire teleported," Riley shouted. "We're clear."

With a sigh of relief, Caleb willed his consciousness into a trance and called to his ancestors for their healing help. He saw them in the colors that swirled behind his eyelids and felt their presence in the heat that immediately suffused his body. Their voices chanted, low and soothing, directing him to keep one hand directly over Mahone's heart and the other over his eyes. Caleb willed the healing heat building within his body to transfer to Mahone. As it did, he took some of Mahone's pain into himself.

He felt his own heartbeat slow.

His limbs weakened.

His body began to shake with the effort of remaining upright, and he forced even breaths, sensing he needed to maintain contact far longer than he ever had.

Come on, come on, he urged himself. Hang in there.

The dizziness came next. Then the nausea. He could feel his lungs filling with the gas that swirled around them and knew his time was running out.

His body jerked as he coughed, and the movement threatened to pull his hands away from Mahone.

They had to get out of there, but if he disconnected too soon, it would all be for nothing. Mahone would die. Hell, Caleb would probably die, as well, too weak from the healing to get out on his own.

But then he felt Mahone's chest rising strongly and his pulse beating regularly, and he knew the healing had worked. The heat slowly left his body, and the voices of his ancestors faded. Caleb whispered his thanks, then opened his eyes. Swiftly, he reached up and unhooked Mahone's chains from the manacles around his wrists. Mahone groaned and slumped over just as Caleb caught him and threw him fireman-style over his shoulder.

Caleb staggered a few steps before he turned, intending

to carry Mahone to the doorway. Halfway there, his knees buckled. He lost his grip on Mahone, and the man slipped and rolled a couple of feet away. Grunting, Caleb fell on all fours, his head hanging, his lungs seizing up.

He'd waited too long. They were both going to die in this warehouse, just like the FBI scientists who'd discovered the vamp antidote only to be killed because of it. He looked up, eyes watering, searching the room, thankful that Team Blue had obeyed his orders even as he regretted the fact no one was going to be able to help him.

But then he saw her. Wraith. Running toward him. He tried to open his mouth. To yell at her to stop.

His heart squeezed. Damn her for putting herself at such risk. He didn't know how the gas would affect a wraith. Since it worked so well on vamps, immortality had nothing to do with the effects. But he couldn't make a sound, and Wraith kept coming. She knelt beside him and pulled him up. She was yelling something, and he tried to make it out.

". . . have to walk! I need to get Mahone. Can you walk, O'Flare?"

She was glancing frantically between him and Mahone, the indecision on her face readily apparent. She couldn't carry them both out of there before the gas ended them.

"Leave me . . ." he tried to say, but again no sound came out. It didn't matter. Wraith understood.

She grabbed him by his shirt and shook him, hanging on when he began to slide, practically keeping him on his feet. "No fucking way, O'Flare. I didn't survive Korea just to come back and lose you in the States. Stay on your feet and move. You're walking out of here. Got it?"

The vehemence in her voice roused him enough to nod. She released him, and although he swayed on his feet, he didn't fall. Quickly, she grabbed Mahone, carrying him in the same lift O'Flare had used. Then, amazingly, she positioned herself next to him and ordered, "Lean against me if you need to. Start walking. Now."

Caleb walked. He didn't know how he did it, but he managed to put one foot in front of the other. At one point, he did have to lean on her, and he sensed how it slowed her down, but she didn't move away. She stayed with him.

Until they made it out into the open air. He heard shouts and the sound of stomping feet just as he collapsed.

When he came to, he was being loaded into an ambulance. Riley's face hovered above him. "Mahone?" Caleb rasped out.

"Still alive," Riley said. "But I don't know if he's going to stay that way."

From the worried expression on the man's face, Caleb knew his own chance of survival was also in question.

"Wraith?" he asked, grabbing on to the man's shirt when he didn't answer. "What about the wraith?"

Riley shook his head. "I don't know. She passed out, same as you. No pulse, remember? No breath. No way to tell if she's alive or dead. They took her in another cab. Your guess is as good as mine."

FROM *NEW YORK TIMES* BESTSELLING AUTHOR OF *ATLANTIS BETRAYED* AND *ATLANTIS REDEEMED*

ALYSSA DAY

VAMPIRE IN ATLANTIS

The Warriors of Poseidon

A vampire's oath, a maiden's quest . . .

Daniel, vampire and ally of the Warriors of Poseidon, has fought on the side of humanity—even against his fellow creatures of the night—for more than eleven thousand years. But the crushing weight of futility and the reality of always being starkly, utterly alone has forced him to finally give in to despair. He took the first step into the sunlight that would destroy him—and instead walked into Atlantis.

And the blackest of magic that could consume them both . . .

Eleven thousand years ago, Serai was one of a group who agreed to be placed into magical stasis to ensure the future of the Atlantean race. When the gemstone that protects her sleeping sisters is stolen, she awakens to a vastly changed world—and the one man she could never, ever forget. And with an ancient evil tracking their every step, the long-lost lovers must battle both the darkest of magic and the treacheries of their own hearts.

penguin.com

M846T0311